Embryonic Legacy

Copyright ©2011 By Bahati

Cover Art done by Ison Design Company
Griot Publishing

Copyright © 2011 by Bahati
Published in the United States by Griot Publishing

ISBN 978-0-692-70386-1

Cover Art by Ison Design Company

I would like to dedicate this book to my family. From my parents, siblings, to my children, without all of you, this would not have happened. A special thanks goes to my sister Yolanda, (YoYo), who is the first person who told me to write.
Inspiring me to do, what I did not know I could do.

Chapter 1

Trouble started as soon as she got off the plane. Leslie, her Cousin, that was more like an aunt due to their age difference met her at Oakland airport.

"Kathy, we need to get to your mother's house as soon as possible. Angela Lynne and her kids are already there rifling through everything. Like a bunch of vultures on a dead carcass."

Leslie had grown up in Texas and still referred to many female family members by their first and middle names as if it were one name.

They almost ran to the other side of the airport to get to the baggage pickup. Kathy was angry with herself for not changing from her work clothes. It was not the skirt suit she was wearing but more the heels she had on. Not really shoes to wear for fast walking. And she could tell right now, it would be awhile before she was out of them, luckily she had spent some money on having them customized inside to support her feet better. So they shoes did not hurt yet, but later on this evening, the pain would be kicking in something terrible.

"My mother just died 4 hours ago and they are already there?"

"You know Angela Lynne and her brood got keys! Surprised they were not there before now to tell the truth. I always told your Sylvia, your mother, she was too good to them folk. They always have been taking advantage of folks. Your mother was just so moved to help her because she felt some sort of responsibility for their mother's death. What gave her that feeling is beyond me."

Kathy frowned as she thought about how her mother *had* helped Angela after Angela's mother died. Let her live with them, because Angela was still in school. Helped her go to college. Later, after College did not work out, helped her pay rent an endless amount of times. Co-signed on a car that she later ended up paying for herself after Angela, quit yet another job. The problems just kept piling up. There seemed to be no end to her mother supporting Angela. Not that Kathy felt in any way like her mother ignored her, because she did quite the opposite. She felt well raised and taken care of. She just always wondered why Angela deserved such coddling. Kathy's mother supported Angela.

Angela for her part, seemed like she felt like she *deserved* the royal treatment she was getting. She never seemed to be bothered in the least by Kathy's mother having to clean up her financial messes. She just kept on like it had never happened. Like she did not have any accountability to the problem she had just created. And for some reason, Kathy's mom, who normally was a strict disciplinarian, would let it go, as if she had not noticed it.

After getting her bags which, thank goodness, were the first few of the bags to come out. Both Kathy and Leslie stroked out of the Terminal to what seemed the farthest corner of the parking lot in what had to be, record time.
The sun was setting, Leslie handed the keys to Kathy, "You know I can't drive when it gets dark. Getting to old, and we need to get

there as fast as possible. But judging from the shocked look on your face, and me still being a young 28.…...I will drive anyway." Leslie said jokingly as she was well past 60. She did decide to drive.

Kathy threw her bags into the back of the aging Saab Hatchback. Once she got in she was surprised at how the car from 1990 felt and smelled new.

Upon arriving in what seemed 2 milliseconds from Leslie's driving, they stepped out doing a run-walk to the house. It was a Victorian that Kathy's mother took great pride in keeping up to date and in good damn near new condition. When Kathy was a child she called it the Chocolate House, because it was only brown and darker brown. The roof was dark brown the window sills were a slightly lighter shade of brown, and the rest of it was a Milk Chocolate Brown. Only shades of Brown from Milk Chocolate to Dark Chocolate. Leslie and Kathy pull up to the curb as they arrive at the house. Exiting the car they walk up to the front door.

Entering the house, Kathy's nose seemed to be besieged by the Stronger than Pinesol smell of Angela's Perfume. The smell never left the room when Angela did. It stained the air like like the moldy walls of a house in New Orleans after Katrina. Better to be torn down than repaired. Kathy and Leslie went straight up the stairs to Kathy's Mothers room. When they got there they saw what Angela and her Brood had done. And it looked like they had entered into an inhouse robbery. Hat boxes were open, Drawers were out of the nightstand, thrown across the bed. Clothes were on the floor. It was as if the world had gone mad, but just in one room. Leslie froze with a look of disbelief across her face. Mouth open, eyebrows furrowed, forehead wrinkled, eyes flashing between rage and hurt. She looked across the room, surveying the damage and also looking for Angela.

Kathy kicked off her shoes, she was looking across the room to the closet as she strode toward it. Inside she found all four on their knees trying to pry open a box that was actually Kathy's Grandmother's given to her Mother before the Grandmother passed. This stopped Kathy in her tracks. She originally planned to come and do damage to each and every one of the of thieving ingrates. Seeing them trying to PRY open this Box that was clearly locked for a REASON stunned her and left momentarily stuck. They actually had a screwdriver jammed into the front of the box trying to pry it open. Angela, turned in light surprise to see Kathy standing there. Her children did not look up to acknowledge Kathy standing there. Just kept their focus on finding what they thought to be treasure in the shoe size tan metal box. But Kathy could see that they knew she was there. Angela stood up in the four or five steps it takes for her to get up. Angela was now an Obese woman with a bad right knee with the left trying to follow suit. Angela went first to turn while on her knees, then look for something to grab onto, then use that leverage to get up making a noise that sounded like she was freeing herself of a constipated bowel movement. Everything from her ugly attitude, worn-out wigs, perfume that seemed to sear nostrils, undersize clothes that highlight every roll, bad skin that used to be beautiful, smooth, and lack of dental hygiene. Literally see the plaque from years of barely brushing her teeth. It was amazing to Kathy men would still lay with her, let alone get her pregnant.

"Kathy?!? We were about to call you." Angela said. A voice that clearly said, I do not know how fuck you got here, but I will distract you while my children keep working on this, because we cannot be concerned with your stupid ass right now. Kathy watched as Angela talked never making eye contact. "

Wanted to make sure you got here to claim all that you rightly deserve. Listen...........”

Kathy could not hear her any longer. She could see Angela mouthing words but she heard nothing but the blood boiling in her own body. It was as if her ears were filled with the sound of blood moving, flowing faster and faster, with a larger and larger volume. The sound became louder and louder with every glance Angela took over her shoulder to check on the progress her children were making. Not once did she look Kathy in the eye. Angela would raise a hand to point at this or that, then casually look over her shoulder to see if the box was open. Clearly thinking she was the distraction for Kathy. As if Kathy was not intelligent enough to see what Angela was doing.

The box started to crack open then busted open. As soon as it did there was a loud crack sound right after the box opened. The children did turn around to see where that came from. Angela looked in shock and some horror at Kathy. Leslie looked at Angela with a somewhat satisfied smile. The box was open, but not without a price to Angela.

“Why did you ......”
“Get the HELL OUT!!!”

Kathy herself, did not know at first, but then it came to her as she felt heat unbridled rage as she stood staring at Angela. Kathy had just slapped Angela so hard she felt her hand beating. And a darker imprint on the side of Angela’s face was forming in the shape of her hand. Kathy had slapped Angela. A hard, slap.

“You ain’t got no right to be hitting me like...”
Kathy could not hear her once again, but said in a low voice, that she herself did not recognize.

9

"If you and those children of yours do not get out of THIS house *right* now, nothing is going to stop me from hurting you and your robbing stealing children. Now, get, OUT!" Wanting to say much worse, Kathy held herself back.

Angela felt something different in Kathy than she had seen before. Kathy's eyes were calm but focused, and she could not move out of Kathy's gaze. She quickly turned and grabbed her children, leaving without a single word or backwards glance. Her kids not saying a word either, (which is rare for them). Her hands were shaking, and she felt a great deal of fear as her heart pounded. Angela had been no stranger to fighting when she was young, but something in the power of the slap Kathy threw made her think better of challenging Kathy. Also something in her eyes was different. It never crossed Angela's mind that Kathy was being affected by her mother's death. It should have but did not register. That is why a thought crossed Angela's mind as she left out the door. "I will be back. This shit is not over. I know there is money around here somewhere."

Kathy watched from the Master Bedroom window as Angela and brood walked down the walkway to the sidewalk. Then down the street to her brand new less than a year old beatup SUV. Dents and missing taillight. Scrapes down both sides with a loose muffler in the back. Angela bumped the cars in front and back of her as she worked her way out of the parking space. Then pulled out right in front of a car coming down the street. The Driver that was cut off laid on his horn, Angela gave him the finger. He gave her one back. She then hit the brakes halfway down the block. Trying to make him hit her. He swerved and avoided her, going around the right side of her. Then hitting his brakes and started yelling at the top of lungs. She then turned toward his car. He gunned it suddenly sensing this might be more than what he wanted to handle running a light turning from yellow to red. Angela pulled up to the light. Her head still moving side to side with her left hand going up and down. Her pointing finger pointing up then down with every other word. Kathy could not hear her, but knew she was probably still talking stuff about the guy she cut off. The light changed and Kathy turned away from the window.

"Lord Jesus what is wrong with them?!??" Leslie asked to no one in particular, looking around the room as she tried to start putting everything back in its proper place. Kathy looked around the room while standing in one place and almost subconsciously started to pick up things and put them up. The box had contained some old jewelry that was not real, and very tarnished. There was one piece of cloth that appeared to have a blood stain with some dirt. Other than that, nothing was there. Kathy disposed of the small wooden box and all its contents.

Both women worked on the room for what turned out to be an hour and a half. After finishing Leslie turned to Kathy.

"You really should not have to deal with anything like this. And I am sorry."
"Don't apologize. That was not you fault. Angela is just scandalous, and I do not for the life of me understand WHY my mother used to deal with her?!?? I just don't understand. She is not even a real relative. "

Leslie came and sat next to Kathy on the bed. A look of concern on her face. She sat next to Kathy but did not reach out, not knowing if that is what Kathy wanted, but still wanting to comfort the young woman that looked so tortured by the thought of Angela and her mother.

"Leslie, do you know why my Mom felt like she HAD to take care of Angela? What is their connection. I know she was friends with Angela's mother. But she did not kill her. Yet she acts…..or used to act as though she owed Angela her life as if she took Angela's Mother's life herself. "

Leslie looked at Kathy. Studying her actions. Kathy just looked at the floor shoulders slumped in defeat. Lost in thought trying to figure out an answer to the question she herself was asking.

Leslie, rubbing Kathy's back said, "You mother, never told me why she did that. By that I mean taking care of Angela as if she were her own. And spoke even less about the relationship with Angela's mother. It seemed like they shared a secret life no one knew about."

Kathy's nose flared and eyes flew wide open. Leslie laughed, not meaning to but it was comical the way the conversation was panning out.

"Your mother was not a lesbian. What I meant is they were deep into something that neither one would talk about. My Aunt, your Grandmother, would always say, 'Those girls do not know what they are doing. They are not listening and one day this is all going to come and bite them. They think it is strength what they do. But you cannot be strong when you are wrong.' She would not say a thing past that. That was when we were young, and I never asked her what she meant. But when Angela's mother died…….."

"What?"
"We will talk about this later. I am not feeling too well." Leslie gave her a tired smile. She was a little tired but she knew that Kathy would let her go with the look she was giving.

"OK. But I would like to know more Leslie. It seems like there is so much I have missed not living here."

Kathy walked Leslie down to the front door. They hugged. Kathy thanked Leslie for the call and all the help she gave her. Leslie said it was nothing, we are family. As Kathy closed the door and locked it, she was suddenly overcome with grief. The house that she grew up in was now empty. The house her mother used to fill with her spirit and charm, as though it were missing something. That something she knew was her mother, but something else seemed to be missing. The warmth she would get from being there was gone. There was a coldness, it seemed almost like a barrier had been dropped and some type of cold joyless energy was slowly taking over the warm family feeling that had always been here for many generations. She could feel it like the cold from a Freezer door left open slowly, reaching across the kitchen on a hot day. You feel the heat, but the longer that Freezer door is left open, the more you feel the cold wisps lightly touching your skin. Almost like invisible frozen feathers. Lightly brushing you.

For the first time since hearing her mother passed away, which was so unexpected, the full feeling of her mother being gone hit her. She could not breathe for a few seconds, almost panicking, she grabbed the back of one of the chairs near the kitchen. Kathy could hear her heart beat. Still unable to breathe she started to unbutton two of the top buttons on her blouse. Feeling constricted, it gave her some measure of comfort, No longer having the blouse buttoned to the neck. She stopped everything and focused on breathing. Still unable to focus on anything in the room her grip on the chair turned into a death grip. Holding on as hard as possible as the room seemed to start spinning around her. Her legs started to shake. The more she tried to gain control of herself the more she lost control. Her legs gave and she collapsed on the floor Kathy with wracking uncontrollable emotion. She cried, until her body gave and she lay on her side, sobbing. Silently shaking, tears

13

flowing, yearning to see, smell, talk and hold to her mother again.

Kathy fell asleep, on the floor in a fetal position. Not knowing she was asleep, she felt cold air from under the back door caressing her skin, slowly wrapping around her body. Too tired to wake up let alone get up Kathy feeling the cold, hibernated on the floor, energy spent, until almost noon the next day.

Chapter 2

Sitting in the backyard after making arrangements with her job for more leave of absence. Kathy sat and enjoyed the sun. Something she rarely had time to do being the Senior Vice President of Marketing. Being back home in Oakland, part of the Bay Area of California usually meant it got warm, real warm, and maybe on or two hot weeks for the year. But usually, the weather was just right. It would keep you warm, but if you got too warm a breeze that had been cooled by the water coming in from the ocean to the Bay would blow through. Bringing your own body temperature down, cooling you off. Kathy sat in one of the lawn chairs feeling that exact breeze cooling her as the sun caressed her milk chocolate colored skin.

Since her Mother's funeral things had calmed down significantly. She was now able to enjoy some time alone, to herself. She looked around the yard. It had been Landscaped since the last time she was there. Her Mother always threatened to change the backyard. Said there was too much negative energy in the backyard. Needed to tear, and she emphasized tear, out all the roots and start anew. Kathy now regretted not asking her why she felt that way. Looking around the yard that used to be her Grandmother's garden before she passed and home to the evil weeds after. Kathy started to think back. Back to when she was child playing in the backyard. Back when there was still a quasi outhouse back here.

Looking around the yard she tried to see something still there from when she was a child. Nothing looked familiar. Everything was new. Almost as if another person's back yard had been lifted and dropped down in the back of this house. There was grass with, concrete pavers down the middle. Large pavers, looked more like blocks of cement meant to go together, but spaced so they did not touch. The grass ran between them. Then there was a thin, but long pond that separated the garden from the lawn. The garden was located against the back fence that separated the neighbor's yard from this one.

Even looking at the layout she was amazed by the intricacy of the yard. The more she looked the more she saw different features. Lights next to each Paver. Which undoubtedly lit up the walk way at night. There were lights that followed the fence, of a type she had not seen before. They were painted to almost work as camouflage to the fence. She almost missed seeing them. Kathy made a note to herself to see this yard lit up at night, tonight, as soon, as it got dark. The lawn chair she was sitting in was one of the ones from her childhood. Actually quite old, remarkably clean, but old. She then noticed the covered sitting area that escaped her view before. It was in front of what looked like a clay baking oven....

"Where the hell have I been not to have noticed all this?"

Kathy said aloud, not caring who heard her. Whether it was people walking by the on the sidewalk or a nosy neighbor she was lost in too deep of thought to care. She began to feel like she must have missed more than she knew about her Mother. The house was different, the backyard was different. What else had she missed, and what else could she have looked over while she was here.

She sipped the lemonade she made from lemons she got off her Aunt Leslie tree in her backyard. Her mother never let her play in the yard again after she had an incident in her youth. Scanning the yard she tried to see where that may have happened. But the yard was so different, the vibe was different. It felt like a place you come to meditate now. Kathy now understood what her mother meant by negative energy of the backyard. It was now inviting. Before it seemed to devour positive energy. Before she felt like that, when she was young. It had a different feel.

Kathy was around 5, maybe 6 years old when it happened. The yard was nothing more than a deeply fertilized and watered garden back then. To her eyes, all the plants were damn near her height. It made for a fun Playland. There were dry walkways for her to navigate between the plants that went around the wet areas. Being a curious child, in a yard full of strange and unusual plants was just too irresistible. Every time she went back there to play, she found some new area, plant, or things she could not describe. She had no idea what her grandmother had in the backyard. But so many things led her imagination to expand to whole new universes. She would make up stories about her dolls being in distress and bring in her fat black boy cabbage patch doll to save the doll in distress. There would monsters, drama, and of course and end with the hero and damsel in distress getting married and living happily ever after.

That one year, she spent many of her days at her Grandmother's house. Her mother and father had split, so her mother had to go out and work again. Not being able to afford Daycare, Kathy was sent to stay with her grandmother. Her grandmother was a woman in her late 60s, but could easily pass for a woman in her late 40s or early 50s, Kathy still saw her as that crazy old woman that would whoop her, and cook up smelly foods like pigs feet, chitlins, and various other vegetables that stank. But she could cook breakfast and lunch good. Young Kathy would never admit that though. She would just wolf down both like she had not had any food in a week.

Kathy was a slender child with a protruding belly. She had long hair that was always kept up by her mother and grandmother. Neither letting her hair get too out of place when she would go play. Kathy had started to make sure she did not let her hair get too out of place, because that meant having to sit in one place for a LONG time. Because her mother or her grandmother would redo her whole head if one ponytail got messed up. And that was boring. She could be playing with her dolls Natasha and Olinga. Natasha is a Supermodel, and Olinga is a college student from Africa. Both dolls were black, but Olinga's hair stayed braided, so she was from Africa in Kathy's little mind.

Kathy and her grandmother would go to the grocery store, post office, or anywhere else to run errands. The only thing Kathy found strange is why so many men seemed to want to help her grandmother carry bags, or seemed to not care who was in line as the cashier, offered his personal help to the car or his personal help to her period. Always looking her directly in the eye as they spoke. Packing bags without looking away the male cashier would offer all this. Patiently waiting on an answer that her smiling grandmother would reply, "No, that is ok."

"Anything you need Sister. I can help. Anything you need."
"Thank you, but I will be all right."

The cashier would then hold the bag he just packed keeping us in line looking like he was thinking of something else to say. Which always led her grandmother to say

"I do need my groceries to get my granddaughter back for her nap."

This would always leave a look of wonder on each different man's face leaving them speechless as she took the bag away from the weak hand pushing it toward her. Young Kathy always wondered why they looked shocked at the statement. She was *old*.

Once Kathy grew up she would look at pictures of herself with her grandmother and discover that her grandmother was a strikingly beautiful woman, and for men that were barely out of their teenage years to be so strongly attracted to her still at the age she was. Made Kathy hope, wish , and pray that type of beauty was something she could inherit from her.

There was one man though. He would come by every so often while Kathy would stay there. He appeared to be an old man. He had a bald head, gray and white beard and enormous hands. Not that tall, and seemed small from a distance, but grew and expanded the closer he got to you. He also seemed to stand straighter than most people. Always standing in a way that looked like he was ready to spring. He moved in a smooth but well oiled manner. He moved like no man Kathy had ever seen. Like a Panther that she had seen on TV, or cats that she had seen walk down the street.

The first time Kathy saw him, he had come by. Knocked on the door. Her grandmother answered. When she opened the door it seemed as if her grandmother turned into a young girl for a moment. A wide smile crossed her face, almost a giddy look. He stepped in. He had on a three piece suit, and smelled strongly of some strange cologne. He walked in and stood in front of her grandmother. He stepped right up to her looking down at her with a small smile. She looked up at him as if some silent communication was happening. They stood in that position for more than a few moments. Even Kathy's young mind picked up on something. He turned and saw her, Kathy, the little girl.

Walking across the room with his cane. It was a thick cane. He was not using it to walk but holding it in one of his massive hands like you would carry a suitcase. The stick itself was a dark wood polished to a glass like finish. It had many, many diamonds across the top of it. Extremely large diamonds. He stopped in front of her. Letting the cane tap down on the ground. Kathy swore she saw a light pulsate inside it.

The man squatted down to her level, both his hands resting on top of the cane. His eyes were gray. As if time had taken away all the color in the iris of his eyes. They looked a little scary to Kathy. He had eyes like those of the wolves they showed on the Animal show on TV. He looked at her and said,

"Well. Is this the next generation in line?"
"She is young. We will not know until she is older."
"No. I know right now. She can *see.*"

The man's voice was so many different things. Like rocks grinding together, but thick molasses running between them to ease the grinding. Harsh as wolf tearing open a deer's stomach to eat it, but soothing as riding in the back of her mother's car when she is playing a boring talk show on the radio.

"You know of my cane, but she does not. Yet she could see it. There is no mistaking."
"Maybe it is just pretty to her. Maybe…"
"Little girl. What is your name."
"Kaddy" Kathy spoke with her child's speech.

The man cracked a smile, which somehow made him look younger to Kathy. She then noticed he did not have skin like an old man. There were very few wrinkles, and his skin did not have all those holes in it. She had asked what was wrong with a Great Uncle's skin to her mother once when she saw it. Her mother said they were his pores. She then said as some people get older their pores get bigger.

This man's pores were small and seemed closed. His skin was a smooth dark brown. He watched the girl study him. Not saying anything. He then stood. Walked over to her grandmother and said something very quietly into her ear.

"Kathy, time for nap."

Surprised by the sudden change in mood, Kathy hurried to do what her grandmother asked, wary of having to go get a "switch", off one of the bushes in the backyard. Her grandmother's tone had changed. Somewhat cold. After Kathy used the bathroom and came into the room set up for her to sleep. She lay down. Her grandmother looked down at her.

"Be careful of letting people know what you see. When you get older you will be taught to understand the great gifts that you have. But for now, we will work on you not letting everyone know what you can see."

Kathy looked up at her confused and lost to what her grandmother spoke of. Her grandmother gave her a kiss on the forehead. Then stood , looking down at her eyes full of love, regret, and a deep look of worry. Then she seemed to realize as she was looking at Kathy, her grand baby was looking back at her, taking it all in.

"Go to sleep. If you don't you will get bit by the bedbugs. They only get bad little girls that stay awake when they are supposed to be asleep. So if you do not want them to bite you, lie still and go to sleep."

Her grandmother tapped her nose, smiled at her then left the room. Then, she did something she *never* did. She closed the door. This fired up a curiosity in Kathy that was almost uncontainable. Straining she could not hear what was going on. Their voices were muffled. She did hear them go down to the basement. But sleep got a hold of her as she tried to stay still to hear any part of the conversation.

Kathy would see that same man come by many times that Summer. Each time watching her like a hawk, even when not looking directly at her, she could sense him watching her. It made her feel slightly uneasy. The man's eyes showed nothing but a curiosity and grandfather like caring. He and her grandmother would speak, he would always make a quiet comment to the grandmother after sometime, and Kathy would be sent to bed.

She began to make her dolls imitate them talking. Playing in the backyard, her secret, magical world.

One day while playing in some of the long dead Rose Bush on the side of the house. She walked passed the bushes. She found a new path she had not seen before. It seemed to lead to a storage shed, which to her young eyes looked like the perfect evil castle for her dolls to escape from. The fence itself was open. There was a concrete path that went down the side of the house. Kathy had not seen this path before. What she saw in her childlike way was a hoe, rusted giant scissors, some icky yellow plastic bucket, and then there was a dark shed. The shed itself seemed to pull her in. It looked perfect to be a place for evil characters she thought once again.

It did scare Kathy, but she was overcome with curiosity, she wanted to see this thing up close. As she walked down the path she felt a cold breeze blow past her like an exhale from someone's mouth. Kathy looked around, sure in heart that she was not supposed to go down this path on the side of the house. Knowing this may well get her a whoopin from grandmother with one of those "switches" she was so afraid of. But she just *had* to see what was in this wooden shed with all the dead and dying weeds around it. There were a few plants growing from inside to the sunlight outside. Today was overcast and chilly, but it looked like the dead plants had been reaching out to the sun at one point or another. They would not be getting any nutrients today. These plants to Kathy, looked more like plants that feed off other plants. Her imagination starting to soar as she felt the thrill of doing something she was not supposed to be doing, took hold of her. The fact that she could get caught and get into trouble, only increased the adrenaline she was feeling.

The closer she got, the longer the path seemed, and the closer the other various plants down the walkway seemed to get to her. Kathy did not like these plants, or weeds. They were dirty and stank like the doorways to buildings smell downtown. Large dry leaves with white hair on top of them. None of the plants were green. All brown, gold, or sickly yellow. Some even had thorns on their branches.

Closer, the shed now looming before her. Kathy reached for the door. It was brittle and old from many seasons of sun and rain. She pulled on the rusty handle, but the door did not move. Kathy tried to see past the door by looking through the small crack that was opened. She only saw the few plants growing out with their thorny branches. Nothing deeper in showed. Again, Kathy pulled the handle. Nothing happened. For something that looked so brittle, it sure did hold its place. She found a, less dirty, patch to put her two dolls down. When she turned back the door appeared to be more open than last time she looked. Maybe she had opened it more than she first thought.

Kathy went to reach for the door with every intention of yanking this stubborn stupid door open, but before she could grab the handle the door flew open. Kathy screamed only to feel dry leaves being pushed into her mouth. They stank horribly and tasted even worse. Kathy tried to spit them out, but they went deeper into her mouth. Now all the way to back of her mouth she started choking. Kathy started to feel scared. Then completely terrified. She could not breathe, she started to panic. Reaching for her mouth she felt and saw a thorny branch sticking straight at her coming from the darkness in the shed. Her fingers lacerated and bleeding freely from her pulling on the thorny branch trying to pull it out of her mouth. She started to heave, the bile of her puke being stopped by the branches that seemed to increase as more time went by. Frantically Kathy tried to back away. Another branch wrapped around her leg. Kathy saw the branch move and wrap around her leg. It looked more like a branch swaying in the wind, then grabbing her ankle abruptly. Digging its thorns into her skin.

Still fighting, Kathy tried to scream make a noise, but none came. Her heart was pumping hard, frantically clawing kicking, pulling, scratching, she could not break free. From inside the shed a mound of what looked like mulch, came toward her. It did not move, more seemed to be blown forward by some soft wind. Kathy's foot that the other branch was wrapped around started to disappear under the mound as the whole mound seemed to open in the middle like a mouth. Wind seeming to blow it open like tall grass swaying in the summer breeze. Only the movements were more of a violent nature. It almost looked like there was a face forming in the center. A face she could not make out as her lungs started to burn and her vision started to cloud..

"Kathy!"

Kathy could hear her grandmother, and felt a searing pain in her foot and also around her ankle where the branch was on her leg. A hand grabbed her and she saw the mound of putrid living mulch move backward.

Everything had a distant sound, and all color started getting darker. She felt a hand grab her torso, it was the man with the gray eyes and cane. He flung her backwards like a piece of clothing.

Her grandmother caught her, and raced around the corner. As they turned the corner. Kathy saw the man that came to visit, watch them turn the corner. He had the branch that was holding her ankle under his cane. There was smoke coming up from the branch under the cane. He had a look of worry in his eyes for her. As he saw they were about to turn the corner, his eyes changing to a cold hard look, turned toward the shed and entered it. The memory ends there, Kathy remembers nothing else.

That was the last time Kathy would ever see that man. It something her grandmother would not ever bring up again.

Kathy, now a good 30+ years older, looked down at the foot that had been caught in that mulch that day. The scar looked like acid had eaten through her skin to the bone, then healed. It was the reason she did not wear sandals of any sort. And only let her feet be bare when she was alone. Kathy does not remember much about the rest of that summer. But she does remember her first time seeing that side of the house again, which was probably a year later. The plants and shed had burned down to the ground. All that was left was dirt so scorched, that some of it was glass. She had looked over in the area for any sign of her dolls. Her mother snatched her and shook the sense out her while yelling,

"Don't you ever go back over there again! You hear me?!?? If I see you over here again, I swear before God that I will tear your little ass up!"

Kathy had never seen her mother have such a wild look on her face before, and had not ever heard her cuss at her. Kathy stayed away from the backyard itself, let alone the side of the house until now. Now she was walking over there. Thirty some years later to see what was there. To see if it had all been just her imagination.

Chapter 3

Kathy had put down her drink and started walking toward the side of the house. From the backyard you would look to the right side of the house. It looked different now. The whole yard had been newly landscaped. It almost looked like a different house's backyard. None of the weeds and overgrown plants remained. After Kathy's grandmother passed her garden seemed to pass with her. Being killed by all the weeds that grew with the plants. Some plants had remained. But most perished. Almost as if they cried out for help as they were being slowly taken over by weeds. The yard on that side of the house looked different, almost as though the old yard had passed with her grandmother.

There was now a full concrete patio behind the house now, then it went into a grass area with the pavers. As Kathy neared the side of the house she started to feel great pressure in her chest. A compounded pressure that seemed to grow as she got closer. All sound seemed to fade away as she walked closer to that side of the house. It seemed the side of the house stretched away from her, with every step she took the side of the house seemed to get further away. Kathy thought to herself, "This is stupid, for more reasons than one. But I am not a little girl anymore. I am a grown woman and that is the way I am going to handle this."

Now feeling, not only apprehension, but some embarrassment because she could not tell if she said that in her head, or out loud. She quickened her pace to the side of the house. And even though it was a mere 70 feet or less to the side of the house. Kathy felt like she had just got through walking a Country Mile. Sweat had started down her back and her legs felt weak. Her heart felt like it was beating overtime while her clothes shook to same rhythm as her heartbeat.

The shed and weeds she remembered were gone. There was a new fence that went all the way around the yard replacing the rickety fence that leaned at an angle that made you wonder how it still stayed up at all. There was now a concrete walkway down the side of the house. The only thing that looked halfway like an old remnant was an old rusted shovel stuck in the ground next to a shallow ditch. There was a mound of strange looking dirt next to the old shovel. The dirt was all types of different colors. It looked like a mix of dirt from different areas. The colors were red, orange, white, yellow, black, and all the different shades of brown. In the ditch, there appeared to be some burned looking rocks. Kathy could see a light reflecting off of some of the dirt. From the distance she was standing at, still hesitant to walk any closer, it looked like a bunch of shattered pieces of a mirror. But as she kept staring, she saw that the pieces were actually glass in the dirt. She started to walk closer to the area. Tried to see deeper into the ditch. There was more glass in there. Not like someone broke a window in it, but more like sand heated to a level that it turned to glass. The dirt looked like it had been dug up in some places, other places were looked hard. Like the dirt had been dry for not just days but years. Only the strongest looking weeds grew from there. And even those seemed to be on the verge of dying.

As Kathy walked closer, the more details seemed to pop out.

There was a smell emanating from the ditch. A stench. At first she thought it was just the smell of mulch. That recycled shredded trash they used to cover dirt on off-ramps from the freeway. Nothing too abnormal for people to use in their backyards. Everytime she went through on her walks when she visited. She would walk some small hills in Berkeley. Every block at least one house had the same mulch smell or something else that seared the nose dry. Many people there loved their yards, so they always were fertilizing it with all manner of things. Constantly landscaping without knowing where they wanted to stop. Almost as if this was their workout. And there was always more to workout, constantly planting new plants whether they matched the rest of the yard or not. The stench she smelled, was not mulch...it was something more rancid.

But there were some smells, Kathy found familiar. She could not put her finger on it. But, there was something familiar to the smell. Kathy walked closer. Standing right near the ditch, she looked in. It was deeper than she thought. That explained why the dirt mound was so high and large. It would need at least that much to fill it in. But the smell. She looked down to the bottom of the ditch. Thinking to herself, "This is not so bad. Maybe Mom was going to put in a Jacuzzi originally and changed her mind."

Some of the dirt at the bottom seemed to move. Kathy frowned. Squinting her eyes to make sure she was not imaging it or seeing a bunch of bugs move thinking it was the dirt. She quickly glanced at the leaves of a tree that stood in the next yard. None of them moved. She felt no wind. Looking back down. The dirt at the bottom appeared to be still. Looking up a little bit higher at a larger piece of glass in the ditch she saw a piece of glass with what looked like a small thin branch inside. It looked smashed and burned, but it was a in the glass. As she moved to reach for that glass, a blast of thick humidity hit her pushed up from the ditch. No wind just heat, hot sticky heat. Like the thick molasses type heat you feel back east or down south in the summertime. But this heat felt worse, and it intensified the rancid smell that was coming from the ditch. Kathy felt as if she could not smell the stench, but felt as if it was covering her. Stepping back she still felt the touch of the heat. Sticking to her. As if homeless person had used a bucket for their waste. Waited for her to walk by and threw it on her on a hot summer day. She started to perspire profusely. Still backing away from the ditch the feeling went away. She could see the waves of heat rising out of the ditch. No where else around it let of the waves of heat, distorting her vision past the ditch. The heat waves seemed to emanate directly from the ditch. First they seemed normal. Then they seemed like they were forming a shape. All the lines seemed to start moving in the consistency of a stream of water flowing in a small stream. In this case, it looked like something was rising to the surface of this stream.

Kathy closed her eyes and shook her head rubbing her eyes. Trying to shake the vision. But when she opened her eyes, the heat waves were still there. But now instead of seeing something emerging, she saw the shape of a face. With features of the face started showing one by one. The forehead, eyebrows, nose, eyes, lips, and chin. The eyes appeared to be closed. The features were so faint, that Kathy thought she was just tired, tripping. Maybe she was sleepy. Turning, to walk away, and too make fun of herself having an over active imagination. She heard boots hit the dirt. Turning quickly she saw a man in a filthy old shirt, work kakis, and work boots. Every piece of clothing looking well worn and faded by the sun. He had quite a bit of dirt on him, looking like he was either a dope fiend, or someone that had been working in dirt all day. Judging from the size of his hands, Kathy leaned toward working in dirt all day. He seemed to be focused on the ditch where the heat waves still emanated, though now, the face in it was complete. The eyes started to open, but then a white powder seemed to hit the back of the heat waves and stop mid air. The mouth of the face flew open in what looked like a cry of pain and rage. Froze in that position then fell down to the ground. The amount of white dirt, powder, whatever it was would not have fell to the ground that quick. It was as if it had been thrown into some water, dropping the same speed as water would fall. Not like heat waves dissipate. The man holding the bag poured the rest of the powder out of the cotton bag he had it in. He seemed very intent on filling the bottom of ditch. Never once looking up at her.

Kathy went to speak to him, but he turned quickly. Snatching the shovel out the dry ground as if it had just been laying on the side of the house. Earth flying in the air behind him from the violence in which he ripped the shovel out. He then started shoveling dirt in to the ditch from the mound. The man was clearly a man that worked outdoors. The sheer power that he worked with showed him to be someone that handled heavy equipment with ease. Kathy, watched him, wanting to ask him who he was and what was doing. She did not want to get too close. He was clearly a very *strong* man. After about a minute went by with him shoveling and seeming to at least be conscious of her standing there. Kathy went to speak, but he spoke before she did.

"Kathy. I know you do not remember me, but I was the one who worked on this yard to get it this way. Your mother hired me. We had not finished this one part over here before her untimely passing."

He kept shoveling with speed and power Kathy had not seen anyone do. It was as if he were trying to plug a hole, or put out a fire. Shoving the shovel into the mound and pulling out a full shovel of dirt, then turning with a strong purpose throwing the dirt down and into the ditch. Like dropping the dirt down there was not enough. He would actually aim the dirt he shoveled at different parts of the ditch. Like there was a method in it that was deeper than just filling the ditch evenly. Kathy feeling more confident moved in to speak with the man, but he started to speak right before she opened her mouth.

"We have known each other since childhood. And I have known you long enough to know that not only your mother, but your grandmother told you not to come on this side of the house."

Thrown off by the man speaking of her Grandmother and Mother, Kathy stopped. And looked at him. He now had a slight smirk on his face that looked very familiar, she still could not place it yet. The man kept smiling as he shoveled a little bit faster. Seeming to get more efficient the longer he went. He continued.

"Your mother and I spoke quite often. She was there for me when my mother passed. She was like the loving Aunt I did not have. So I feel for your loss. I sent flowers I hope that you approved of them."

Kathy had seen many flowers at the funeral. She made a note in her head to go back over who sent what flowers. Her Mother was well loved and respected in the community she lived in. It was not uncommon as a kid for other children to say they wished their Mother was like hers. She always knew how to make any child laugh no matter how scarred, or spoiled the child was she would find the inner light in them and bring it out. No one was her enemy, even people that were determined to hate any, and everyone. Kathy kept thinking to herself, who the hell is this. But once again, before the words came out her mouth.

"You know, we went to school together. From Kindergarten to High School."

He has to be lying. Kathy thought. I would remember something about someone that I went to school with that long for.

"Who are you?" Sounding a bit timid. Kathy then said in as strong a voice as she could muster. "I would think I could remember someone from school." Hitting what she considered her power stance. One hand on her hip and the other hand pointing down at the ground. Making a point pose.

"You left a doll in this area some years ago. Your Mother put it away for safe keeping. She told me it was in the basement in the box without a label. It is the only box without one. We went through this house top to bottom clearing and organizing it. She did not call you because she did not want you to worry about it. Besides that she said she was not ready to show what you needed to know."

Kathy thought to herself, "What do I need to know? And what the hell is he talking about? My Mother did most of the organizing herself, and did not need anyone to help her. She had watched this all her life. From the time of her Father's passing the woman had been a one army machine of organization."

"She normally did mountains of work alone. But because most of the things in the house were from her mother, your grandmother, she needed some support, for the heavier things. Heavy lifting."

The man kept shoveling with a machine like efficiency halfway through the pile. She did feel like she knew him, from school like he said. But she still did not remember his name. Kathy felt floored by the fact her Mother had someone else to help her with all the work. There were so many things she just has not thought about before her Mother passed. It is as if she took her Mother for granted and did not recognize her for the intricate woman she was.

"She spoke highly of you on a daily basis. She always felt you would be highly successful. She said you had, vision, could see." His squinted after the last word, as if he said something he did not mean to say. Trying to hide the fact he felt that way. But his eyes told a different story.

"What do you mean?!?"
"Shit I don't know. She just said you had vision. She always said that. Said something about you could see more than most people before you reached the double digits of your life."
"But what do you mean?" Slight tension, frustration, and confusion came into her voice by accident.
"Lady." Jamming the shovel deep into the ground with what looked liked a building frustration. "I know we have not seen each other in quite some time. But I will tell you right now. Talking to me like you are about to have a nervous breakdown is not going to get any more of an answer out of me than asking me with the home training I know you received. In fact, will probably get me to give you less of an answer. "

He stared at her dead in the eye. Kathy looked at him right back. Then recognition hit her.

"Jerome!"
"Damn! Took you all year." Smile breaking out across his face, "Now I know, I am in my work clothes, but damn! I thought you would never recognize me. Took you all the hints in the world to

finally guess?"

"No. You look different. I would hug you but…."

"I understand. A little filthy. Had to do some work under a house today. Lost my Electrician to some big project taking apart a car plant down in Fremont. He was a new expansion to my business, but really just a friend helping me out for the low pay I was giving him."

Jerome kept on working while talking. Kathy never would have figured he would be the type to be working outside. When they were younger he was always immaculate in his style. Never dirty. Seemed like he could keep a white outfit white even playing basketball with friends. He had definitely gotten bigger. His hands must have been five times bigger. He always had hands that looked manicured. Now they were giant size. They looked like two rocks with metal under the skin. As he shoveled she watched him. He was almost done. Kathy went back to her chair and sat down.

"Jerome"

"Yeah."

"You want something to drink?"

"Nah, I am all right. Gotta get going. I meant to do this days ago. And don't worry. I will jump back over the fence I jumped over to get in when I leave."

"You don't have to do that."

He kept on working without answering. She looked over to see if he heard her. But his face looked more intense than last time. So she let him work. Sounds of the shovel going into the dirt then coming back out taking away the fear she was fighting just a few minutes ago. She started to feel sleepy. Fought it off by taking a drink and then stretching. A couple of minutes later. After she got through stretching Kathy noticed she did not hear any more shoveling. She heard Jerome moving and picking up his stuff. She went to check on him, but all she saw was him grab the top of the fence and jump over with one leap. He grabbed the top of the fence and looked as if he threw himself over. He did not say bye. Or seem to see what she saw in the ditch. Kathy decided to go into the house and look in the basement for that box he talked about.

Once she got inside, Kathy grabbed a glass and poured some water. She downed it like people down shots on Spring Break. She then went to the sink and washed her face off. She then headed for the doorway to the basement, which was located under the stairs to the second floor. She opened the door, turned on the light switch. To her amazement it was not the old looking, dusty dark, place where her Grandmother kept her jars of Jam, hat boxes, and other stuff. It was now dust free, fully lit, the stairs were new and there were new storage units built against the walls. New carpet was on the ground and there were vents from the heater pointed down into the room, and insulated walls all the way around. It looked like a new room, not a basement.

Kathy walked down the stairs in a state of shock looking around. Why she had not come down here in her week of staying here was beyond her. But now looking around the room she started to look through the wood shelving that had been built against the walls. Everything was labeled. So to cut time searching, she started looking for a box that was not labeled. She found it. It was not on a shelf. It was on the floor. Right next to a shelf. It was a small box. It had been opened recently. All the other boxes were taped shut. On this one the tape had been cut. A doll's head stuck out the top.

Kathy grabbed the box and put it on the nearest table in the room.

She then opened it. The doll was the one she had been playing with the day she had the incident. In Kathy's mind now she still thought if it as her imagination. In the box, there was the doll, a dress, and two shoes. The dress was smeared with mud and something else brown that she could not quite make out. One shoe was in perfect condition. The other looked like some type of liquid had eaten away at it. The top left side of it was gone. The side all the way down to the sole of the shoe seemed eaten away. The inner sole of the shoe with the name of the company that makes them had the same brown stain as the dress.

Kathy stared at this. Slowly it dawned on her that the stain was blood. The shoe was the one that was burned through when she was being held. The blood must have come from the lacerations. But it could not have been some dirt, leaves, and thorn laden branches that grabbed her. That did not make any sense.

It was beginning to feel like she was in the middle of some bunk horror movie that teenage boys would take girls to just to try to get them to react it.

"I refuse to believe this mess."

Kathy said aloud, more to help herself to believe in the words she spoke. As if hearing them aloud would make her feel better. And it did, were it not for the fact she felt something hard in the blood stain at the bottom of the dress. The blood had dried there making the dress stick together. When she pulled open the stained part of the dress to see what felt that way. She found a thorn, stained brown by the blood that covered it and the dress.

Kathy looked at the dress, the thorn in it. She started to wonder how much blood had she lost. And why did she remember the events like she did. There were too many unanswered questions. So many things she should have asked her mother when she was around.

Kathy spent the rest of the night in thought. She sat in the house thinking. No music, no drinks, no food. She just sat on the couch watching the rest of the day turn into night. From everyone coming home, to kids playing in the street, to families eating and couples walking together talking into the late of night. She fell asleep in the dark with the curtains open. Her sitting on the couch, covered by her mother's blanket. A blanket that still held the smell of her mother. Giving some comfort to how confused and lost she felt. Was she crazy? If Mom was around, would she tell me about what happened if it was true? Was it just my imagination going wild, or did some type of accident happen to hurt my foot like that?

Those questions and many more swirled in Kathy's head even in sleep. She could hear voices, but discern no words. Not paying attention she kept asking herself questions.

"Kathy. Kathy! I know you hear me."

The voice sounded familiar. Young, but confident, maybe even wise.

"I hear you."
"I would have told you everything."
"Everything about what? Who are you?'
Suddenly realizing she was dreaming, Kathy started to wake up.

A face appeared, young, and beautiful. Kathy almost thought she was looking at herself. The woman's skin was beautiful, her hair was done perfectly. Her eyes looked young physically, but seemed to have the a very wise look to them. Kathy felt the dream slipping and her waking up. The face seemed to move back futher away from her getting smaller. As the face got smaller due to distance or a return to conciousness, Kathy heard the woman say,

"Your Mother."

Kathy woke, to find the sun shining in the window. She immediately got up, took a shower and went off for a long walk, not just to get some coffee but to clear her head. Crazy dreams and memories need to be cleared as of today.

Later that day, Henry , the family Attorney, called to find out when Kathy would be able to come in for the Viewing and Reading of the Will. She would have to be there with a lady that she refused to name in her head with her brood of imps. Imps because she was the Mother Demon, by the name of Angela.

The next day came like skipping to the next chapter of a DVD. Kathy was walking out the door when Jerome called to her from across the street. It was yesterday when he stopped her from going down the side of the house she had been ever more curious about him. How did he know about the scorched side of the house? Did someone let him see it, or was he being a bad kid and jumping the fence to get into the backyard? Jerome did run with a few kids that loved to, "get into something", that was the term that they and many others used to describe the trouble they get caught or not get caught for doing. Always hopping fences, getting chased by dogs, neighbors, old people, college students, older kids that would later become thugs, and last but not least the police.

No one thought of Jerome as a bad kid back then. He was just mischievous. Not harmful. And as much as he got into trouble

during his preteen years, he rarely got into a fight. He would fight.
He was just not that good at it, but he seemed to *will* his way into
winning. He would not stop until the other person stopped, gave
in, or ran away. But most of the time, Jerome was the one to stop
fights from ever happening.

He was a dark skinned child with short hair. He was not very tall,
slim, but seemed to be pretty strong. Even the fat kids had a
problem throwing him around when they boys would wrestle. As
he grew older, he began to be aware of his appearance. Going
from all day dirt smells, with grass or dirt in his hair to always
smelling and looking clean. Asking Kathy if she wanted to go
swimming in waves of his short hair, meaning the hairstyle he had
was wavy. Perfected by the do-rag he wore at night. Something
he took great pride in. Often telling people with larger curls, that
his, "good hair", was, "Better than that mixed hair the some of you
fools got. This hair on my head is straight from Africa. Your shit
is lost without a place!"

Girls started to chase him by the dozens, by the time the time they
got to High School. He wore all the newest styles in clothes. No
one knew where he got the money from to buy all that, but most
did not care. Maybe the kids that went to school together from
elementary onward did. But the kids who had just met him in High
School loved him. The guys respected him and the girls seemed to
want to fall down all over him. He would flash his perfect tooth
smile, and all the girls, including a few teachers, would get weak.

By High School, Kathy herself had started to see him in a different
light when they spoke from time to time. He seemed much more
relaxed around her. Around others he would usually be telling
about this or that incident and everyone around him hanging on
every word. With her, he was much quieter. Always asking her

about her mother and how she herself was doing. Kathy would talk and he would look her in her directly in the eye. Making sure she knew he was listening to every word. More than a few of her friends would tell Kathy that Jerome liked her, but she refused to let herself believe it. There were girls falling all over him, and he was letting them fall right into his bed, if, they fit what he liked. And as far as Kathy could see, she was a little too dark for him. Most of the girls he slept with were very light skinned, and always had long hair. Kathy was a milk chocolate brown. Her hair was long, but her skin tone definitely did not pass the paper bag test.

This fact Jerome liked light skinned girls angered many of the girls at school that were of a darker complexion, which was most of the girls there. Many made comments like, "Light bright and damn near white! That is all that boy likes!" But they always made sure they knew exactly where he was before they said that. Because if he was near them, the flirt games went into full effect. Laughing at anything, comments made on his outfits, skin, hair, etc..... Kathy was usually walking off by then. Always with Jerome asking

"Where are you headed to?"

Cutting off any female talking to him to find out about Kathy. Looks of murderous, seething hate, coming from each and every girl around him, directed at her. She did not ask him to ask her anything. She did not try to get in the way of their flirtation. But Kathy knew, that was exactly why they would stare so hard, openly showing hatred and total contempt toward her. Because she was walking away, and here they are begging, for attention from a man they do not know, but desperately want to know.

"Class. I will talk to you later. Tell your mother I said hi."
"Kathy…"

"We will talk later. You live across the street."

Envy would cloud the eyes of every girl in the area while they watched Kathy walk away. Hearing that she, lived right across from Jerome. Knowing that last statement would irk all the girls in the area. She had grown tired of being hated on for something she had no control over. But that last comment was just enough to let them know that there was at least a relationship there between the two. That could not be taken away by their hate. Her best friend often said, he only paid special attention to her. Kathy did not openly admit to herself then. But she knew she liked Jerome. And in fact had fantasized many times of them being together as boyfriend and girlfriend. She just refused to let herself believe, that her fantasy could be reality.

Now, here he was coming across the street, umpteen years later. Not as the man-child he was, but as the full grown man he is now, in an Italian suit. Dark blue with light blue lines running down the jacket and the pants. Not loose fitting, like what her Uncle referred to as Cartoon Suits. Jerome's suit was tailored. And matched and enhanced the look of the strong body beneath. His shoulders and arms showed through the his jacket. Slight outlines of the muscles that lay beneath the dark blue fabric. Some very nice Italian shoes of an Azure Blue color. Light blue shirt, with a tie that matched perfectly with the shoes. He strode across the street as if he was about to grab the car at her curb and move it out the way of them. Kathy found herself putting an extra sway in her hips as she walked toward him. Felt as if she was floating toward him. It was just yesterday he had stopped her from going down the side of the house. The clothes he had on made him look as though he had dug himself out of a grave, with his work boots a very dirty worn out shirt and khakis. He was so dirty she thought for a minute she was about to be jacked by some crack addict. Now here he stood before her clean, and looking very much like a grown man about to do some grown man business. Impressed, and feeling to old to pretend she was not feeling him, Kathy spoke.

"You look nice! Looks like you are a man made for suits Jerome."

Jerome smiled clearly enjoying Kathy's reaction to him.

"Just about to go to the bank then a meeting. But had to try to steal some attention from this lady who came back to town. She is quite the looker herself. As a matter of fact, I have to dress like this to match up with her on her worst day. That lady's style is perfection." Sly smile spread across his face revealing perfectly straight white teeth. The smile was the same. With more of a grown man's edge to it. He had aged, but only in looking far more solid, stronger. Very little age showed on him.

Kathy felt her face warm as he spoke to her. They hugged tightly. To her, it felt as if she was hugging a stone statue with a suit on. His body was hard as a rock. From his shoulders down to his stomach. He, on the other hand, felt her soft body melt into him. Soft, supple. They both stepped back from the hug, not knowing just how much the other liked it. But neither wanting to make assumptions or cross barriers.

They spoke for a small amount of time after the hug, both feeling teenage levels of nervousness after the hug. They agreed to find a time to get together soon. Jerome, not wanting to miss an opportunity immediately said he would check on her later that evening. Maybe do dinner. Kathy replied that would work for her. She had absolutely no plans after the reading of the Will. And would be more than happy to have dinner with a drink, because she was sure it would be needed.

Kathy drove over to Lake Merritt which was a large lake in Oakland, about three miles total if you walked all the way around it. There were small restaurants and shops all the way around. People would exercise there, take their kids, or walk their dogs. When the season changed from summer to fall, and it got dark earlier, small white, Christmas lights would glow on the trees and in between lamp posts. Encircling the entire lake. Many couples, from Teenagers to Senior Citizens snuggle up next to each other. Using each other to warm from the nippy breezes that always seem to give a nice night a frosty bite. The parking however, not so romantic.

Kathy finally found a parking space in a two hr parking zone. She walked what seemed a half a mile to the office. Entering the building, which never had an elevator, she climbed the stairs to the 3rd floor. As she entered she saw Angela and her ill mannered children. Angela was the only one sitting. Her children were picking up and examining different pieces of anything. Magazines, books, pens, paper, pictures off the wall....etc.

"Hi Kathy." Angela said with the most sarcastic and fake tone of concern.
"The funeral was so beautiful. And the way you had her dressed, the Eulogy, all just so lovely. You know. I think that is the way she would have wanted it to be." Angela sat back legs together but turned to the side, hands place ever so properly in her lap over her skirt. Back as straight as she could make it, which was quite the feat for someone normally slouched down in her seat with he legs spread wide open, belly and private parts seeming to burst forward for all to see through her clothes.

Kathy guessed this was the same Angela that was at her mother's house not too many days before, a very grown woman, trying to sit properly, and, "Be good", like a child that has been bad all year, then come Christmas, and she wants to be good to get all the gifts she *thinks* she deserves. Like lying to someone about a court date, they get a warrant and are arrested because of that lie. You go to church and repent your sin of lying to clear your name and conscious of what you just did. Hypocritical. As if God will not see through your sham.

Kathy suppressed all the seething hatred she felt toward Angela. She reached in to herself.   DEEP, into herself. Took a deep breath and said.

"Why thank you Angela."

Angela almost let a the shock she felt from the sincerity of the statement reach her face. Angela, by nature, being scandalous, had to say,

"Those boots you got on are raw girl, how much they cost?"
"I really don't remember. I think they…"
"But, I did notice they had a scratch on the side of the right heel . And I don't mean to hate but…."
"I see your children are not starving, maybe if you fed them less, you too, could afford these boots and not trip on a minor scratch because there many more to choose from in my walk in closet."

Angela rocked back in her chair as if she had to suck in air and swell her chest to get started with a comeback. But it was too late. Kathy had turned at the last word and stood to greet Henry with a warm shake of the hand with words of gratitude too low for Angela to hear over her children talking at volume 10 in an office setting.

Henry was a man in his sixties. Bald as a bowling ball with a halo of gray hair around his bald spot. He had grown a gray beard to the same length as his closely cropped halo of hair. His suit was a throwback to the 1980's. Probably fit him loosely back then, but now fit him very snug in the midsection. He had a stance closer to that of a Mortuary Worker than that of an Attorney that represented a good portion of the black folk with any decent level of money in Oakland. He had no lack of clients, and all of his clients were through word of mouth. No advertising. Five Foot Eight inches and about 220 pounds. He would be easy to take him for a joke, except that he had sharp eyes, and an extremely strong grip in his little hands.

"Kathy, how are you holding up?"
"As well as I can. As you know it is not easy."
"Yes, I do know. But take solace in the fact that this is the last time you have to deal with such needless dramatics." Looking past Kathy directly at Angela and brood, then back to Kathy. He added an extra squeeze to her hand. Sending a message without saying it aloud of, I am as sick of them, as you are. A look of genuine feeling for Kathy crossed his face and cleared just as quick as he said in a solid, but confident tone of a man that is not to be trifled with.

"Angela, you come in. All the children stay out here. Ms. Johnson."
"Yes Mr. Chenault"
"If they cause you too much of an issue. Have them go outside the office, if there is a problem with that, come get me. Too much damage has already been done from on past visits here."
"Yes Mr. Chenault."

Kathy was shocked. Not about the damage Angela's kids had

done, or the fact the Henry had asked his young Receptionist to have them escorted out by Security. But the fact that Angela had been here many times before. What was she here for? And how long ago? Was it before or after her mother died. If it was before, things would be getting more personal. Henry, looking at Kathy could see what she was thinking.

"Angela has been by in the last week almost everyday. Isn't that right Angela."

Angela, standing a few feet to the side of both of them, looked at Henry with unbridled shame, fury, and hatred. From what Kathy could see, Henry did not back off and seemed to be daring her with his eyes to do something more than stare at him. Seemed that Henry could be quite assertive. Kathy had never seen this side of him before.

Angela looked down at the ground as Henry stared at her for a few more seconds as he made the statement,

"We will go to the conference room at the very end of the hall to the right. It is the only doorway there."

Henry stared at Angela until she understood that was an order for her to walk down the hallway in front of him to the conference room.

"Hold all calls for me. This is going to take awhile."

As they entered the conference room, Kathy noticed he had all his paperwork laid out already. Waiting for them. There were three folders. One for him and two for them.

"Kathy, yours is the larger folder."

As they sat down, Henry's personal assistant came in offering coffee, tea, bagels, or donuts. Angela, true to form, acted as if she was on stage for an Oscar for placing an order at Mctonall's.

"Do you have Starluck's or Wheet's coffee?"
"Neither"
"Do you all have Ethopian Bean coffee?"
"No."
"Well what is it you have?!?"

Henry sensing where this was going, cut her off.

"Bring Angela the Coffee, with a cup. Also bring in all the sugar, non sugar, cream of any type. Dairy, Non Dairy. All the donuts and Bagels, with all the butter, cheese, and whatever else we have. Put it all there in front of her and she can put together whatever she needs."

Angela looked offended but said nothing. Henry said, "Now, lets get down to business."

Henry started to explain all the basics of what this meeting was for. Explained all the paperwork page by page. He then stopped and told them before they completed all the paperwork there was a video for both of them to watch.

Chapter 4

Henry got up. He then grabbed a VHS tape and inserted it into a very dusty VHS player. "Had to dig this player out of the storage room." Henry laughed nervously, avoiding all eye contact. Once the tape was inserted he made sure it was rewound all the way. The VHS Tape looked new. But the TV and the VHS player looked dusty. Just like he said, out of storage. Probably in the back of the storage area. Untouched for years. There were signs that he tried to dust it. But the dust on it was so old it was the kind that is like grease on the fan cover over the stove in kitchen that has fried years worth of chicken, pork chops, steak, and an assortment of breakfast foods. Thick and sticky. The dust was not what you would call sticky like the grease. But it sure did hold to the surface with similar consistency of grease. You would need to use some type of chemical to clean it all off.

An image of Kathy's Mother appeared on the screen. She was younger. Judging by her looks this was shot at least 30 years ago. Right here in the conference room they were all in. The wall to her mother's back looked the same, but the rug and other furniture seems to have been upgraded over the last couple of years. Kathy watched her mother asking Henry if she should start speaking yet. Kathy herself would have been I in preschool at the most when this was shot. Her mother's hair was shoulder length, and curled up at the ends, a style she maintained by sleeping in giant rollers to maintain. Out in they wold come in the morning. Her face did not yet have the lines of age, or life quite yet. Her eyes were just now showing the beginnings of what Kathy would call the, "You can lie to me, but I see straight through you.", look. Her brownish yellow skin was smooth and her makeup was minimal. Looking at her, Kathy was struck by how much she looked like her mother. Their noses were both slightly round but not flat. Both have full lips. Kathy's skin was darker. More chocolate to her mother's caramel color. She was taller and bigger woman than her mother. Her legs were long and her shoulders were wide, but her hips more than matched that width. Her breasts were prominent. Kathy's mother had gained weight before she passed. But even with the extra weight, she had been just average on top. Her arms had gotten bigger, but her shoulders and her torso remained small. Her hips and legs had gotten bigger, gained a small stomach, but no where near as much as the other women she knew in her age group.

The original camera view, was from far back. The cameraman, Henry, zoomed in closer so that the shot would only show her mother from the shoulders up instead of her whole body on the stool. As the camera zoomed in she could see that her mother was focused more and more as the camera framed her.

"Kathy and Angela. If you both are watching this, it means that I have passed on."

She paused and seemed to look deeper into the camera. It almost felt as though she was looking through the camera then and seeing both of them sitting now, looking far different than they did as children. Kathy now toned and grown. When she was a child, chubby, and very much the child. Angela was skinny, and seemed mature. Now so overweight you would not be able to tell who she was if someone put her 5th grade class picture up, then asked you to find her on the picture. Angela used to have long healthy hair. It is not short now but, it is now filled with gel to slick it back into a ponytail. Dirty enough to be smelled when she walked by. Hardly every washing it. So you could smell the dirt, sweat, stress, and children in her hair. Kathy, also had long healthy hair as well when she was younger. Always had barrettes in her hair of different colors on different days. Her mother took pride in taking care of both of their hair. Kathy however went off into life keeping on taking care of not just her hair, but her body and soul. Angela ate any and every thing. Allowing her kids to do the same. She did not work out, or even try to stay in decent condition. It seemed that she was so disappointed in her life that she took it out on her own body. Somewhat knowingly. Denial seemed to be not just her motto but her one triumph. Ignoring just how bad she had done in life. How much of a scavenger she turned into. Always trying to feed off of anyone she could take from, if they believed the tragic exaggerations she told them. Never considering any but herself, not even her own children in some cases. Even though lately, she seemed to be more of a true mom. And less of the woman that used to drop of her kids at the drop of a dime at Kathy's mother's house with no notice. Because she, "Needs a break. Got to go get myself together." Which would not be so bad, if she would call and ask ahead of time. But she would pop up at the door with kids and bags in tow. Soon as the door was answered, the piglets were pushed in and she turned around and left many times without stating when she would be back. Kathy would chastise her mother for letting Angela do that, even threatened Angela one time in front of her kids. If it were not for her mother she would have gotten Angela to pay physically for what she put on her mother. But her mother would just tell her,

"I know you do not understand. But this is what I have to do."
"What!?!? Take care of *her* kids?!?? Momma?!?? "
"Stop…… You may not understand. And one day I will tell you why. I have made some mistakes, and you will too in life. But just understand this is something I have to do."
"Momma I cannot understand for the life of me *why*, you have to do this. She is disrespectful, conniving, and definitely does not appreciate the love you show her. And it has always been that way!"
"Listen. That is enough Kathy! She may not be your sister in blood. But there is something you both share that will bond you as sisters for as long as I draw breath. It is the only way to protect you two."
"From what?!?? Angela's desperate need to end up homeless with all her children? Just how does that affect us?"
"Look. I really do not have to explain it. And stop with all the attacks. You are a grown woman now, and if you would come visit or talk to me more often when we both have time, I could tell you everything. But not right now."

Kathy's memory faded, looking back at the screen she saw what she could swear was her mother looking directly at Angela through the TV. A look of pity, and loss of understanding as to what happened crossed her face for the most brief of moments. She then centered where she was looking to the center of the screen.

"Angela. Your mother and I were best friends from what seemed like birth." She looked down and smiled as if lost in the memories what Angela's mother.

"She was the best friend I ever had in life. Her passing ripped a piece of me out. It was a pain I never quite recovered from. Our relationship as friends was more like having a sister. A sister that was far from perfect in every way. But I loved her, and I want to believe she loved me in the same way."

Her face fell. She stared at the ground for a few seconds. Both Angela and Kathy thought she might cry for a moment. Angela looked as though at any moment she was about to say, "Fast forward this shit and get to the money I am getting!"
Kathy sat trying to ignore the intensification of the hatred she was feeling toward Angela. A woman who was not her blood sister, but raised by her mother as if she were. Angela did not appreciate any of the help her mother had given her. The cars, buying a home, helping her with bills, childcare, or money issues period. Angela always wanted more. Always needed more. There would never be enough. Kathy felt as though her mother would have died soon one way or another supporting this GROWN WOMAN sitting across the table from her.

Henry watched the two sitting across the table from each other. Watching the tension mount between the two. The tension filled the room. Even though the conference table was wide and sturdy. To look at them, or even be blind and feel them in the room, you knew that these two needed more room between them. It seemed as if he was not here, two would go in this room and one would come out. There would be no yelling. No cursing back and forth. No screams. One would be dead and the other would not. So deep was their hatred that he wondered how it had started. Kathy was a good person. Had not been in a fight in her life, as far as he knew. No one he knew disliked her. Angela on the other hand had beat and been beat several times due to her mouth and attitude of getting over on people. He stepped closer to make sure they stayed separated. There was a silent war going on. He looked up back at the TV. Sylvia, Kathy's mother, so beautiful when she was young. Never opened up to him on a personal level. She was remarkably intelligent. Had a way about her that seemed downright magical. Any time she did say OK to lunch with him, all the men in the restaurant would take a couple of glances. No one would drool, but she was attractive enough for men to check for her. Her beauty was just right to him. All the Divorcees that came into his office that were extremely attractive, enjoyed attention too much. Seemingly willing to do anything for the attention. Which is something he did not like. And since he was their lawyer, they would reveal just about everything in how they set up the divorce to go their way, not all, but far too many in his opinion. Meanwhile they were doing everything their supposed worthless cheating husband was doing, and some. Including flirting with him. He would sit and not pass judgment, but in the back of his head he loathed some of his clients. But it was because of them he was able to afford to do his pro- bono work with women that were truly in need. He worked free for abused women, Sexual Harassment suits, Hospital lawsuits where Doctors messed up and ruined a child's life with the wrong decisions, or in some cases ended up killing a child because they were not treating these black babies like what they were, babies, young children. Instead ignoring pleas from the mother of the child to do further checks on their child because they feel something deeper is wrong.

These were the women he respected. And Sylvia was definitely one of those. Many were so poor and did not even have money to get around like they needed to. He would help with all these things until the case was over, or even longer in some cases. Sylvia's young face looked up, as if she saw him. He let himself think that she was looking dead at him. Her face turned cold, stoic. She then said.

"Angela, I paid my debt to you while I was alive. Now that I have passed, I would like for Kathy receive my full estate. The only thing I leave to you is your mother's quilt she started but did not finish. Henry will have the information on where you can find it." Her face softened, and she turned slightly. Her eyes full of emotion, tears immediately welling to the rim.

"Kathy. There are so many things I want to tell you. There will be another video I leave for you. And it will be for you alone."

Sylvia looked into the camera like she was looking through it and into the room Angela, Kathy, and Henry were in. Giving them all a moment of tension, and a slight amount of fear. This was the woman they had all just attended the funeral of. Yet it seemed like this tape was some sort of gateway, working like a video conference. One where she dialed from the Death Side, and they answered on the Life Side. Abruptly, Sylvia stopped looking around. Her eyes looked down at her hands. Her voice full of authority and finality, she said.

"That is all."

The Video snapped out of focus and a loud buzz tore out of the speakers like a chainsaw at its highest setting. The TV went off. Henry standing holding the remote, finger on the power button to turn it off. Looked somewhat shocked. Angela's mouth was open. Hand on the table like she lost all strength. She turned toward Kathy. Henry immediately cut in before a word could be said. His face drawn tight. As if he was trying to hold back feelings. Kathy could not tell if those feelings were because he had to deal with Angela, or something else. She would have to ask him later.

Because it did not take a psychic to tell he was deeply troubled…..or perplexed by something. Henry then said,

"Angela, come with me. Kathy. You go to my office. I will meet you there."Angela looked like she was not going to move, but Henry was by her side in an instant helping her stand by pulling her up gently but firmly by her elbow. Angela was quite surprised by his strength. It snapped her out of her disbelief. She then started to walk out. Henry and Angela leaving Kathy alone in the conference room. Where Kathy sat for a couple of minutes before getting up to leave. She wanted to watch that tape over and over again just to see and hear her mother again. The fact that she seemed to see them in the room was of secondary importance to her. She wanted to hear her again. To make up for all the times she had not called her mother back because something she felt was more important had to be dealt with. When in truth she just simply did not feel like speaking to her mother at all. Was she really any better than Angela? Kathy pondered this question for a couple of minutes. Then stood, and walked to Henry's office.

Henry's office had not been upgraded since the 1980s. He still had some of that cheap wood panel wall with a desk that looked like it was rickety when he first bought it. It too screamed 1980 something. The wood look wallpaper peeling along the bottom. The chrome steel legs, and the rug that was thick, but old. It probably was a beautifully rich green color when it was new. Had to be expensive to last so many years and still seem thick. The color however, had faded to a camouflage look. It was brown in some areas, green and tan in others. There were files, law books, and paper everywhere. Stack high on the desk, built up on the ground. Oddly, you could see there was organization in the way all the books and paperwork had been placed.

Henry's receptionist Kim came in and asked if Kathy would like some water. Kathy replied no. Kim smiled and gave Kathy a look that said she felt for her pain. She had known Kathy's mother Sylvia for years. Kim herself was pushing 50. But looked to only be in her late 30s or early 40s. She was not tall 5'4". But she was solidly in the size 16+ group. She kept her hair weaved up in the newest of styles, done so well it almost looked like it was her real hair grown from the root. Her outfits were classy but sexy at the same time. She kept a pair of high heels on. Kathy had yet to see her out of heels in all the years she had seen her. And thinking about it, meant she was even shorter than she originally thought. Everything about the woman was impeccable. She was one of the ladies that would always attract men through her sheer femininity and poise.

Henry entered the room as Kim was leaving. They exchanged glances. Kathy saw the pure fire of that split second the two passing each other. Kim and Henry had been getting together! Too funny the thought of shiny bald, and sexy plump together. It was all too cliché. The boss and the receptionist.

"Sorry about that. This video...... What's so funny?"

Henry looked up from the DVD he was carrying, forehead wrinkled and a look of pure confusion, but yearning to know what was funny written all over his face. Kathy noticed only his forehead wrinkled up, his bald spot stayed smooth.

"Kim say something?"
"No. Just thinking about something. You were telling me about the DVD."

Henry studied Kathy's face for a second while she tried not to laugh in his. For some reason that little moment was taking her back to childhood in High School. When something funny happens and the teacher has no clue. Everyone trying to not say a thing. But the urge to laugh almost too much. Usually someone would fall out, then everyone else, like one domino falling on the next. A chain reaction. But Kathy thanked God, there was no one there that could start laughing other than her. Henry picked up on the fact that Kathy was really not going to tell him and broke out a nervous grin.

"Ok then. Your mother made a DVD two weeks ago. She felt like she needed to update this video for you every 3 years or so. She had just made one last year. But she just made this one recently. Something must have changed. She never told me what, but I am sure you will hear first hand."

Henry's looked down at the DVD like a man trying to figure out the hardest puzzle of his life. Perplexed, a look he had after the other Tape had played. Kathy took this in. She did not say a word.

"She would come to me and ask about when I was available to make a new one. This is the only one she did not make with me. She made this at home. She gave it to me and told me this is for your eyes only. I have not watched it."

Henry then pulled up the biggest laptop Kathy had ever seen and turned it around so it faced her. It was already on. Her pressed the eject button for the DVD player.

"I will leave the room. All you have to do after I leave is place the DVD in the drive and it will start automatically."

Kathy nodded her head in acknowledgment as the man got up to leave. The door closed, and for a moment, Kathy was frozen. This DVD was heavy in her hand. Not from the physical weight of it. But from what she was about to do. She had lifted it but refused to take it further than that. She at a mental impasse trying to put it in the computer. She was consciously telling her hand to put the DVD in. But it would not respond.

Kathy's head dropped for a moment. She then took a deep breath and pushed the DVD in the slot. After several seconds of the software loading to the play the DVD, it started to play. Kathy's mother's face popped up on the screen. She looked tired. Like she had been up several nights in a row. Sylvia was a strong woman, and normally seemed almost jovial through any type of stress. But now, she looked downright worn to the bone. Her eyes were red. Her hair looked like it had been freshly done at the shop, but limp. She had on a nice business suit, but Kathy could see that she was worn to the bone tired. She looked smaller than the last time she had seen her. And this was over video which normally makes someone look lager. The weight loss was something Kathy had attributed to her passing. She had an Aneurism. But she could see now that the weight loss was due to something else that was going on. Her mother's face, eyes, and manner seemed to state it.

"Kathy. I know you are sitting there. Reading the look on my face. Taking in what you are seeing. I probably do not need to even talk for you to know what I have been going through."

A sudden vision of Kathy's mother's face sweating, her hair flattened by perspiration. Her eyes pointed down like her head could not move, just her eyes. Her mouth moving in rapid fire, saying words faster than Kathy had ever seen her mother speak. She could not hear her, but she sensed there was a great deal of heat. Kathy could not see the whole scene, but she knew there was a fire burning in front of her mother. The flickering yellow light reflected of her face and eyes. The colors changed from yellow, to blue. Kathy then noticed her mother was staring right at her. Mouth still moving, but a pleading look had now crossed her face. Slowly she started to hear a voice talking. Then she remembered where she was. Her mother was still talking from the computer. But it seemed as if Kathy herself ended up going somewhere. Like a dream but much more real. Kathy then focused on the computer in front of her to hear the rest.

"You have a gift of sight. Vision. It will not always manifest itself as a vision. Sometimes it will be a feeling. Other times it will be you just knowing something. Not a guess. Not feeling as though it was from something in your past leading you to believe this is the outcome. It will be as much fact to you as you sitting here and watching this DVD play. You know the DVD is playing otherwise you would not hear or see anything I am saying. That is not a guess, it is a solid fact. And that is what you will experience from time to time. What you will see in your mind's eye will be a concrete fact to you."

Kathy took in what she was saying.

"Your Grandmother used to tell me to educate you on this. But I felt like there was no need for you to know any of this. Your life was so different than mine, let alone hers. You did not have to deal with the troubles or have to worry about protection too much. Out here in California, there is less to worry about. its not like Louisiana was when I was young."

Suddenly looking to the side of the camera. An action her mother did so quick it looked unnaturally fast.

"There is not much time for me to tell you. Hopefully we can talk, and you will not see this DVD. But just in case we do not. Here are a few things you need to know. You do not know your father because he does not know you were conceived. Your Grandmother was Priestess of some kind but she never told me what. Angela's mother and I found out I possessed a control of the unseen. Magic, or a control of things, around me. I can sense them but cannot see them all the time. There are many things that are older than any known religion or children's tales. My friend, Angela's mother, Natalie, and I. Both explored what I could do. But in that process we gave away ourselves to being attacked. Natalie had very little gifts or powers. She believed she had more power than what she truly possessed. And it is because of that she died. She thought she could control things that were not natural to this world. Those things are more vile and wretched than anything that I have seen before or since. I will tell you what happened."

In the mid 60s, there was a shop down the street from where we lived as teenagers, in Lousiana. Natalie was a little wild. She loved boys and that is how she ended up with Angela. Angela was only a couple years old by then. Natalie's mother used to take care of her. Natalie herself was not that pretty of a girl. She had all right features and did not keep her hair up. Her clothes were always a little faded, and always well worn. She had cotton shirts, and every last one of them had the little cotton naps from being washed over and over. All her colored clothes were faded, and her whites dingy. Natalie's parents were not rich but would offer then force her to go buy clothes. She just did not care too much for them or her appearance. What she had that was so appealing to boys and men, was a body that came straight from the motherland. She was a curvaceous girl. Not thick. Everywhere they walked men would stare at her. She knew it and would give them something to watch. Many women would tell her to stop walking like that, and she would speak right back to them in the most snappy tone possible. Leaving them saying something like, "You would think your mother taught you better than that!" Women would leave the area before they snatched her up by her neck for her attitude when they were trying to help her to be a young lady instead of the fast girl she was. One of her male cousins told her if she keep walking around like that she was going to get raped. She laughed at him, told him he should wish a girl like her would give him some play.

Rodney, Natalie's cousin, was in his early twenties. Sylvia had always liked him. He could fix anything, did odd jobs all over the Louisiana. A man full of adventure. His accent was thick, but when he would come up from under a car on a hot day with half his coveralls open, Sylvia would feel a tingle unlike any other she had felt to that point. He was not a big man. Small actually. Not too tall. About 5'9" but he had huge hands. Looked like they were thick enough to grab steel pipe and squeeze it with one hand. Leaving an imprint of his fingers.

After Natalie made her crazy comment to Rodney just stared at her. All emotions crossed his eyes. But none more than the look that said, You don't hear me now, but when them boys come for you, don't call me. It was nothing he said. But the look in his eye said it all.

"Come on Sylvia. Let's get away from this fool."
"Do you ever think he may just be trying to protect you?"
"From what? A lugnut on a car? A broken Toilet?!??"

Natalie fell out laughing. She was looking at Sylvia with tears in eyes she was laughing so hard
"You know he probably like you too. I see the way you look at

him. He like girls like you. Quiet. Nice. Good 'home training'."

With that she fell out laughing some more. Sylvia was slightly
hurt. But she knew Natalie was feeling extra good today. She had
went and got what was supposed to be some what some people
referred to as 'enticing smell' to attract men to her. An old woman
made it from knowledge handed down to her from her people. No
one doubted it worked because this old woman had a man half her
age, not only that, he was good looking.

Natalie met a man named Charlie. He refused to lay with her.
Saying that he would wait until she was older. Because she was
special. Natalie did not feel special in that way. She wanted this
big man badly. He was a cook down at some white folks mansion
about 13 miles away.   He was big, brown, and burly. Natalie
liked that. And had told Sylvia she was going to be with him, and
if he was good at it. She might find him to be that type of man to
stay with for life.

Sylvia had always marveled at how many men, even knowing
Natalie's reputation would state how much they wanted to take
care of her, and how much they cared, not just saying it, would
prove it. Treating her as if she was the Virgin Mary, even though
she was quite the opposite. No one came up to Sylvia with those
proclamations. And she *was* a virgin. It was amazing to her that
they gave Natalie all the special treatment that she had heard many
boys and men say was reserved for girls or women that were quite
the opposite of her. Sylvia gave it up to Natalie. She knew how to
work men.

Sylvia and Natalie parted ways. Natalie going home to freshen up
and put on some of that enticing smell. After Natalie had
freshened up, Charlie came by and picked her up. He did not have

a car, so they walked. Charlie asked to come in, but Natalie did not want him to see her mother laid across the floor. Bottle to chest, throw up on the side of her mouth. It was an embarrassment to her. So when he tried to step in saying that he wanted to do the right thing and ask her parents if she could come out with him, she walked right up to him and caressing his head softly. Speaking softly,

"My mother told me to let you know she thinks you are a fine man."
"Well let me speak…"
"SSSSHhhhhhhhh!!!! She is ill and is not allowing anyone to visit her right now. But from what I told her about you she said you must be a mighty fine man. She says she will meet you when she is feeling better. Right now she is asleep. Her medicine has worn her out."

"Ok. I guess we can leave. But I prefer to do this properly."
"Oh baby, you are as proper as proper gets. You will meet her, because she wants to meet you. Let go now."

Natalie gently pushed Charlie backward toward the few steps up to the entrance to the house. Charlie looked over her shoulder, but then he went down the stairs. They then went to the road and started walking toward town.   There was a celebration going on. It was starting early. Around 3PM. The town folk wanted to end it early. Around 8 PM. So all the grown folk could go out without worrying about too many children seeing what was going on.

Charlie and Natalie arrived. Her arm wrapped around his thick forearm. They talked and ate. Natalie was surprised by how much she loved the conversation. They were only interrupted once by a boy she used to sleep with. He was angry about seeing them together. Tried to stare down Charlie. Charlie tensed like a pitbull about to kill something. The boy, being young and much smaller, looked away in acknowledgement that this might not be the path to travel if he wanted to grow into full manhood.

The sun started to go down so fast it looked like minutes instead of hours. As it started to set they went down to the water. An area slightly sloped toward the lake with all itsalgae and moss covered trees. Charlie holding Natalie close. Going from touching her lightly at the beginning of the day, in all the respectable places like her shoulder, elbow, upper back. Those touches began to be more solid imprints from his hand with more weight and strength to them.   He started to touch less areas that are less respectful. Like the side of her breast, hips, and finally inner thigh as they sat and talked. Charlie could feel her soft body getting softer to him with each touch. He found himself wanting to feel more and more of her. It was as if the more he smelled her, the more he wanted her. Something her was aware of, but seemed to not be able to control. Trying to control himself as much as possible, As they walked toward the water he stopped her by some trees. Out of site of everyone. With the sun going down it would be hard to distinguish them from any of the plants and trees around them. Neither one of them had on anything bright to stick out in the fading light. Both had on off white and tan clothing.

Charlie stood, lifting Natalie up with him, holding her with one arm, as if she weighed the same as a sweater that he had just thrown over his arm. Not really being a muscular man, Natalie felt his strength more than any muscle flexing. It was just raw strength. His hands gripping the whole right side of her rib cage. Charlie could feel Natalie's body relax. Still holding her with one arm, her feet dangling off the ground. Charlie pulled her in close. They stared each other in the eye. Neither moving, both taking in

and giving out a building level of lust. Suddenly Charlie pulled
Natalie in closer and kissed her like he wanted to taste everything
inside of her. He brought his left hand around, sliding it over her
spine then down the the split between her legs, squeezing her
behind, and also sliding a finger across her womanhood.

A sharp thrill of pleasure ignited Natalie. She felt weightless and
was completely at Charlie's will. She felt his mouth move from
hers to the side of her neck up to her ear. His hot breath, his voice
rambled his deep for her. She could not understand a word he was
saying, but she could feel his lust overtaking both of them. After
he stopped talking he lifted her more, and pulled her shirt and bra
open in an impossible way. But just as she was going to protest his
treatment of her clothes, Natalie felt Charlie's warm mouth and
snake moving tongue take in her whole breast as his tongue
lathered her nipple wetly and ferociously. Her right nipple being
tasted, licked, breast consumed made her grab the back of his head
pulling him in tighter. Wrapping her legs around him she could
feel his manhood pressing against her. She felt his thick, hard rod
pushing through his clothes, through her dress, and into her
panties.   It felt as if his member would push through all of their
clothing and into her.

Charlie tasted her sweet nipple. It was as if she had put some type
of fruit juice on herself. The small round breast, and thick brown
nipple tasted good. He felt her nails digging into his neck. Her
breathing strongly into his hair. It was hot and humid already, but
her breath made it even hotter. Slight moans came from her a she
wrapped herself around him like that was the only way she would
stay alive was the intensity. He felt himself growing toward her.
It was as if she had a magnet between her legs and it was pulling
him in. He was beginning not to be aware of anything. Just the
sensation of her body violently pulling down on him as he pulled

up and in to her.

Natalie felt herself snatched off of Charlie. He detached from her breast and swung her around so quickly she did not know what was happening for a moment. Then she felt him holding her with one hand. Her feet slowly touched the ground. There were sounds of his belt coming jingling loose and then silent as his pants dropped to the ground. She could not see Charlie but she could feel his breath as he stood close behind her. He was slightly to the right side of her. His left hand was raising up her dress slowly. Natalie did not know it was risen up all the way until she felt his long, solid, thick manhood press up against her soft bottom. She tried to push back, but he was so hard she could not move any further back. His right hand let go of her rib cage. He grabbed her panties and ripped them off as if they were a worn thin sheet of paper.

Charlie saw Natalie's lower body ripple from her panties being torn off. This took away his last hesitation and he pushed into her. Her lips and pubic hair catching the sides of his manhood. She was tight. Some of the head was in, and with the head only, he could feel the wetness within. Juicy, warm, wetness. He had never wanted to plunge deeper into a woman in his life. Normally he would take his time to make sure he did not hurt them. But right now, all he felt was the deep need to feel every millimeter of this pussy. From the entry to the womb. He wanted to feel all of her. Pulling back a little his pushed back in deeper. Feeling her pubic hairs go in with him. Pulling back and pushing in again. Doing it again and again penetrating deeper each time. Seeing and hearing Natalie tremble while reaching back and pushing on the right side of his leg.

Pushing him because he was hurting her, but scratching his hip deeply because she loved the feeling of his solid penetration bringing out more wetness with each stroke. Natalie felt him stretching her inside as he went deeper. She was wet inside, but it had not gotten outside yet. And he was wide, thick. Even if she was ready he would have been something to get ready for. But as her eyes rolled in her head, and all vision faded. All she could do was feel his systematic penetration. He went deeper and deeper inside her. Each time bringing more wetness out than the last. She could no longer feel her pubic hair being pulled in with him. All she could feel was the deepness of his stroke. Feeling him stretch her insides with his thickness.. He was so long she could feel him in her stomach too. It hurt, but pleasure was outweighing the pain. And the transition from pain to pleasure, made it all the more enjoyable. He sounded like a starved bear eating as he breathed behind her ear. He held her in place while his pace quickened and intensified. Ever stroke deeper, harder. She let his right hand, wrapped around her shoulder hold her up, while his left hand held her waist and hip. Her breast rotated on rhythm while she felt her lower body tremble with each stroke. He felt as though he was pumping ever more intensely. With an intensity she had not felt before. It was more than lust she felt. His great love want and need of her drove him further into her. It was not just physical. He wanted to feel her in totality. Leaving nothing unfelt. He wanted to feel her body, her soul. Natalie now wanted to give him all that he wanted to now take.

He moved her body to his rhythm. Natalie let him. His control was total. Her body gave to his will. He pulled a different pleasure out of her than she had ever felt. No trees, water, sun, moon, existed around her right now. All she felt was his piston like drive. So consistent, so intense. Charlie felt the beginnings of him reaching his peak. The feeling of her nails driving deeper into his hip, hurt, but intensified the feeling. He watched her body, limp, completely submitting control to control. A woman known for being wild and unruly, in complete submission to his will. A wave of pleasure hit him, his member swelled larger inside her. Natalie felt the change, "Mmm!" . Charlie felt himself getting closer. He stroked deeper, harder, deeper, harder.

Natalie, felt a wave of new pleasure and had an orgasm that seemed to spread to every limb as she felt Charlie push in harder than he had before and hold it there, deep inside her. Stretching her, she felt his powerful hands almost crush her shoulder as he started to throb inside her. The feeling of him throbbing, inside, made Natalie squirm and move.

Charlie saw and felt Natalie writhe in his hands. Moving his member inside her as he came. Sending him to obscene levels of pleasure. Even though he felt like he was going blind with pleasure, he could see and hear her peaking to another orgasm. She kept going and stopped right as he was about to push her off.

Natalie felt a second orgasm come. Being filled with his seed turned her on. So much, that even with him still in her, it ran down her inner thighs on both legs. She held herself up with one hand on the tree in front of them, still moving ever so slowly bending his shrinking member inside her. Not doing enough to make him want to pull out, but just enough to get more enjoyment out of him. Her legs were weak and shaking. Her breath came out sounding labored.

Clap. Clap. Clap.
"Now that was damn fine show! You two ought to take that on the road!"

Mason clapped again. Charlie and Natalie both snapped their heads in his direction. They were both startled by him. Natalie tried to cover up, while Charlie pulled his pants up.

"No, don't get dressed for me. Just start up again. Maybe this time I can join in."

A devious look of someone in need of mental help crossed his freckled face as he grinned. Mason was a slim light skinned man, with a balding head. He was only in his mid 20s but looked to be pushing 50. His stomach wide and he was slim everywhere else. He had thin ghostly hands. No hair on his face and he always wore a constant smirk. Women were afraid of him, including his own mother. As the story goes. His mother was raped by a lynch mob. They all took turns raping, beating on her. Then left her beaten and bleeding from every orifice on the side of a dirt road. He was the offspring of that hellish day. Father unknown other than the fact that it is guaranteed to be a sick piece of shit. Mason had always made any woman or girl uncomfortable when he walked past. Men just did not trust him. He had a gray eye and a brown eye. A nervous twitch in his right hand. He would shake it like there was something that needed to come off it.

Charlie walked toward him after tying his belt. Mason, squares his shoulders toward Charlie. In a way that clearly states he is not going to just submit to the bigger man.

"Mason, you know that ain't right walking in on me and the lady here."
"Shit, this here is public land. That means, both of you are in public. It is my right…"

Charlie moved to hit Mason in the head, with a blow that looked powerful enough to knock out a horse. But while he was swinging, Mason sidestepped him and hit him with a thud in his chest. There was a flash of something in Mason's hand. Charlie seemed to know immediately. He stepped back clutching his chest. Mason flashed a smile with a silver tooth in the front. Making him look like a deranged child with an old man's face.

"Got some bone on that one. Sure you want some more of that? 'cause I got more where that came from."

Both men stared at each other. Charlie looked to be calculating. Mason seemed to have a gleam in his eye, like that of a child about to open a Christmas present. A freak like anticipation. Almost giddy. Mason's body seemed to be totally relaxed compared to his eyes, staring at Charlie who was at least double his size. But clearly a little bit slower. Charlie had now dropped his look of shock at being stabbed. His looks of calculation gone too. The knife had been stabbed with had ridges in the back. So he could feel his skin rip, and some of his insides had been ripped. His face turned into emotionless stone. He had decided he was going to kill Mason.

"Now Charlie. I do not want to hurt you no more in front of this fine piece of pussy you got. But I will kill you here and now if you come at me again. You too big for me to be fighting. "

Charlie's hand dropped down from the wound he was clutching. It was clear he had made a decision to beat this man to death. And Mason could see that. There was a resolution in his eyes. And for a moment it looked as if Mason might waver. But it was a trick of the evening light.

Charlie moved quick, actually grabbing Mason's knife hand, to which Mason dropped his knife and caught it with his free hand slicing Charlie's other hand that was reaching for Mason's empty one. Then slicing the forearm of the hand holding Mason. Charlie had raised his foot and kicked Mason as if he was trying to kick in a secure door and then proceeded to kicked Mason off his feet while Mason, was slicing his forearm.

Natalie was so scared she could only stand and watch. Mason landed off balance trying to stand, but found Charlie lunging toward him. Mason rolled to the side out of the big man's way then stabbed Charlie's left shoulder, slicing down through the muscle into bone and cartilage. Charlie, screamed out in pain. His left arm now useless he rolled away from Mason. Both men stood. Both men looked dead set on the other having to go.

"Shit, you kinda quick for a big man. Shoot, we could have been friends….."

Charlie threw a rock he grabbed while on the ground with his good arm. Narrowly missing Mason's head. Mason was dodging the rock and almost did not see Charlie come in with his foot trying to kick out his legs. But he did. And in that moment. Jumping over his Charlie's foot, Mason sliced across Charlie's throat and blood shot out instantly. The amount and how fast it was coming out looked unreal.

Charlie slumped grabbing his throat. Trying to stop the bleeding. Mason did not even look down at him as he walked straight past looking at Natalie like a meal he had been waiting to eat all day. Natalie tried to run over to Charlie but Mason grabbed her.

"Oh no no no." Mason wagged a finger in front of her as he grabbed her. Paying absolutely no attention to the fact that she was still trying to reach Charlie.

Mason cut open the rest of her dress with two cuts. Natalie startled out of trying to reach Charlie reached back to hit at Mason. Mason's eyes changed, the pure insanity she always knew in him burned. He back handed her with his knife hand. Her lips swelled immediately. The handle of the knife getting her on both her lips. Suddenly he was on top of her he yelling something Natalie could not understand, he then licked her face and hair. Natalie felt a revulsion like she had never felt in her entire life. His breath rank, the rest of him smelled like a man that stayed in the swamp all summer with no bath. To have him licking her, was just too much. She tried to push him back, but he was stronger. He did not look that strong, but he grabbed her, turned her around and slammed her down hard on the ground. Hard enough to knock all the air out of her. As she tried to inhale she heard him behind her laughing. It was the sick sound of madness. It was a

laugh not because anything was funny. But because he knew he was about to do wrong and the thought of it brought him overwhelming joy knowing the harm he was about to inflict on her. Knowing she was powerless to defend herself against him.

Natalie tried to push herself up but he had his hand in the middle of her back, and was pressing her into the ground so hard she felt as though her would be harmed beyond what they could heal from. That was until she felt him push himself between her legs.

"I don't like sloppy seconds, so what we are going to do right here is explore another way!"

Natalie had heard people talk about doing this and had been asked to several times in her young teenage life, but it was always something she felt was too nasty. Though she knew if Charlie would have asked her she would have done it. But this demented man, the child of rapists, racist terrorists, and killers, was now on top of her trying to get a good angle to rape her. She kept moving her hips from one side to the other so that he could not get in. She was held down so tightly by his hands and the position of his legs held her own. He was determined to get inside.

"I want your dumb ass boyfriend to watch as I do this to you. "

Natalie was looking straight at Charlie whose light in his eyes seemed to be fading fast. The life in his eyes seemed to be getting more distant. Natalie looked at him. Reaching out to him with her eyes. It was right as Charlie looked up and locked eyes with her that she felt a tearing pain behind her inside. Mason had purposely distracted her. She had just inhaled her first breath from getting the air knocked out of her, while looking at Charlie. Now she tried to move away from the jack rabbit pumping that Mason had started doing as soon as he entered her. Tearing her apart inside. She felt so much pain from the pushing and pulling he was doing she had to detach herself, mentally. The pain was so overwhelming that she started to go inward. Away from the situation, away from what was going on. She could not escape her tormentor in body, but in her mind and spirit, she would find solace. Her detachment came easy to her. The same as it had come to her when her godfather had first started to "play" with her in the back of the church. Making sure she was "developing right". She started to feel like she was leaving her body, watching this all happen from another location. Watching this man savagely pumping away behind her, as her eyes turned empty, distant, dead.

Charlie, seeing Natalie, wanted to reach out to her, save her. Mason had the look of a maniac demon on his face as she looked up to look at Charlie. He could feel his life slipping away. But something in the way she screamed out when Mason first entered her, made him gain back some strength. He started to move toward them. Slowly. His body felt cold. One arm was dead. He pushed toward them mostly with his feet. He remembered he had a little swiss army knife his back pocket and pulled it out slowly. Mason was too into raping Natalie to see what was going on. His face buried in her back as he savagely pumped away. Yelling incoherent words that made no sense and may not have even been real words. Charlie was getting closer. He just had to get close enough to make one last lunge. The knife was now out. He had it hidden behind his hip. He could see the fight fading from Natalie's eyes as he edged closer and closer. Natalie's eyes were open. But you could tell she could not see.

Natalie looked down to see if Charlie was still alive. Hoping he was not. She knew if Mason saw him watching it would only make this torture last longer and get even more sadistic. But what she saw was Charlie looking up at her. Much closer than he had been. Then she saw his hand. Mason was grunting and yelling some type of sexual code that only Mason himself understood. Natalie could feel the blood and fluids run down her legs. She could feel he was tearing her apart, and she could barely stay coherent the pain was so high. Just as she started to fade away, Mason yelled in her ear,

"You always were a little slut bitch weren't you??!? You little ass probably enjoys every stroke. Used to see you walking. Switching that little ass of yours. Swinging them little breasts. Hell I was planning on tearing your little ass up anyway."
"Fu....fuck ,..."
"What's that? "
"Fuck you...."

Natalie was only able to say it with a weak but clear voice, that Mason actually stopped. He then put his head down and bit into the area between the shoulder and the neck. Biting hard and breaking through some skin. Natalie screamed as this maniac tried to tear her shoulder with his teeth.

Charlie had enough. He was dying but would be damned if this was the last thing he saw. Right after Natalie started to scream he stood and buried the knife deep into the side of Mason's neck. Mason reacted quickly. He tossed Natalie out of the way and hopped on top of Charlie stabbing him three times in the heart as fast as he could move. Charlie was alive for a second, then died. Mason left the knife in his neck knowing that maybe it was keeping him alive. It hurt something terrible. It felt as if the little rusty knife had hit a bone in his neck under the skin. Charlie had buried it deep. He would have to go to his nurse cousin. She could tighten him up. Turning to look for Natalie he found she was gone.

Natalie felt Mason come down on her hard when Charlie stabbed him. Charlie must have put all the strength he had left into the blow. Strangely, Mason did not cry out. He just took it with a small grunt. She then felt Mason throw her from under him and jumped on Charlie. She knew Charlie was about to die, so as soon as Mason was off her, she ran full speed toward Main Street . Running around tree after tree trying to get as many behind her as quickly as possible. Kicking as hard as she could toward the road. She did not hear any shouts behind her but she was not waiting to hear any either. She felt like she had been split open. The pain was severe, but the thought of being caught by this loon was inspiration enough to run through any pain. Because he did not just offer pain. He wanted to abuse her in the most sick and vile way possible. She could feel it. Just like she felt like he may be catching her so she was constantly trying to run faster. Even as she got onto Main St she kept running. Only daring to look behind her when all the people on the street looked at her with looks of shock.

As she slowed down from a run to a fast walk looking every direction in obvious fear and terror. People were all around her now. No Mason in sight. Her clothes hung off her and most of her body was revealed in its violated nudity. Bruised, bleeding, and sick looking. She looked beaten, used, on her way to dying. Several people came up. One man tried to put his jacket on her.

"Get away from me!" Natalie squealed in a high voice that displayed her true age. Her nakedness, how scared she was, was too much. A plump woman with calloused hands but kind eyes, but the hard look of a middle aged woman that had lived a hard life. Took her. She walked up with open hands, slowly taking off her own coat. Then wrapping it around her shoulders.

"You got people around here?"
Her voice was melodious.

"Yes."
"We are gonna take you home to your kinfolk. "

Several older people came up to her. One man opened a door to his car. One woman got in the back. The lady with her coat and arm around Natalie eased Natalie in next. Then she sat next to her. Natalie then told them how to get to Sylvia's house.

When she arrived Sylvia was so shocked by the way she looked that she started crying. The big hard life
looking woman spoke with Sylvia's mother. They seemed to know each other. Sylvia took her into the house.

"Sylvia. I need your help." Tears streaming down Natalie's face.
"Whatever it is, I am here for you."

Sylvia stared into Natalie's eyes with the full belief that whatever they needed to do. She was willing to do. However she needed help. If she needed to cry, scream, fall, run, jump, whatever was needed. Sylvia was down with it.

"I am going to kill Mason. But I need your help to kill him the right way."
"Is he the one that did this to you."
"Yes…. Can I count on you?"

Natalie's eyes burned with a searing hatred. A hatred that had been burned deep into her soul. Her body radiated heat from the hate.

"Will you help me?"

Sylvia stared at Natalie. Then nodded her head yes, and that was where the problems truly began.

Chapter 5

Sylvia felt a great deal of pressure immediately after agreeing to help Natalie. Natalie had a swirl of angry energy around her. It was understandable. But something seemed off. It seemed as if something had been opened up and Natalie, was trying to pull it through. She was like a walking magnet of negative energy. The energy itself felt more unnatural. Almost perverted. You could feel something moving through the energy trying to make its way out. But for some reason it could not. Like someone you could hear, see, feel. But you could not see their total features because they were talking to you through fabric of some kind. Pressing their face against it. And even though you can touch, hear, and see them, there was no way to see the exact details of their face.

Natalie and Sylvia had learned together as young children that Sylvia could feel things around her. She was able to manipulate things. It started with being able to move plastic teacups they used play House with. Then as they grew older and found out different things to try, they could scare dogs away, then rats, to gators.

Controlling and manipulating animals was the latter stages. Sylvia could bend objects and create wind where there was none.

There was a boy that liked Sylvia. He was not so much a boy as a young man. He was 18, and had always been attracted to Sylvia since she was young. One day he started trying to push up on her. It was in the evening. Since he was a friend of the family, almost a family member, her mother had found no reason not to let him take her into town for an ice cream. He always seemed to have good intentions. Always attended church faithfully every Sunday. Worked with all the young children in the area. He was considered a Youth Leader. Destined to become a preacher when he got older. He was tall, and had a solid upright stance that showed that he had a confidence most grown men would never possess. But the Leader of a Congregation would need. His hair was short, skin was light brown. He looked everyone directly in the eye. Spoke with clarity, and gave the feeling that he did not know how to speak without sincerity. If it was not sincere then he would not speak.

Sylvia must have been the only girl in the little town that did not find him attractive. Girls, Teenagers, Women, Older Women, and even Married Women all found James attractive. The slim young man with power in his stride. They walked together after leaving the ice cream shop. Sylvia wearing her Sunday clothes still. James wearing his gray slacks, tie, polished but worn shoes, and his best shirt with his gold Cuff Links. He was sharp. Older people could see where he was going by his style alone. He did not own a jacket to go with the two pairs of slacks he owned, but he would get there.

"What did you think of today's sermon?"
"I thought it was nice."

"What was nice about it Sylvia?"

James looked her directly in the eye. Sylvia was still young. Her body was now starting to change, her emotions too. She had been able to avoid answering questions like this for so long. Now at this age she found everyone wanting direct answers from her. She did not like how these questions made her feel bare. Like someone put up a sign pointing toward her that said she was did not know anything. That may not be what people thought. But it sure is the way she felt when trying to think of an answer.

"The way the preacher said that life is a constant circle between birth and death. How God created this. And how it all works together."

James had not expected that kind of answer. He expected her to dodge the question and say something without any thought. Her answer showed him she did pay attention. And that what she paid attention to held the most weight out of all the things said in Church on this day.

"That is a good answer. Walk with me over here for a moment."

Sylvia looked up and saw where James was pointing. It was behind a closed down warehouse. The warehouse itself had started to rot. And the boys in the area had kicked in some of the doors. After the doors got kicked open and no one boarded it up, all the adults started to use it as a haven out of the sun. The sweltering humidity of Louisiana could make you feel like you were drowning under hot water some days. So many people, especially old people would find a chair inside and sit. It was their resting spot before they left town back to their houses. Preparing for the walk down the road or just people watching.

Today, the building stood empty. Everyone seemed to be preoccupied talking, or just not over near the building. As they approached, James walked straight into the building.

"Come on in here for a minute. I need to cool down a little bit before we walk back."

Sylvia felt funny about it. But quickly pushed the thoughts to the back of her head. It is just James, she thought. James, was watching Sylvia in a different light. Sylvia noticed as he motioned to her and talked to her he did not look her in the eye.

James mind was spinning. He tried looking away from Sylvia as she talked and walked. But she no longer gave off the little girl impression he had seen when she was younger. Her voice had changed. More melodic and smooth. Even gaining a rich tone. Her hair was still in a little girls style, but her eyes and body were different. He kept looking down at her legs. Her neck seemed to have gotten a little longer. Her lips were so full to him. He felt himself stirring, and he tried to fight it off. Trying to fight off the easiest thing to do. Give in to his desires.

Sylvia, did not know what was going on. She kept seeing James staring at her when she was not looking. Then turning away quickly to look at the ground or down the street whenever she saw him looking. He even stuttered a few times during conversation which is something she had not heard him do. It was as if talking was something he wanted to make his job. Which was something she just did not understand. Most the men she knew worked with their hands. And a few black men worked using paper, but none she knew used their conversation to work. James seemed to be the only person on a mission to make speaking his prime occupation.

As James paced he kept clenching and unclenching his fists. He seemed nervous. James could see that Sylvia noticed a few things but for the most part could not tell what was going on. As she walked in, he watched the sunlight on her skin, and lips. He felt a powerful pull toward her now. As she entered the doorway in he offered an outstretched hand.

"Come with me over here. It is cooler."

Sylvia took his hand and felt a slight shock at its cold, sticky clamminess. But she left her hand in his and followed him. Once they got in the area he took her to. Sylvia could see that it would be hard for someone from outside to see in. She looked back the way they came in and saw that where they were was slightly blocked from a street view. As she turned around she felt James other hand slide around her waist pulling her in toward him. It startled her. She started to scream but felt his mouth on hers instantly. His tongue darted all around her mouth like some type of slimy slug that moved quicker than a small birds head when looking around.

She tried to pull away, but he tightened his grip and stuck his tongue in deeper, groping her behind with the hand that was holding her hand. He was grabbing so hard she felt herself getting more and more bruised with each grip. She could not breathe, could not react. She was trying to push him off, but her 12 year old strength was no match to his late teen/ early manhood strength. He seemed to be getting stronger the longer this went. She could feel his manhood pressing into her stomach. Stiff, like a broom handle. He seemed to want to press it through her stomach and into her.

She was squealing trying to push him off, all she could see in his eyes was a overwhelming desire to take her. Something was welling up inside her. She could feel the room around her. It was as if a radar had been turned on inside of her. She now felt where they were in the room. Struggling against each other. Almost felt as though she was guiding some unseen force. She felt it move in from over their heads and flow out from her hands pushing James off and slamming him against the wall directly across from her.

James had let go of all his inhibitions and gave in to desires he knew was wrong. This was a little girl and here he was about to take her. He had never been so hard, so possessed by pure lust. It was to the point that he was ready to take from this little girl, what was not his to take. And he did not feel a thing about until now. Pressed against the wall by some invisible force pressing him like a giant hand. Looking at Sylvia. The iris in her eyes was reflecting a gold color, instead of the brown that it normally was. It was a reflective gold color. It made her eyes look like they gave off their own light. Her fingers on one hand moved slightly. He felt his right arm slowly get more pressure on it. First his skin felt pressed, then the muscles started to feel crushed. The pressure kept on with the slow raising of her finger. When her finger slowly raised up to pointing directly at the arm, he felt the bone snap.

Screams filled the room for a split second. But her right hand came up and silenced him. He was not being choked, nothing was different. He knew he was yelling but could not make a sound. Sylvia made a movement with her left hand like stop. But as her hand moved forward, James felt pressure on his chest mounting. It grew higher and higher. His lungs, heart all felt the pressure. Then ribs started to crack one by one. The middle of his chest getting the most pressure. He could feel it being pressed in, harder and harder. Fear rising to a level he had not felt before because the amount of pain he was feeling was already high. He could not yell for help, and felt like he was going to die a very slow and painful death. His heart felt as though it had stopped when he saw her turn her hand to the side. As though she were going to do some type of karate chop. She moved her hand down dropping her hand like someone being blessed in the Catholic Church.

The pain as his sternum pressure to the point it ripped from the ribs was excruciating. And he could see that Sylvia was just getting started. Her face showed no emotion. All he could see was focus. Then,

"Hey! Everybody all right in there?"

James fell to the ground. Whatever force that was holding him up gone. His sternum and broken arm both jarred so violently, he wanted to scream, but still could not. All he could do is hold on to consciousness as the most pain he had ever felt in life, tore through him. He saw Sylvia climb though a window on the side. Then he saw another girl he could not raise his head to see her face come running toward him. She had a stick in her hand. He could only see up to her waist. As she ran up to him, she pulled back the stick and swung it at him. That was the last thing James remembered. The older man asking if everything was all right, came in to the building and found him. Laying in a pool of blood, from the injury his head got. There was no ambulance. He was put into the back of a truck owned by another Church member and taken to the nearest hospital. Once there. The hospital originally said they would not take him. But after one of the Doctors walked by, he checked on James. He then stated.

"This young man may lose his life if he is not operated on right now!"

He ordered all the nurses around as to what to do. He then fashioned himself the Savior of the Negro type white man. Even though he clearly could not stand the sight of so many standing in his hospital right then.

"All you people wait outside this hospital. Someone will tell you when we are done."

All that happened was he cut off James' right arm to nub, instead of resetting the bone. Stating that the break was too bad to fix. As for his Sternum. It was never checked, so James never healed right. He walked stooped down, and was very fragile looking for the rest of his life. The town thought it was a scandal. Everyone tried to find out what happened. Who would do such a thing to James. He was the Town Standard as to how a young man should be. And here it was he looked to everyone like he had been beat by several people.

Sylvia had run all the way home. Her mother knew something was wrong when she got there. Demanding answers from Sylvia, she finally started to talk but it all turned into hysterical crying. They ended up in each other's arms consoling each other. When word got around the last person seen with him was Sylvia, her mother did not let anyone speak to her or get near her. She told anyone that asked the experience was too traumatic for her to talk about. Going on to state that if you have any decency, no one would pressure a little girl into describing what went on that night. It was a horrible, horrible thing what was done to James. Even though she knew there was more to it than Sylvia stated.

After awhile everyone in town simmered down about it. With James not saying a word other than he did not remember. And

Sylvia not saying a thing to anyone, not even the sheriff, the subject was dropped.

But then there was one person who had seen it all. From beginning to finish. The person who had gotten two good hits in on Jame's head. Natalie. She had seen it. She waited. Right when they got back to school. Natalie pulled Sylvia to the side.

"I saw what happened. I saw what he did to you and how you got him back!"

Sylvia's heart went into her throat.

"You don't have to worry about me telling nobody. But one day you are going to have to do that for me too. But your secret is safe with me."

Natalie smiled and walked off to the restroom. It had been months. No one had said a word. Natalie was her best friend but she knew this would be the beginning of something she would regret. Only time would tell. But in her heart. In her Soul. Sylvia knew. This would be going down a negative road. A road that Natalie herself was going to pave straight off of the road that Sylvia planned to stay on. Time would tell. But this is how Natalie gained Sylvia's loyalty. Through that one secret. Natalie would form a pact with Sylvia. Ensuring her loyalty. Sylvia would hold up her end throughout, not really understanding or wanting to accept that Natalie was using her more than being a friend. Denial could be strong for people who did not believe in themselves. Sylvia had all the doubts that most teenagers had, but some more than others. Things like believing people wanted to be friends with her. Natalie was someone she knew the longest. That longevity allowed Sylvia to feel more comfortable with Natalie. More comfortable than she should have allowed herself to be. But that is the thing about youth, you do not know until you experience some things.

Chapter 6

Several months went by after Natalie had been attacked. Mason had not been seen in that whole time. Charlie had died where he took his leap at Mason. Natalie was convinced Mason was hiding in the swamps down the road. He had been known to stay out in the swamps for long periods of time. It was said he had such a mental problem, even the animals sensed he was off. Leaving him alone because of his aura.

Townsfolk had started whispering rumors. Since Natalie was well known for being overly flirtatious to put it nicely. Many said she caused the problem that befell her and the death of Charlie. No one thought she did it on purpose, but many of the women said her trampy walk was the cause. She had walked by too many other women's husbands or boyfriends catching too much attention, on purpose and not caring who she offended. Even though it was known she had been raped and hurt severely, many of the women just could not feel for her. Some of the men did. And the elders of the town definitely felt for her. Truth be told, she had started behaving more like someone with some sense, since the event. She no longer displayed parts of her body for attention. She no longer added a extra bounce or switch to her walk when going by men.

Sylvia was actually beginning to feel less of a burden being Natalie's friend. She did not know just how much Natalie was a weight until Natalie went through her transformation. Natalie had always been pressuring her to do things all the time. And now that she had one focus, and would open up to Sylvia about how she felt inside, her thoughts and feelings. That made her seem far more human to Sylvia. More someone she could look to as a true friend. Before it seemed as if Sylvia was almost her pet that was made to follow her everywhere then clean up her messes. Now, Natalie would cry every now and then. She was far more sensitive to Sylvia's moods and needs. As tears would stream down her face. She would often tell Sylvia, how she would have married Charlie. How he was the most strong and right man she had ever known. A man that liked to do, more than say. A man of action not words. All the men like that around the town were all married. Even more than that, Charlie seemed different in some way to all the other men in town. When he looked at her, she felt bare. Charlie seemed to be able to see her soul for what she really was. Not all the extra things she did. And she did do a lot less when around him. He calmed her. Made her feel as if his vision narrowed to just her when she was around. He knew her history, but did not care. She remembered how powerful he was. Yet had a tender caring soul. He was not the twisted murderous demon inside that is Mason.

"I talked to the lady about finding Mason." Natalie said out of the blue as they sat on Sylvia's steps to her house.

"What lady?"
"The one down there at the edge of the swamp."

Sylvia thought of the woman. She had seen many people talk to her. Including her mother. The woman had bowed to her mother as if she were some type of queen. She never had understood that. The lady looked dirty. Her clothes were rags sewn together. She clearly did not care about her appearance. She had two braids lazily done down both sides of her head. By the way she looked, you would think she smelled. But normally she smelled like sweet incense. She hid her hands. She was missing most of her teeth. One eye seemed to wander, then move back into perfect alignment. There was something about her that reminded you of a piece of paper that had been dropped in the garbage full of wet half eaten food, then taken out and stepped on in the mud. All the kids had always tried to sneak over by her house to see what she was doing at night. Making up stories about her eating children.

Those adventures continued until she brought a white dog with gray eyes back from a trip. It looked like an Eskimo dog, but bigger. It was quiet. She let it roam around her house freely. It would sneak right up on kids. Getting right up to their ears and letting off a growl as its nose almost touched the unknowing child's ear, sending them running for cover or to just get away from the dog. Some people ran back to town, others ran into the swamps. The lady would catch most before they got into the swamp, and tell them the next time they came she would curse them, maybe even eat them. The funny thing about all this, is the dog would run into the water to get at people or half way up a tree like it could get up there like a cat. Even though it was always in the brown water or mud, its white fur was *never got* dirty. Strange. An all white dog whose fur never got dirty in the middle of the swamp. So strange in fact, many believed the dog was something else. And by its actions, it was something else, or the most intelligent dog that ever lived. its owner must have all ways washed it to keep it so clean. But no one believed that, due to how dingy the owner herself looked. Something in the eyes of the dog, did not look…. normal.

As the kids grew to be teenagers most of them decided that she was just an old woman who wanted to be left alone. She did cook up all manner of concoctions. Many people went to her for medicines. She would go off into the swamp. Find whatever plant that was needed and make a home remedy for whatever was ailing people. Some people went to her for other things. Things that can be put in food, and work on someone slowly over time. This is what Natalie was referring to. When she had a talk with this woman it was surely not about healing anyone. It was about finding and killing someone. That someone being Mason. Sylvia knew Natalie had been violated and defiled by him. But it seemed to Sylvia, that Natalie, had been getting over, or dealing with what happened. She did not seem as though she was so intent on killing Mason anymore. Natalie had seemed to fall in a more peaceful place. But now she that all the peacefulness she saw in Natalie may have been just Natalie focusing on how she could find and kill Mason.

"She said she has something to find someone."
"And you are going to buy it?"
"I already have. She said I need to mix it with something from him. I kept my own fingernail from that day. It has the skin I scratched off of him with his blood too. Something told me to keep it. When I mix these two together, we, are going out to find him."
"Natalie….."
"You remember our pact?" Natalie spoke turning to look at Sylvia.

Locking eyes with Sylvia so there was no misunderstanding as to how serious she was. Ending the look with a definitive, you owe me this. As much as Sylvia wanted to say no she could not. She did not feel like this was something she owed Natalie, but she did feel

Looking at Natalie, Sylvia felt that negative energy she had felt before. When she had agreed to help her. But now it was stronger deeper. The feeling like whatever it was needed to be free was overwhelming. It had been feeding off of Natalie's feelings of hatred, violation, shame. The feeling hit so hard, Sylvia had to steady herself, even though she was sitting. Her vision became blurry, like she had tears welled up in her eyes. But she knew she did not. She could hear Natalie's voice, but could not understand her. The sound was muffled, like she was underwater. It was as if Sylvia was under water and could hear Natalie, who was out of the water. Speaking.

"Sylvia. Sylvia!"
"I hear you...... I just had a feeling that..."
"No feelings. No feelings other than ending that demonic motherfucker's life!"

The feeling of this other being hit harder than ever this time. Luckily Natalie had gotten up and started walking to the road. Taking the feeling with her.

"Be ready tomorrow. Remember, I know what you can do. And you made a promise to me!"

Natalie stormed down the road. Walking with a set purpose. Sylvia followed her all the way home. It was rare that Sylvia went to Natalie's house. When she got there she saw Natalie's Aunt holding Natalie's child on her lap. She spoke to Sylvia, but did not say a word to Natalie. Natalie was not disturbed in the least by her Aunt not acknowledging her. She seemed very content not to be acknowledged. Her daughter was asleep. A young Angela was sound asleep. Without a care in the world. Sylvia did notice Natalie glanced at her child, not her Aunt, her child.

By the time Sylvia started to take in all this, Natalie was in the kitchen trying to boil some water. She was using a tea kettle. The cup she had some what looked like dirt and torn up foliage in it. It had a powerful smell to it. To most folks from around this area it would just smell like smashed up plants. But to people from a city environment it would smell more far more offensive than just some smashed up plants.

"She told me if I put this in some warm water and drink it like tea, it will give me the ability to find Mason. All I need to do is put in something of his and drink that down with the water from these herbs she gave me."

Sylvia looked at the smashed up leaves, dirt, and whatever else. Thinking to herself, if I was that determined to find someone, I guess I would drink this dirt out of a cup and look at it as nothing but "herbs". As she was about to turn away from looking at the cup she saw a fingernail in it. The fingernail had blood, and dried skin connected to it. Natalie had said she scratched him, but there was more skin on the nail that there was nail.   The thought of her drinking something with that in it, made her sick to her stomach. It was hard enough she was about to drink what was basically dirt. Add this on top of it, Sylvia felt like throwing up.

"You really going to drink this?"
"What did I say?!? I bet this works and we are going to be down

there slicing that nigga up! Wherever he is at!"

Angela walked in rubbing her eyes. Probably awakened by her
mother's sharp tone and increasing volume. She walked one step
into the kitchen and froze. Natalie went toward her, but Angela
took one quick step back. That step stopped Natalie from moving
closer. She could see Angela's face frozen in horror. Sylvia felt
that Angela, being a child could feel the sick perversion of feeling
around her mother. Sylvia felt it but it felt distant.   But for a child,
with or without any special gifts, the feeling may be
overwhelming. Children in their innocence and newness are far
more sensitive to things than adults.

Natalie tried to move toward her daughter more gently this time,
but the look of horror in her eyes only went higher. Natalie feeling
stuck, scared, and confused by her daughter's actions froze too.
Sylvia quickly went to the girl.

"Angela, you still asleep? You look like you are still asleep. Your
Mom and I just want to…"
"Not my mother."
"Yes it is. Who else would it be?"
"Not my mother."

As Sylvia got closer she felt the raw energy coming from Natalie
to her daughter. It was the same overwhelming negative energy as
before. But now it felt like it took a tubular form and stretched out
toward the child. Like it was reaching for the child but could nor
quite reach. Little Angela's eyes stayed locked on the end of the
snake like figure. Making sure to stay a good distance from it.
Natalie, sensing the absolute conviction in her young barely
speaking age daughter's voice and actions decided to not go any
closer. But she had a face full of concern. Sylvia moved closer to

Angela.

"Let me take you back in the living room where you can lie down on the couch."

"OK" Angela answered.

Sylvia lifted her up and took her to the couch, lying her there then covering her with a quilt. As she walked back into the kitchen Natalie drank her concoction. She coughed the cough and gagged, forcing herself to drink it all. After she recovered, Sylvia could see that Natalie had been crying. She had tears running down her face even now. She drank some regular water then went up to Sylvia and gave her a hug. Then she moved close to her ear and whispered.

"If anything happens to me tonight. The only person in the world I trust her to is you. You two seem so close and I always admired how you could reach her when I couldn't. Please tell me you will take care of her if I am not here to do so."

"I will take care of her as if she was my own. For the rest of my life if that is the case. But I don't think it will be. We do not have to do this."

"Yes we do."

Natalie backed away from Sylvia's ear and said,

"Thank you for letting me know I can count on you with Angela. But we need to go. Follow me. And grab that shovel over there."

After Sylvia grabbed the Shovel they were off on their way, leaving out the back door. They started their trip into the wooded swamp land. Natalie leading the way.

It was late in the evening. If it were not summertime it would be dark by now. But since it was summertime, the sun, heat, humidity, and bugs, were all out in force. Natalie was walking like she was in some type of trance. She walked straight toward the woods. Her eyes wide like she was seeing some type of trail that might disappear if she blinked. Their first stop had been to where Charlie had been killed. She stopped there for a moment. At first Sylvia thought Natalie was in mourning, but it turned out to be she was picking up on something from the area. Natalie was not sniffing anything but she was taking in some type of feeling or essence. It looked similar to when Hunter's dogs get the scent of something. But Natalie, unlike the dogs, was not sniffing anything. She stood perfectly still. Right on the spot where Charlie died. It seemed as if she was pulling in every experience around the area, and siphoning it down to just Mason. She then then crouched down close to the groundf. Touched the dirt that was still stained with Charlie's blood. Her eyes were closed. It looked like she was sensing something from the very dirt she was touching. She closed her eyes, frowned, and then made some strange whimpering sound, that stopped, as soon as it started. Her eyes flew open, with an intensity that seemed twisted, and burning from the inside out. Not only did her eyes look wrong but, that swirl of negative energy, now felt like a living, breathing, creature swirling around her. Natalie's eyes looked of a woman possessed. It was still pretty bright outside but her pupils were so open it looked as if the whites in her eyes were disappearing. There was white left on her eye, but it would be easy for someone to think her eyes were onyx colored. Fear stung Sylvia's heart for the first time as she took several steps backward. The fear passed as she saw Natalie turning.

Sylvia went to say something but found she could not get too close to Natalie. There was some type of invisible barrier around her. She called Natalie's name, but she could not hear her. Sylvia felt like there was some type of divide between them. More than just a few feet, it was more like Natalie was hundreds of feet away. Natalie then got up and started walking at a very fast pace moving away from town. She made one statement.

"I can see where he went. I know where he is."

Sylvia could swear she heard more than one vocal tone in her voice.

"Come on. We need to hurry. I want to get there before dark."
"Natalie, something is wrong with you."
"I don't want to hear that shit right now! Now I am going this way. If you do not want to help, give me the shovel now, and I will do this alone."

Sylvia stared into her friend's face knowing that what they were about to do is wrong. But nodded yes, like she was with her. When really, she wanted to run a million miles away from this place. Whatever was surrounded Natalie was real. And it did not take a person versed in the occult or anything else to see what was going on. This mysterious force was feeding off her misery and desire for to reap vengeance on Mason. Nothing was wrong with wanting Mason dead or even to wish something horrible on him since he had already taken such a large piece of her away. Her soul was torn, like fish after a shark has bit down and through the bottom of it's body. Looking just as gruesome, and a lot more painful. But this presence was manipulating her in the same way as Mason. Sylvia did not have the skill or knowledge to reach through it to Natalie. All she could do was feel it. She could not see or affect it. But the presence was well aware of her. And it toyed with her by blocking her from Natalie. Playing its own game knowing that Sylvia could do nothing to stop it.

Sylvia did a walk/run to keep up with Natalie's pace. It was as if she had grown to 7 ft tall. She floated over the roots and bushes in their way. They went through certain parts of the swamp, but where Sylvia would stumble and sink, Natalie floated and seemed to speed up. Sylvia feeling a growing apprehension as they went deeper into the swamp, felt as though she was losing her friend with every step. She did not know what she was going to do when Natalie got to her destination, or even if that destination had anything to do with Mason. But she knew she had to stay as close as possible, because Natalie, was going to need her.

Sylvia kept catching back up only to lose more ground. Foot getting stuck. Stepping into water and sinking further than she thought. She willed herself to go faster regardless of environment, and still was losing ground on Natalie. Natalie was getting farther and farther ahead. She almost appeared like an apparition. A woman with clothing flowing behind her in the dying light of the day. Sylvia had accepted the fact that Natalie was floating away from her. It did not scare Sylvia to her amazement when the acceptance of the thought hit her. She could almost hear the presence laughing in her direction. Taunting her. I know this for sure: that thing is not human, she thought. And it was taking more of a physical form the closer it got to their destination.

Sylvia could now see the outline of what looked like a giant snake's body, constantly moving in a circle around Natalie. Surrounding her and seemingly carrying her. But the form would change, to what looked like various shapes of heads all through its body. Then it changed back, after this happened a few times, she noticed these were heads inside of the body. Fingers arms legs all pushing at the skin. They where trying to get out. As Sylvia got closer she began to other shapes and forms that were far too hideous to pay any more attention to than she already was. The more she looked the more she saw, and the more she saw the more she began to fear what she was seeing. This was no trick of light. This was some form of demon. It is something Sylvia just knew.

Natalie stopped moving. Sylvia hardly noticed as she was now keeping her distance, and not trying to get any closer.

"That shack is his. He is in there." A voice, foreign. Sounded like it was coming from something big and inhuman. Old and new. Its voice was labored. Like someone speaking who needed to clear their throat. Full of mucus, wheezing.

"Are you sure?" Natalie replied
"Yes child! Hurry. He will know we are here if you wait any longer. Go!"

The presence unwrapped from Natalie. It seemed to not want to get too close to the small rickety shack they were across from. The shack looked hardly big enough to fit one bed. But it did have a make shift front porch. A door and good roof. The best part of it was the roof. The rest looked like wood taken from the swamp. Natalie pulled a knife and went running toward the house. Full speed. They were some 100 yards away and Natalie was running toward it with complete and total abandon. You could see no thought of the danger she may be in was going through her head. She was caught in the madness the creature had built up so high in her. Driving her to insanity.

Natalie was a fast runner, but right now she seemed to be faster than she had ever been. Maybe it was the adrenaline or maybe it was her sheer will to kill Mason. Whatever it was she was making quick work of the ground she was covering to the house. Mason opened the door and walked out. His step was calm, light. He looked like he was drunk, but he did not sway or seem to be unbalanced. As a matter of fact, his balance seemed to be more perfect than ever. It was hard to see his face with the sun as low as it was. To make it worse the sun was setting behind his little shack. So Sylvia could only see the silhouette of Mason and his home.

Natalie ran full speed toward him knife drawn and looking like she was going to drive it into him with the full force of her speed. Mason stood, motionless. Natalie lunged straight at him with the knife pointed straight at Mason.

Mason moved to the side in a way, that did not look right. The speed and the way his body moved when he did it just did not seem right. Natalie missed him and the pure speed she was doing caused her to slide a short distance in the dirt. But she turned and sliced at Mason with a quickness that Sylvia had never seen from Natalie. The way she swung the knife, you could see she was trying to kill someone. Everything about Natalie's stabs and swings was meant to connect in a fatal way. You could tell if she connected she would try to slice or stab again and again until Mason lay unmoving, dead. Mason, on the other hand, was contorting and moving out of her way in a manner that was unbelievable. It almost as if he would leave his body in position for her to try getting him but then move at the very last second leaving Natalie off balance. She would recover quickly, leading with the knife every time. It was her recovery that seemed to keep Mason from being able to grab her. It almost seemed as if Natalie herself was trying to bait him into putting a hand on her so that she could slice something.

Sylvia was running toward them but they seemed to get further and further away the harder she ran. Mason dodging and Natalie slicing. Normally the speed at which Natalie was moving would have gotten even the fastest man. But tonight, something was different about Mason. That trademark sneer of his was not on his face and as he dodged Natalie, Sylvia caught glimpses of Mason's face. And he looked as possessed as Natalie. There was no facial expression. His eyes were blank, and he did not have his typically look of insanity or off-ness to him. He looked calm, confident, unfazed by Natalie trying to kill him. This was not his normal look. He normally looked like someone fighting inner demons, and definitely was not calm. There was a madness, an insanity in his eyes normally. His eyes now looked the same as a person laying in a casket. Dull, glazed over. He would look around and follow Natalie's movements, but Mason was not in there.

This made Sylvia stop from running any closer. She was between the fight and the entity that brought Natalie there. It watched from a good distance away. Near the trees beyond the small clearing that the shack sat on. Sylvia could not see its head or eyes, but the movements of its body looked as though it were trying to see past Natalie and Mason. As if it was looking for someone, or something. It could not quite see or detect anything, but it knew there was something there. The fact that this creature, or whatever it was seemed to be, stopped its taunting and laughing to see what was past the two people fighting, spoke volumes to Sylvia. So many volumes that she felt her heart seizing up as it beat faster. She watched the creature moving from side to side, up and down. Like it could not see past something. Or its sight was being blocked. This creature that scared Sylvia initially was now looked jerky instead of smoothly moving, antsy......scared. Sylvia could not breath. Suddenly she felt like she was overwhelmed with fear. She was starting to loose control of herself, fighting the urge to scream, run, do anything to shed herself of the fear building up inside her. She steeled herself as much as she could. But the terror she was feeling was intense. She did not know what was going on or what else could happen.

Suddenly there was an anguished scream. Sylvia turned back to see Natalie's left hand, which was not holding the knife, dangling at an awkward angle off her wrist. Blood was pouring out.

"I tire of this. Kill her, and her friend." An older male voice stated. On hearing the voice, Sylvia could not see who it was speaking, but the monstrosity that had led Natalie here could see. It froze. Only the people or souls that seemed to be reaching to get out of its body moved. They continued frantically trying to tear out of the body that anguished them.

Natalie still swung her knife at Mason. But more to keep him away. Natalie was losing, and she knew she was in mortal danger at this point. Sylvia had not seen how her hand had gotten that way. What happened to cause it. But she was seeing bugs come out of Mason's skin and over his hands shaping themselves into clawed fingers.

He then grabbed Natalie's knife hand while she was in full swing. It was done so quickly, Natalie had not registered the hand was being crushed. As his other hand grabbed her by the ribs. Natalie watched as his fingers grew and dug into her skin. Piercing her back and cracking ribs. Her hand smashed so hard the handle of the knife started to bend in the middle. The thick metal helping to break the rest of her hand under the pressure. Natalie did not make a sound. Tears rolled down her face, eyes focused with a determination to kill Mason. He held her tightly. She could kick, and hit him with the useless hand. But nothing she was doing fazed him. She then tried to bite his arm closest to her mouth. But as she went to bite him, something whipped off his back with the sound of a whip cracking. It tore through the back of his shirt and pants flashing by the front of Natalie's body.

Natalie's face had a look of shock. She tried to speak, but she only coughed up blood as she looked toward Sylvia. The creature that in inhabited Mason tossed her several yards across the clearing as if her weight were no more than a baseball. When he turned he tore off the rest of his clothing. He did not look human anymore other than some of his torso and his face. His eyes were empty. They moved like he could see through them, but Sylvia knew Mason was no longer behind those eyes. His skin looked like it was covered in some type of liquid, that was moving like water, but looked more like blood. The only problem was, liquid flows down the body. This was moving up the body. There were things opening and closing all over him. It was as if his body had become a hive to some type of unknown bug. That is what this liquid was. Bugs. Tiny bugs. Had to be thousands on thousands. His back was to her, and it had an open wound. In that open wound, bugs came out of his ribcage and flowed out to the rest of his torso. Then there was the middle of his back where his spine was. Only there was no spine there. Sylvia stared at it too scared to move, as she saw so many bugs smash together to form a spine of some sort. As she watched she saw the bugs move into a shape. An oval shape. Then forming a face that stretched out toward her. Reaching toward her with its tongue out. It was too far away to reach her, but the face was that of Mason. He was still in there. Sick as he was it looked as if he was enjoying what he had become. The face did not have eyes, but the movements of the face and the empty eye sockets conveyed the feeling of pure madness that was Mason. Perhaps this is what he really was the whole time. This form matched him better than what he did look like. Which is , a regular person. He always looked like something crazy was ready to burst forth from him. Now, he looked like the insanity everyone saw in him.

There were several cracks that split the air. It was the tail, made from his spine, whipping around in the air. It moved so quickly that Sylvia could not follow the path. Stretching ever longer. The face in the back of Mason's body stared with its open sockets where eyes should be. Bug pus oozing from each one. The tail grew with each crack it got closer to being able hit Sylvia, as the body walked backwards toward her. His face grinning out of the back of the body, tail made of the spine, cracking across the dirt and sky. One more crack and it would be long enough. That crack happened out of rhythm with the other ones. And Sylvia found it coming straight down toward her. She instinctively raised the shovel head and blocked the blow by sheer luck.

The tail however pierced the metal. Snatching the shovel away from her. Mason's body turned around facing her and leaped forward toward her. Sylvia back pedaled, but he was moving by milliseconds, while she felt like she was moving by the minute. He came forward, his mouth opening, then stretching open. Inside there were rows of bugs moving at a frantic pace, eating away the bottom part of his face. Creating a new jaw formed by them, with teeth made to tear flesh. All this happened in less than a second, but was so intense that Sylvia saw everything happen as if it were in slow motion.

A sick sound of Mason's body yelling, with a throat full of bugs could be heard, but Sylvia's disgust and fear hit a maximum. She was back pedaling as fast as she could, turning her face and screaming with her palms out. She felt something inside her come out through her arms to her hands. She screamed as Mason's body closed in on her throat. She knew she was about to die a sickeningly painful death of being eaten alive. But that was not what happened. When she opened her eyes, she saw Mason's body.

His body and bugs looked to be locked outside of time in mid-air. It had started to transform into something unspeakable. Sylvia watched as the bugs started to move again and change Mason's body into something she could not describe. The torso remained the same but the rest of it was blood and pus of the bugs multiplying and manipulating the body. Far too much to look at, and Sylvia crushed her hands into two fists like she was squeezing something.

What was left of Mason, and the bugs that took over his body mashed into smaller and smaller circle as Sylvia, squeezed each hand into separate fists over and over.

"Ah, you are the one.......many years have passed, since we have seen!" The once invisible creature that was wrapped around Natalie spoke.

"But you did not see her first. Come child. Away from, such a demon, as you would call him."

A hand reached around the shack. It was misshapen and appeared to be slimy. The fingers looked from half an inch long to one that was a foot long. They looked more like slugs connected to a hand. The pointing finger rolled instead of bent when the thing beckoned her over. There was clearly no bone under the skin by the way each one moved. The way each one would bend.

Sylvia stood, frozen in place. Terrified. The boneless creature on the other side of the shack beckoning, the creature across the field unmoving, focused on the hidden one behind the shack.

Across the field there was a flash, Sylvia did not see of what but the creature that was there crossed the field heading straight for the shack. Masses of bugs flew from behind the shack straight at the creature. Large and small. A swarm so thick nothing could be seen. But over the den of the bug's wings you could hear what sounded like a thousand screams. Nothing could be seen. Just noise, the sound of pain.

It was over, as soon as it started. All the bugs flew off in different directions.

"Now chiiilldd. Come here." Several mucus filled coughs followed the statement.
"What are you?"
"Does it matter!?!? If I showed you, it might kill you. If I described myself, it would only make you sick. It is clear that you do not know the presence you are in. Such childlike questions will not be entertained."

The swarm of bugs came back, straight for Sylvia. She screamed. But none touched her, as she opened her eyes she saw that they seemed to be up against an invisible wall. Once all the bugs pushed on the invisible wall, they burst into flame.

The heat was unbearable. You could smell the bugs burning. A hand was laid on Sylvia's shoulder, she spun in terror to see her mother standing there. Her mother was looking past her at the shack, toward the being that was hiding itself. The hand was still all that could be seen of the creature.

A man with a gray beard and bald head came walking up behind Sylvia's mother. He was dark brown, he had on an off white three piece suit. A white shirt. Gold colored Tie, handkerchief, and shoes. It was less gold than a deep shade of tan. He carried a dark colored wood cane. It had large diamonds at the top of the cane. They were placed randomly around the thick round top of the cane. Almost looked like they had grown out of the cane.

The man glanced at Sylvia as he walked by. Never turning far enough to cutoff his sight line to the shack. He nodded at her. Then turned back to walking toward the shack. The hand of the creature was still. It did not move. Each finger had been slithering up and down each other in very vulgar ways. As if each finger was humping the next one. But now, no movement. They were still.

The man in the white suit walked with a confidence and strength like every step he took rooted him to the earth like the trees surrounding them.

"You have traveled far to get here. Why?" The man in the off white suit asked in a deep baritone voice.
"You should know. Or have you been here so long that you have forgotten?" The creature stated, voice full of mucus. A sick wet sound accompanied pauses between every word.

The man in the suit walked over to Natalie's body. He looked down at it, looking at what had been done. It had been ravaged by the bugs. There was not much left but the torso. The rest was bone with freshly eaten flesh sticking to it. Sylvia let out a gasp. She had not looked over to where her friend had laid dying just moments ago. Now she was gone completely. The sight of her body and what the bugs had done to her was overwhelming.

"I have not been here too long to forget. But there was an

agreement made. Do you not remember how you ended up in the state you are in? Hiding yourself from us, not because you do not want to scare the girl, but because you lost the vanity you once had, and want to return to that vanity. To have a woman give herself to you as they used to long ago."

"Silence!"

"Oh. I see it has not been so long for you. You, gave it all up, knowing that you would pay a price to shortcut your way to power."

"All shall bow before me again."

"I never did bow before you. And never will."

"Then you shall die"

Dirt, bugs, plants, all in unison stretched toward the man in the suit. He did not move, his eyes were locked on the other side of the shack, where Sylvia could not see.

A plant touched the man before anything else could touch him. But as soon as the long plant's vine touched him it caught fire along with everything coming toward him. It was as if a bomb was set to explode, but somehow where the fire burned, how wide the explosion was completely controlled.

As soon as it spread it was over. The flame went out, only one section of ground burned. That was Natalie's body. The color of the fire was not normal. It had almost a red color. The skin then bones started to disintegrate. The man in the suit took a couple of steps forward. He seemed calm. Very collected. The creature however, let off a feeling that even Sylvia could feel. He lacked confidence now. The last creature it killed with no problem. No fear. But this man was something else. His air of confidence was solid. Sylvia felt instantly like she was safe.

"It is time for you to leave. We will finish this later. Unless you prefer to finish this now?" The man in the suit said.

"Your power has grown, from our last meeting. So much, FIRE!!!!". A mucus filled laugh could be heard from behind the shack. One long finger tapped the ground while he laughed. But the man in the suit was not amused. He did not look angered. But he did look serious. Sylvia could hear a low buzz in the air. Like big speakers give off when they are turned on with no music playing. Just high volume with nothing playing. And she felt as if there was going to be a loud noise, just like if she put on some music with the speakers already at volume 10. The man did not move, staring at the creature from a vantage point she could not see. Laughter filled the air, as the creature laughed heartily.

Then the buzz stopped. All the grass in the clearing around the man laid flat, as if something heavy and large had sat pushed down on every strand. Some trees near the clearing leaned back away from the man. The shack itself leaned back away from him, revealing more of the creature. Now, seeing its arm, Sylvia realized it was not human at all. It looked like two branches intertwined, but not wood, skin. They met at what would be the hand. The arm to the hand and the way it fit was wrong, and disgusting more than anything else. Skin that was covered in some type of thick slimy fluid.

As more things laid flat and moved back, Sylvia, felt where this emanation of power was coming from. It was a power emanating from the man in the clearing. It felt like heat, pressure, humidity, and most of all it made you feel insignificant compared to it. That is the level of power she felt coming from this man.

The laughter stopped, only to be replaced with the sound of

choking. Then the hand in view started to disintegrate. A scream was heard, a scream so piercingly violating that it could not be of this earth. The sound pierced the ears so deeply you could easily imagine your ears bleeding. The sound literally seemed to fill the air. Sylvia and her mother covered their ears but the screams were so loud, and violating that it was as if they were not covering their ears.

Around the man in the suit and he as well as the shack were hidden from view. A powerful gust of wind hit Sylvia and her mother almost knocking them off of their feet. The flames where Natalie's body was, almost went out from the force of the wind. They heard the screams go up into the night sky.

"He is gone. But we need to leave. Others will be converging down here. There is a power down here that is untapped. And the things that are coming are so old they have no name. They are from another time, and other places, before humans were here. Even though they have no name, each was considered a god of something at different points in time. You and the girl must go."

Kathy stared at the screen watching her mother look back at her in silence. Must have known that would have been like taking a trip back in time all that information. Sylvia, the now deceased mother of Kathy, continued.

"I know that is a lot to take in. But it is all true. Surely by now you could have seen some of the signs. Angela's mother was not the best of friends, but I did make a promise. A promise I meant to keep my to her about her daughter."

Sylvia's eyes darted around again. Scanning the room behind the camera. She was in her own basement in her own house but seemed on edge, tired, nervous.

"There are things here now. One reached out in your childhood. I have run out of time. Cannot tell you it all, but you have a power. A woman loses this power when she has a child. This power might manifest in her child, especially if it is a girl child. You have my gifts plus more. It is your legacy given from me to you, and countless other generations before us."

So many questions raged in Kathy's head, that she could hardly concentrate. She saw her mother look up, she stood. Her mid section was the only thing showing on the camera. She was speaking to someone but Kathy could not make out the words. It was a man. Very deep voice, but his words were not clear. He walked to her side. Perfectly tailored suit. Big strong hands, and a cane with diamonds in the top of it. The video abruptly stopped. There did not seem to be a quarrel happening when it did. They did not seem to be arguing. But it was something urgent and important. It just seemed like the video recorder was turned off. The DVD was now at the main menu.

Kathy tried for another 30 minutes to find more on the DVD. But that was it. She would have to learn about everything on her own. That was the most she was going to get from the DVD or her mother. And she felt woefully inadequate in the information given and what she knew herself. At least she knew more about her mother, and why she helped Angela so much. She was now even debating talking to Angela about past incidents. But she was going to have to feel her out first.

Chapter 7

Angela walked out of the office upset. Her every thought was of how she was sick of being treated like some type of diseased prostitute. Angela thought to herself as she walked, that bitch Kathy her stuck-ups, high siddity ass has another thing coming to her if she thought this shit was over with. Angela got to thinking to herself, hell, I was as much a daughter to Sylvia as Kathy was. I came by more, helped out more, (even thoughts on what she helped with evaded her mind at the moment). Yeah, she gave me money and helped out. But isn't a mother *supposed* to help their daughter out. Yes, I am not her blood daughter, but she treated as though I was. Hell, I got kids, that bitch Kathy only has a job with no one to take care of but herself. What the hell makes her so special?

Angela was strutting down the street so fast it shook her whole body. Several men looked at her, with a look of, "I would hit that." Angela noticed, but knew that most men only met up with her at night since her weight gain. Rarely would a man take her out to eat. And in most cases she had to contact them to spend any kind of time together. When she had her first kids she was still somewhat vibrant and youthful. She was in decent shape and many men liked her shape. They would look at her, and lock eyes with her to let her know they were definitely interested. Now, men looked, but when she looked back they turned away. As if they were saying, "I would have sex with you, but no one could know."

This very thought crossed her mind as she crossed the street and a large man, working construction, looked at her. For a moment, Angela felt some hope that this man. Large, tall, brown, with a strong build was interested in her. But as soon as he noticed her looking back at her, he turned away. Not a turn because he was embarrassed she saw him looking. More of a, I do not want to give you the impression that he wanted anything more than sex. Even then. He was not going to pursue her.

Angela felt everything coming down on her. Her doubts about her mothering skills, the weight she had gained, Kathy's hatred toward her, Sylvia's lack of leaving her anything......ANYTHING!!!!!! She was overcome by emotion, she walked to the closest darkest place she could see. Which being in an area people like to walk around at lunchtime, was hard to find. There was a 5 story building with a pillar near a wall. All the shops that had inhabited the first floor were closed and had been for sometime creating a dusty dark area. She aimed for it and walked that direction as the tears welled up in her eyes. They welled up so high she could barely see the pillars through the distorted vision that her tears caused. But she could see the shadowed area she was trying to get to. That was all she needed to see as she rushed over to the area.

As soon as Angela got around the pillar away from the sidewalk, she broke down. The building looked as if it had been abandoned, but it just turned out this was an area not many people came to judging from the dust on the ground. All the pressures she had put on herself to get money, and to do things she thought was right. She was trying to change but it was not going to plan. Angela had finally hit the age where she had to start admitting, all the problems she had were for the most part, caused by her. And to come up out of that, she would have to make a change. That change would mean she would have to stop lying to herself about her weight, romance issues, ignoring problems developing in her children. Most of all, she would have to stop blaming any and everyone else for her own self inflicted problems. Now that Sylvia was gone, there would be no one to fall back on. She was truly, on her own.

"Excuse me. Are you all right?" A smooth even male voice asked from behind Angela
"Do I look alright?!??" Angela answered with venom.
"Look. I saw you come over here, and I know this is not the safest of areas. So, I had to come over and check on you. You do not see many chocolate colored Sisters like yourself in a very sexy Business Suit break down crying. It must have been something to spark that."
"Who are you and why…"
"You are clearly in pain. I know you want to tear someone's head off. But that is not me. I merely came over here to make sure you are all right. *Are*, you all right?"

Angela turned around, the first thing she saw were his shoes. Clearly an expensive pair of Italian made shoes. His slacks were of a fine cloth. As Angela slowly looked up his body and into his eyes, her mood changed immediately. When she looked into his eyes, her first feeling was to turn away. But she did not turn away.

He seemed to stare deeper into her eyes than she had ever felt. Angela felt as if he was slowly licking the wounds on her soul. Healing them while creating an erotic feeling from deep inside. She felt all those things from just one look.

He was pretty tall. He wore a blue slacks that fit perfectly. A black sweater with a white shirt and dark blue tie. Professional. His head was bald, and his eyes were friendly yet piercing.

"I happened to be walking the other way and saw you duck over here. Thought I would check on you to make sure you did not need medical help."

Angela, barely hearing what the man was saying, struck silent by how attractive this man was. It had been years since anyone attractive had talked to her. And no one as refined looking as this man is had ever approached her before. His voice made his words hypnotically smooth. She felt at ease with him immediately.

"No. I was not in need of medical help. But I appreciate you coming over to check on me." Angela's voice was now less of an anger strain and more of a feminine flirt. She stood a little straighter and wiped her tears quickly. Smile spread across her face. She almost looked girlish.

"I must look a mess. I just probably seem like some fat drama queen with the way I was crying and talking to you."
"No. I saw you come across the street. Wanted to talk to you the moment I saw you coming. That suit you are wearing is sexy. Your feet are nice, hips inviting, and face is fit for royalty I would think any man could see that."

Angela was stuck for a moment, was he joking, or was he serious.

Looking into his eyes she did not feel he was joking.

"My name is Dominic. What is your name?"
"Angela…."
"Well Angela, would you like to join me for lunch? itson me."
"Yes." The word popped out her mouth so quick, Angela barely registered she had spoken.
"Excuse me?"
"Yes. I would love to join you for lunch."
"You said it so s I barely head you." A smile flashed across his face. Perfect teeth.

Angela had to get a hold of her self. She was started to feel the heat of embarrassment.

"I know a nice place we can go to. It is just two blocks away."
"Well, I will let you lead the way." Angela said a little awkwardly.
Dominic did not seem to notice as he tapped her by the elbow and started toward the restaurant.

They talked briefly as they walked. He asked if she liked Vietnamese food, and she replied she did. Dominic kept information flowing out of Angela for the next two hours. She found out very little about him other than he was an Entrepreneur and was not originally from America. That was enough information for her. The way he seemed so interested in her life, Angela did not need to know anything else.

"Let me say something. This has been one of the best lunches I have had in a while. We should do this again. "

Angela could not hold back a smile.

"Yes. We should. Did you have a date, in mind?"
"Tomorrow 6 PM. We can meet somewhere or I can pick you up."

Angela was not ready to have Dominic come to her house quite
yet. He was attractive and seemed intelligent, not crazy. And if he
would whisper in her ear and touch her in the right way he could,
definitely take her right here and now. But Angela stopped the
thoughts as best she could. It was time for a change in her life. No
more being used and abused. She needed something new, that was
real and lasting. And if this man was real. He would definitely be
a big spark for the fuel that would light her fire to change.

"Lets meet up-"

Dominic cut in quickly, "There is a place in Jack London, called
Rinaide's. Do you know of the place?"
"Yes."
"We can meet there at 6PM. "
"Ok."

6 would work out perfectly. That was enough time to get the kids,
buy them dinner, freshen up then get over there, not too early. But
right on time.

"It is a date then."

Dominic stood taking Angela's hand as he did, helping her up from
her seat. They did not let go of each other's hand until they got to
the door out. Dominic opened the door and let her out. They said
their goodbyes and each walked separate ways. Angela feeling
good put a little extra swing in her step as she walked toward her
car. Desperately wanting to look back and watch him walk away.
But in control, she steadied herself by looking at the ground.

Steady hoping someone opened a door that reflected enough behind her. Allowing her to see behind her without turning around. She needed to see this dream man one more time. Like a miracle from God. A mirrored door opened and she was able to see behind her perfectly. The person coming out worked for ShipEx, so he was holding the door open to get packages out. This allowed Angela to find Dominic in the reflection. She did find him. She slowed for a moment, just a moment, as she found his reflection. What she saw was that he was standing in the middle of the sidewalk staring with a pure focus on her lower body. Angela could see pure desire in his eyes. A look that was deep, like she had not seen directed toward her since she was a teenager or in her 20s when her body was in full bloom.

Angela stared at the reflection with an overwhelming urge to turn and run to him, but she held. The longer she saw him staring the more she wanted to turn. As she got to the door she remembered she needed to drop a letter in the mail. There was a mailbox in the parking lot in the back of that building. If she happened to see down the street as she held the door, then she was not being weak and looking back. She merely saw him through her peripheral vision.

She walked up to the door never taking her eyes off of Dominic's reflection. As she turned to go inside she looked down at the door. The angle was good enough for her to see down the street. But she did not see Dominic. Shocked, she turned her head more, then just outright looked down the street. Dominic was no where in sight. He was not halfway down a block with no where to turn and walk into. He was not crossing the street nor was he further down the street. He seemed to have, disappeared.

Angela stood staring for a second. Then a car came to the stop sign at the corner. It turned and started down her way. A horn blew twice. It was Dominic. He was in a dark blue convertible Jaguar. Cream colored interior. He waved as he went by and drove off down the street. A slight rumble could be heard as he hit the gas to get on the freeway. Angela watched until he was out of sight.

Angela thought to herself, if ever there was a perfect man, this is the one. She immediately started forming plans on getting a gym membership, hair done, facial......a complete makeover. She vowed to do everything she could to lock this one in. Not knowing him for more than an hour, her mind was made up. Turning and catching her own reflection in the mirror reflection of the tint in the door she let shut. She wondered why her? What did he see in her? She was fat, hair was a little matted under the ponytail she had clipped in. She wore no makeup, and was rude to him when they first spoke. Whatever the reason, Angela was about to give him even more reasons to like her and if things went right. Love her.

Chapter 8

Kathy walked down the street away from the Law Office with her head in a fog. She just could not seem to grasp all the information. There were too many open holes and no way to get the rest of the story. She would have to speak to Angela at some point. There was much they had to discuss. Did Angela know any of this history? And if she did know, why hadn't Kathy's mom shared any of this with her? Angela was not the type of person you confide in. Quite the opposite. For years she was known as the person to put your business right out in the street like it was the thing to do. Very few people had checked her on it. Angela would get real quite with that around people that would check her, hard, if she did that. She knew exactly who to do it to, and who not to. Angela knew Kathy's mother would have taken care of her no matter what.

Kathy had found her mother's diary and read every page. There were many things in it Kathy had not been told. One of the tales was the trip and all the circumstances involved, from Louisiana.

It had been a long road from Louisiana. Angela was old enough to remember it. Kathy herself could not remember, because she had been conceived, (barely), in Louisiana, but born and raised in California. So Angela was old enough to remember the trip. Sylvia, Kathy's mother had said it was a long trip north. They had to travel with a Preacher who himself was trying to get out of Louisiana.

The Pastor, or Preacher as he was known on the road. Preacher Jones as he was called by most, had been working at a rather large mansion on a small plot of land. The home and land were owned by a white family that had been there for generations. The family was French in origin. But over the years became distinctly American except for some of their eccentricities . They would invite people over and do things none of the workers there could have imagined. From Rituals to outright orgies. If you were a woman and wanted to keep your job there, which many did because of the higher than average wages black people women were getting paid. You had to give sexual favors on command. This did not happen all the time, but when it did, things had to be done. The men, for the most part, did not, the white women were off limits. All the men working there joked when away from the grounds that the women there, who had sex on the regular, were not satisfied at all. Some of the men there were too busy pleasing each other and screwing all the young maids they hired to notice the burning need of the women they called wives. Being in such a sexually charged environment the women too stayed charged with raw sexuality. Seeming on the verge of either running out to the fields to tear off the clothing of a field worker picking cotton, or falling out from being overwhelmed by sheer untapped sexuality.

But Jones, like everyone else saw these women were undernourished sexually. He did not like the wives of the lower cousins or younger siblings. The parents had passed on so most of the family left there was younger than him. At 51, he was still a strongly built, young looking man. He could be working pulling cotton, but he was now a driver. Being a driver had its perks. It was not hard work and it gave a lot of downtime that he filled by working on the car and cleaning it. It also allowed him time to observe and find out everyone's schedule. Like the Head of the Household's wife. Jones could have been wrong but he swore she had black in her. Looked like one of those people that came from a family that went lighter and lighter until they achieved the fantasy of being white. What is called "Passing". A fantasy that so many black people, not all, but far too many dreamed about. And some, actually lived. She was slim, but slightly bottom heavy, which sparked his attention and got tongues to wagging amongst the staff that she may be black. Her hair was a dark brown and just a tad bit thicker than any of the white people there. Her lips were full. She seemed to have far more restraint than the other wives in the household. She was quiet and kept to herself. While the rest of the wives gossiped and openly flirted when no white men were around, knowing full well if anyone touched them, and some white person found out, including the white women they were sitting with, the ones that were flirting just as hard, would scream rape. This did happen on occasion. Sometimes just because the man did not accept their advances. Making these white women that just KNEW they were superior, feel worthless. In their mind these heathen Negroes should be begging for what they were offering. The false accusations would fly. Accompanied by real tears from the rejection, but done more to get the white men riled up into a murderous rage. Killing any black man that seemed like he might be the problem, along with the one man the white women claimed raped them. Torturing them in the worst way possible trying to keep these innocent black men conscious so they could feel as much pain as possible. Before being lit on fire, having their privates were cut off and stuffed in their mouths as these men died a terrible death.

Rebecca, the wife of the Head of the Household, Jean-Marc, would always stay away from the other wives unless she had no choice. She passed time knitting or reading. Even though her husband spent the least time of any of the husbands with her. She still maintained a discipline of not showing too many emotions. The other wives were so shallow, that they did not notice how she would maintain this on purpose. Jones saw it, but kept it to himself. Until she started going on shopping trips in town to get away from the 20 Room House she lived in.

At first he just made sure to do as she said. Becoming more and more helpful with each trip. Feeling out just how much she had resistance to him physically. He worked his way closer over time. Because if she was just a white woman. A white woman that did not want his attention, then it could lead to a long, drawn out, death. He started first with typical conversation.

"Fine day today. Where would you like me to take you ma' am?"
"Take me to the Main St. Shoes on Main St. Park at the corner of Main and Duhaney."

Rebecca kept conversation down, by being very precise. Over time Jones noticed that she started to ask for more rides. Sometimes not buying anything. They would drive to other places than downtown. They would go out by the bridge or near a lake, where she would have him park the car while she stared out the window in what looked like deep thought. Jones made sure to not say a thing during those times. He just sat. Every once in awhile glancing back, looking at her features for less than a second each time. Until one day as he looked in the rear mirror he looked for a second too long at her lips. She caught him, they locked eyes for a moment. She looked offended, angry. Something in Jones made him hold the stare, then look back down at her lips, then back up to her eyes. The tension in the car was thick Rebecca looked back at him and tried to maintain her offended look. But she could not. Instead her eyes dropped, and he continued to stare. His mind told him to look away. But something in him kept his eyes locked on her. He could see she was feeling deeply insecure now. She bit her bottom lip.

"Ms......"
"Take me home."
"Ma'am.."
"Take me home!"

Jones looked in the mirror.   His hesitation giving her more confidence.
" Drive Boy!"

The word boy was said with virulence. He could see he had overstepped his bounds by quite a ways. She was now upset and no telling what might happen. She stared at him with open aggression. Jones tried not to look in the mirror, but could not help but to glance every now and then. She stared in the mirror all the way back to the house. Even though she stared with open aggression, she seemed more angry at herself than at him. There was something else there and Jones could see it.

As they drove up the driveway to the house, Jones noticed her husband come out the front of the house. Rebecca was still in the back seat, glowering at Jones until she noticed her husband walking up.

Seeing her husband walk up made Jones break out sweating all over his body. He started sweating profusely under his shirt, and across his face. If this woman said a thing about what just happened, he was going to lynched, and would consider it a blessing if just shot and killed. It was too late to do anything, but see how it played out. As soon as the car stopped the man walked up to the back door and opened it.

"How was the shopping?"

"Fine. Did not find anything today though."
"How did Tommy Boy here do driving you?"

Jones heart was in his throat and the sound of it beat in his head. He kept his eyes straight forward looking at the garage doors. It was better that way because any reactions to him being called Tommy, which was not his name, and Boy, which he clearly was not, would only get him fired at a minimum, and lynched at the maximum. And right now he was waiting to see if he was going to have to pull off in this car to get away with his life.

"He was excellent, we have not a had a better driver. As a matter of fact he was going to drive me over into the city tomorrow to find some real clothes. I want to go visit that French Tailor as well as my relatives."
"Well your wish is his command. I have been waiting for you to get home for some time. Get on out, so we go inside out of this hellish heat. Tommy. Park the car, and clean it up."
"Yes sir."

Jones pulled into the garage, and watched them walk up to the house. Right as Rebecca got to the door with her husband, he reached for the door, back to her. As he reached she turned and gave a look that showed a deep longing toward Jones. She knew he was looking in the mirror. And she wanted him to see her. As quickly as she looked she stopped. Turning to her husband to continue the conversation without him knowing she was giving a look of yearning toward another man. He sat in the car for 30 minutes saying praises and saying thank you to God for sparing his life. The Relief was thick. But the desire was deeper. That last stare and the way she complimented him let him know how she felt toward him. He knew it was wrong but he also knew he would be back to trying to open her up soon.

The next day. In the morning. Rebecca came out and got in the car. She was carrying a suitcase, which Jones grabbed quickly, as he opened the door to let her in the car. It was a 2 hour drive to the city. 30 minutes of it on some of the unpaved roads that lead to the highway. Many times, the residents of this strange household would spend the night if they had to travel more than 1.5 hours away. So her suitcase grabbed no one's attention. She had even asked some of the other wives if they wanted to go with her, but they all declined. Her husband was off on "business" before she woke up. He would not mind either. So the stage was set.

Jones did not know if this was something she was doing to be alone with him. Or if she really was going shopping and visiting relatives. He did not know one way or the other. What he did know is, this time he was going to be far less bold. He was planning on being far less forward. Truly feel her out this time. She had not told anyone about him or revealed what had happened. This told him a lot. For the first part of the ride, Rebecca looked out the window. Watching the landscape go by. After they got on the highway she began to speak.

"My mother is black. She was a whore in New Orleans, or so I was told. You do not know how true or false that statement is seeing who it came from. I was given to a well to do white family. They could not have children, after they saw how I looked close enough to a white girl they adopted me. My mother was very light skinned, and my father I assume was some blonde blue eyed man. I was 2 when they did. It something I do not remember, but they told me and all the Servants, who are of course, all black. I have always been told and aware that I am black. Very few people are able to tell. As seeing my hair can be straighter at times than some of these white women and my skin is a very light shade. That is why I have as little interaction with anyone as possible. No one needs to know."

She was looking directly at Jones in the mirror. He glanced back but kept watching the road.

"I could tell by the way you, and a few other people watch me in the house, that you knew I was, or at least thought it was possible. But it is mandatory, that no one finds out."

A look of severity crossed her face. Its meaning was clear.

"When we get to the city, you will act as if you are merely a servant, driver. Then we can talk later."

Jones continued driving without saying a word. He still did not know if this was some elaborate hoax. When they got to the city he did everything like a driver and servant, arousing no suspicion. Once the day was over and they got to the hotel room things changed.

"Put that down over there"
"No."

Jones stared at Rebecca. Unmoving. She glared back at him. He had gone by the agreement. But they were no longer in public. If she wished to carry on this charade of being a white woman, and not the black woman with a secret that was every bit as dangerous to her as him being accused of rape by a real white woman, that would be her choice. But there was no way he was going to continue to act the part.

Rebecca walked up to him and swung to slap Jones, but his thick hand caught hers. He turned her around. Holding her with one hand on her right shoulder. She could not turn around, or grab him. Jones pulled up her skirt and slip as she tried to reach back and grab him. He ripped off her panties watching her butt shake from them being torn off. The movement he saw turned him on more. He then undid his pants with the same hand while still holding her in place. As soon as he pulled himself out, he pressed himself against her. Rebecca, was struggling, then stopped feeling his heat behind her. Jones did not move, he did not want to rape her. He wanted to be sure she wanted to do this. Rebecca did not say a word, but her shoulders relaxed, and she bent forward slowly, then turned her head to look over her shoulder, Jones felt himself inside her before he could give his body the command to enter her.

The shock of feeling him inside made Rebecca gasp. He was extremely hard. Longer and wider than anyone she had ever felt. He did not wait to see if she was ready, he just started pumping into her, deeper with each stroke. It was as if he was not just inside her. But pulling and pushing her inner thighs. He felt that thick to her legs. She felt him push inside of her and pull out. But it also felt as if he was moving her thighs in and out with every stroke. Still holding her by the neck and shoulder, she was unable to move, he had somehow gripped her in a way where she was almost being held up by him. Jones entered her and felt how wet she already was. It was like entering a deep ocean. He wondered how long she had been this turned on? He could not help himself, she was so wet, and it was so thick that he started to pump inside her with abandon. No thoughts of technique or worry to how she was feeling. He could hear her go from making sounds of a fight, to sounds of deep pleasure. She moaned in a way that almost sounded like crying, a low whimper. A whimper that could be heard by the rhythm of each stroke. The one hand she put on the front of his thigh to push him back, to keep him from going inside, was now grabbing him, and scratching him savagely. Pulling him in with each thrust, hunching and unhitching her back. Taking in and grinding each stroke for all it is worth. The harder or deeper he thrust into her the harder she scratched his leg.

With each stroke Rebecca fell deeper into lust with Jones. She had wanted him since before the incident at the Lake. Ashamed and scared, she had lashed out at him. But now feeling him deep inside of her, she could only feel the pleasure he was giving her. She could hear him pumping inside her. The sound of wetness being squeezed in and pulled out. Almost every stroke could be heard. She could feel his grip tightening on her neck and shoulder. He was strong, and hard. She wanted him in as deep as he could go. She wanted to feel every stroke to its fullest. And she was. Her thighs were now shaking. Bringing her closer and closer to a peak. She could feel it coming down.

Deeper each time. It felt like Rebecca had endless sensations inside her. The deeper he went, the more he felt. Even when hitting in a far as he could go. Pushing so deep he felt her inner wall, but that gave it's own sensations. There was more to be felt the more he pushed the deepest part of her, stretching her deeper inside. Now, he wanted to see more of her body. Her blouse was still on, he let go of her neck and shoulders. Pulled himself back, halfway out, maybe more. Watching Rebecca stay in the same position whimpering, trying to slide him back in on her own. He grabbed one hip, watching his thumb go deep into her soft flesh. He used his other hand to rip the buttons loose of her blouse with one quick tug. Rebecca gasped, her body pushing back on his, trying to be penetrated deeper again. And again, he held her in place by her hip. Slowly slid her blouse off. Her bra was all that remained of her clothing. He grabbed it, tearing it apart from the straps to the clasp with one pull. Her breast falling forward hanging over the bed. Jones could not see it but knew they were there and knew she could feel them hanging. He was close to his peak as well. He felt himself radiate pleasure inside her. Listening to her moan as he swelled more inside of her.

Rebecca felt her breast fall after her bra had been ripped off of her. She was turning to see him, to look at him, so she could take him in, but as she turned pushed all the way into her. Feeling larger than he had felt before. Her head dropped, only to see her own breast move to each stroke. He pushed harder, and stronger, with each slow stroke. The sound and sensations bringing her to her peak, faster, stronger than before. Her inner thighs were ablaze with sensation from right above her knee, straight to him inside of her. She felt an electric current intensifying with each stroke. Her body, shaking more with each stroke. Her thighs, her breasts, his body, his manhood inside her womanhood, all of it taking away any sight, sound, just feeling remained as she went over the top. An explosion of feeling inside of her as he stroked two more times, past her peak, then throbbed somewhere deep inside of her. She could feel him, filling her insides full with his creations.

The feeling was overwhelming for Jones, each stroke taking him closer and closer. The harder he pumped the more he wanted to feel. Seeing her body shake in front of him with each stroke. Seeing her give more and more to him, to the point that he had to hold her up as her body went limp. Clearly enjoying every stroke. She got more quiet instead of making more noise. She seemed to be loosing strength with each stroke. This in turn turning him on, that much more. He was feeling a second strength come in to last longer when he felt her, reach her peak. It gave him a swirling feeling around the head of his manhood deep inside her. Like a whirlpool encircling him inside of her. He could only push two more times and then he felt the deepest ecstasy that he had felt in his entire life. He felt himself throb out, all of himself, inside of her. Like multiple explosions of pleasure shot up his shaft and out into her. Unable to pull out of her. Not able to move , frozen. Stricken by how powerful the moment was, finally finishing collapsed on top of Rebecca on the bed. Unable to move, he felt her start to squirm under him seeming to pull more of his essence out into her as she moved her hips in a rhythm he had not felt before but was powerless to stop.

A few minutes later, Jones rolling off of Rebecca. Fell asleep instantly. Spent. While asleep he felt a growing pleasure on his manhood. As he awoke, he saw it was night time, he saw Rebecca's head going up and down between his legs. The pleasure was intense. So intense, he began to wonder if he could take it.

But when she looked up at him it was not Rebecca he saw. It was something else. The hair looked like Rebecca's but it was not her. It had a slug's consistency to the texture and color of the skin. It was dark and Jones had just woken up but he could swear that it was what he was seeing. The mouth was open, there were no teeth just an open hole with some type of thick liquid coming out. It seemed to come out with the same consistency of a heartbeat.

Jones jumped back. Quickly pulling up his pants, and tightening his belt. As he stood he could see it was Rebecca's hair on its head. Rebecca lay on the other side of the room, still alive, barely, with her head scalped. She was bleeding out profusely on the floor, from a wound on her neck. The amount of blood coming out of her and the speed in which it was coming out, made Jones know it was only a matter of time. A minute at the most before she was dead.

Looking back at the thing that had been sucking on him, he could see it completely now. The head of it was slug like, but the rest of it looked like a bunch of leaves and dirt. It had Rebecca's scalp on itshead. The scalp fell off as it saw Jones grab one of the bed post, kick the base of it and pull it off.

Jones was scared, he did not know what this thing was but it was, but he did not to intend to die easy. Jones jumped down off the side of the bed and ran toward the door. He was beat there by the mound of dirt that was under the head. The mound of dirt then surrounded him encasing him. He was not able see, hear, or breath as the dirt wrapped around him in an instant, squeezing him, like an anaconda, slowly getting tighter while the dirt was trying to get in his mouth, nose, and ears. Just as he thought he could hold his breath no longer, that slug skinned face with human features appeared in front of him, giving a rectangle size space with room to breath. Jones took in long breaths of air in what was the space of air between him and the inhuman head. It opened its mouth and spoke.

"There is a girl. When you find her we will find you. You will give us the girl, or you will suffer a fate that even death cannot save you from."

Her voice sounded like 10 women speaking at once. Every voice full of a seething hate. The smell coming from her mouth was like a thousand people with food rotting in their stomachs.

"You have no choice in this matter. You will be our vessel."

its eyes, two large black orbs, stared deeply into Jones. Its mouth opening. Jones unable to move could only watch as the face spilled a liquid out the mouth. The head deflating as the fluid flowed out of the mouth. It turned into an empty shell when all of the bile looking fluid formed in a puddle in front of him. To his horror the dirt around him clamped his head in place. He could not move, could not reach for his face. All he could do was look around with his eyes. But with his eyes, he watched the liquid rise into a slightly humanoid form. It was only as tall as his head. But the head of the creature cocked to the side as it walked up to him. It then put an arm, or what would be the hand under the nose. Then started shooting liquid straight in. Unconsciously Jones yelled, and the rest of the creature jumped into his mouth. The taste was of a bitterness never known to Jones. The liquid itself was not soft. It stretched his mouth and throat open as it moved its way slowly down his throat. Choking him into unconsciousness.

Everything went black. When Jones awoke he was face to face with Rebecca. She had no hair. Her dead eyes stared at him with sadness. There was a trail of blood over to him from where she was. She was stronger than her thought she was. She had died with her hand touching his chest. Judging from the blood marks on his shirt, she must have tried to wake him up.

Accepting the situation with remarkable calm. Jones could see that this was going to be a problem. He was in a hotel room with what everyone would see as a dead white woman. He had to leave, and had to leave now. He cleaned himself up as much as possible. Thanks to having to wear a coat for his job the clean up was made easier by being able to cover up most of the blood and dirt.

He walked down to the main floor carrying bags, making himself invisible to any white people around him. Other black people that worked in the building would glance at him, knowing something was wrong. But all it took was a short look toward the other and it was understood. Something has happened and it was to a white person. Please do not bring any attention to me. It was all understood in a look. As so much was during those days of blatant terrorism of the black people by white people for fun.

When Jones loaded the car and drove off to the highway. He did not look back. He went on to the highway.

Sylvia also said she and her mother ran into him when they were all at a house where people went to hide out when on the run. Sylvia and her mother were there because things were starting to get out of hand around their house. Too many people were invading their privacy. It would get worse and Sylvia's mother decided not to deal with that at all, they were going to lay low, then leave.

Sylvia's mother left Jones and her alone to often. He was a man on the run feeling like any day is his last. In telling the story to Sylvia about what happened to him. He gave full details to her, a teenage girl. He had written off the liquid that entered his body as a dream. Nothing ever happened to show that anything was wrong with him. Which in turn, got her physically curious about this big man. It took two days before they were both over-come with lust, Sylvia was a virgin. He took her virginity and more satisfying her in a way few other men would be able to. He also got her pregnant with Kathy.

Kathy read why her mother rationalized not telling Kathy. Sylvia said it was not proper to tell her about all that when she was a little girl. All she needed to know is that her father had passed. She did not tell her he was killed until this full story was told.

On the trip to California, Jones had gotten captured by some rednecks when he stepped out to take a smoke outside of a Church Members home in Arkansas. They came and put guns on the few people there, which were mostly women, old men, and took him. They did not find him for three days. When they did he was hanging from a tree, with half a leg missing. Face so beat you could not make it out. There was blood on his pants in the groin area, with his privates stuck in his mouth.

There was nothing supernatural about his death. He was a black man. That looked like he had some pride about him. The drunk rednecks that picked him up just wanted to kill someone for fun. They did not know him from anyone else. It was just what would happen in the south. The last thing Sylvia heard as they drove off with him was, "Teach this uppity nigger something about respect to the white man!" And then he was gone.

The memory of what she read read popped in her head so suddenly she almost did not see the connection. Kathy thought on it for a minute. It was because she felt like her mother had not told everything there was to know. And at the time it seemed like much of it was just straight out delusional at the time. Which is what probably kept her mother from telling her so much more. But, now, she believed anything. There just seemed to be something in the air that was calling to her. But from two totally different places. Kathy hopped in her car with a mind full of thoughts after leaving the Law Office. Just as her mind started to clear, she noticed Angela standing talking to a slender well dressed man. They seemed to be pretty deeply engaged in conversation. The man, who was looking at Angela, seemed to sense Kathy driving by. It was almost as if the man's whole back turned to look and follow her as she drove by. It was as if his back was a face and was looking dead at her. He was steady talking to Angela. And Angela was enraptured in the conversation. His hands and head positioned so it was clear he was really speaking directly to her. But his back was squared up exactly with Kathy's car as it went by.

Kathy wrote it off as her overactive imagination running away with her. Maybe some jealousy in the back of her mind on Angela talking to a well dressed man. But as Kathy thought about it. She said to herself, she would keep that memory in mind. The one of his back seeming to watch her. Because right now, there is no telling what was going happen. She would catch up with Angela at another time. Her phone started to ring. It was Jerome, Kathy smiled as she answered.

"Hey"

Chapter 9

Kathy had almost forgot about Jerome with all the events of the day. The video, Angela, all the questions that Kathy herself had. But hearing Jerome's voice was just what she needed. He added a calmness to her that she so desperately needed right now.

"I thought you might forget about me after your meeting, so I decided to call you."

"Well, I did not forget about you.......well maybe a little, but I remember you now."

"Ooooohhh I see. You remember me when I am here. But forget me when I am not around. That is twice now. Once at your house now on the phone. I am counting. "

Despite her stress, Kathy could not help but laugh. "You are not supposed to be keeping track."

"Just getting to know you again. We have not been around each other for many years. You might be a Crack Addict, I don't know?"

"Oh, if I was an Addict, of anything. You would know. There

would be no doubt. Besides, you are the one hopping fences like you are straight out of Mad Max and the Thunderdome. Maybe *YOU* are the one that should be watched and tested. It took three hours to clear the dust that came off your clothes when you landed in the back yard."

"Ok, well..."

Jerome could not finish, he was laughing too hard. Kathy too. They both laughed for awhile. Then continued talking. They agreed to meet in an hour and half. Jerome would pick her up. That seemed to be enough time for Kathy to be able to soak some of this stress off and then get ready to go. She was almost home and the first thing she planned to do was go straight to the bathroom and run the bath water in the tub in the master bedroom. It was an old tub. The type with feet on the bottom of it. Deep and long. She would be able to get a good soaking in there. She could not wait. This would get the night started right.

Kathy enjoyed the feeling of the warm water, and the smell of the fragrance her mother had used from the bath and body store. It was soothing. After a day like today she needed something to exfoliate everything she was feeling. She wanted to make sure she was good and relaxed when she met with Jerome.

As she settled into the bathtub, finding the perfect position. She felt her body relaxing. Water up to the bottom of her neck. Carefully keeping all the water away from her hair, which was up in a shower cap and wrapped perfectly under that to maintain her hair from losing its style. Her phone charging and alarm on. It was set to wake her up so that she would be able to get up and get ready in time. Everything was set. Kathy allowed herself to fall off to sleep. Lying in the bathtub with only candles lit made it easy to ease her way into sleep. She felt like she was in warm cocoon, what was soft, but airtight. Smelling the sweet scent of the bath water mixed with the relaxing smell from candles. Looking forward to seeing Jerome, nothing could be more perfect than what she was feeling at this very moment.

A cold gust of wind blew across her face. Extremely cold. It felt like a winter wind. The bite of it hurt. Kathy went to look to see if a window was open, but she could not move. She could not turn, she could not raise her arms, or even open her eyes. She tried to move, tried to scream but nothing happened. It felt as if her eyes had been sealed shut with some type of adhesive. The cold air still brushed her face. The water was still warm but her face was starting to get numb. Kathy was panicking. She could not move, but felt the need to not only move, but to run. There was something in the room. Watching her. Maybe even more than one. She could feel it in the room somewhere. Somewhere close. She could tell, because the air got colder as it got closer. She could not hear breathing. The only thing she felt was the air getting colder as it got closer. Her cheek, ear, and neck getting colder at a rate she never felt before. The water itself was starting to cool at an alarming rate. To her left, was a wall. But to her right, was the rest of the bathroom. A large open space that led straight to the door out. It was on the right side she felt her exposed neck, face, and ear, freezing. The cold was so intense it might as well been a fire, burning into her skin as she felt it grow ever colder. There was no breathing, but she felt like there was a nose inches away from her neck. Slowly, agonizingly slowly, getting closer, and closer. She could not move, scream, or even look toward what was getting closer.

It was starting feel is if the very blood in her veins was starting to freeze when a loud noise suddenly exploded in the room. Kathy sat straight up screaming her head off. Her back slammed against the wall as two candles fell in the water. Looking around frantically trying to see something, but she found nothing. It was warm in the room without any trace of the ice cold air she had felt. The water itself was still almost hot. The sound she heard as her own alarm going off on the chair she had put next to the bathtub. Slowly she came to the realization that it was just a dream, a nightmare that had passed. Kathy quickly turned the light on in the bathroom. All of them. She then proceeded to turn on all the lights in the room. The closet light could be turned on while still in the bedroom and she made sure to turn that on before she opened the door. After feeling satisfied that everything was well lit, and constantly telling herself to calm down it was just a dream. Kathy, finally started to calm down. The feeling of pure helplessness still fresh in her mind. The mind numbing cold she felt still could be felt on her neck as if it had just happened. But when she touched her neck it was warm.

Kathy continued to get ready. Turned on the Radio, and let it play rather loudly, just another way to get rid of the nightmare feelings she was experiencing. And after awhile she fell into her own rhythm to each song being played. The DJ seemed to be playing good song after song. Which is rare. Normally it is one good song, followed by several played out songs, or just bad songs. But tonight, it was commercial free and song after song kept hitting. The doorbell rang and she barely heard it, and in fact, had gotten so caught up in the music had started to have her own little private party. Luckily, she was able to do her hair, and all she needed to do was put on some shoes and her shirt.

Jerome was standing to the side of the house, trying to see where Kathy was in the house she was taking so long. He had his cell phone in his hand, staring at it with a frown on his face. He had not noticed that Kathy was standing there watching him look for her, calling her cell phone that was still in the bathroom.

"If you are wondering where I am, you can find me right here."

Kathy said smiling as Jerome turned around obviously surprised that she was standing there and looking a tad bit like a kid that had just been caught doing something bad.

"Well, I was just on the phone trying to reach you, but you did not answer. Tried to call you to let you know I was running late, but you did not answer. And hearing how loud the music is you are playing lets me know exactly why. You ready? 'Cause you look ready."

Jerome smiled. A big smile, showing perfect teeth. Kathy and he embraced. This time neither felt awkward. It was a mutual desire. Jerome one stair step below her, so they were eye to eye. His arms wrapped around her waist, her arms wrapped around the top of his shoulders and neck. They stood for a moment in that embrace. She enjoying the rock hard feeling of his body. He, enjoying the soft, supple, feel of hers. Both looking each other deep, in the eyes. Finally, Jerome released her, and Kathy turned toward the door still looking him in the eyes.

" I will go get my truck and pull it up here. That will give you enough time to grab what you need and we can take off. The reservation is set for 30 minutes from now. You with that?"
"Oh, I am *with*, that!"
"Well let's DO, this!"

They both looked at each other smiling. Then she turned to go into the house as he turned to get his truck. Both could pass on the dinner, but they were both hungry. The sexual tension was high.

This was something they both wanted. But the waiting would make it all the better.

Dinner went well. The food was excellent, and so was the service. Jerome was surprised by how good the service was. Normally at a place like this, he got the "Nigger Treatment". Which normally consists of being ignored as far as service goes. Servers would either look directly at him and serve someone else. Or just ignore him outright. People always say that type of thing does not happen anymore. But Jerome and many of his male friends had the same complaint. That is why he usually ate at home, or went to small black owned mom and pop restaurants. They may not always have the "ambiance", but they served up a full plate of food. Kathy, however, hardly ever had any issues when she ate out. And right now she was enjoying the ambiance of the place. The lights were not too low, but also not too high. You could see clearly, but it was dark enough to get comfy with whoever you were speaking with. The bar on the other side of the restaurant was full and loud enough to carry over the sound to this side of the restaurant. Jerome and she were watching the sun go down on the other side of the Golden Gate Bridge. They were seated right next to the window. The restaurant itself was above a harbor, over the water in the Bay. There was a clear view of San Francisco, the water from the Bay, the Golden Gate Bridge, and the mountains that were the background past the Bay water. There were mountains to the North and South of the Golden Gate Bridge. As the sun got lower the hues in the sky changed from blue, to yellow, to red, then finally, black as the stars shown in the clear night air. The water itself reflected all the colors of the sun, as it set on the other side of the mountains. As they talked and drank waiting for their order to come, both enjoyed the view.

Kathy watched Jerome as he spoke to her while watching the

sunset. In that moment she found herself exhilarated by his conversation. She no longer saw the young teenager that had all the teenage girls chased after. He was now a full grown man. His face, eyes, now had the look of a grown man. He had the definitive look of someone who had made a way where there probably was none. His body though powerfully built seem to have an elegance to his movements. He was bone crusher strong but, he moved with a preciseness she had not seen in many people. Every hand gesture, when he lifted his glass to drink, was controlled, not robotic, actually quite smooth. He sat up straight, and seemed to have no give in his posture. She glanced around at other tables and found many women at other tables sitting with a look that said, "I wish she were over here, and I was over there with him." Indeed many of the other men in the area seemed to be lacking in one area or another that Jerome was not lacking in at all. After they finished their third round of drinks after dinner, with the sun gone all the way down. They both decided it was time to go.

Jerome recommended they go for a short walk. Help burn off some of the food. Kathy had no objections to that. Jerome told her he knew of a Park down by the Port that was not too far from where they were. It had a grand view of San Francisco. Kathy thought it was a great idea. It was not too cold out, and the night was clear, which was rare. Usually the fog rolling in from the ocean would block the view of San Francisco completely. They both stopped at the restrooms that was to the right of exit. Then both put on their coats before heading out of the restaurant. As soon as they walked out the front door, they were caught by a slicing wind coming off of the water. Jerome took Kathy under his arm and squeezed her close. He had wrapped his jacket around her. The heat from his body filled the coat and kept her warm as well. She noticed Jerome get a little extra pep in his step as they got closer to the parking lot. Maybe it was how close they were, but Kathy wrote that off as she saw the gleam in his eye as he stared directly at his truck.

Jerome was proud of his truck. It was a Tahoe, '09, an SUV, but he still called it a truck, and thought of it as a truck. First vehicle he ever bought brand new. Everyone said they would not buy brand new. Loses too much value, but Jerome had outright bought his truck. There was no loan. If there was an accident or he ran into extra lean times he would get all the money it was worth, and with no Lien holder to pay for the loan he owed them. On top of that, he was tired of buying cars that had belonged to someone else. He wanted a new vehicle, customized to what he wanted. Nothing else would do. The only thing he did to it after buying it was add a full exhaust system which improved its freeway acceleration noticeably. Besides that, he like the sound. Glancing out the side of his eye to see how Kathy reacted when he started it up in the parking lot. She had just put her seatbelt on. When the bark turned rumble of the engine started, she paused, then seemed to visibly melt deeper into the chair. That is the exact reaction he hoped to get. Knowing most women could care less about anything to do with performance or trucks as a whole. He knew if Kathy reacted to the startup, she was very sensitive to him, and things were going exceptionally well. She was reacting because she knew he was watching. For her to give him that meant she was open to him, and willing to give. Smiling and watching her from the corner of his eye. He could not help himself and said.

"That sound good to you?"

Kathy just smiled while avoiding eye contact with him. Jerome now felt things were going perfectly. He pulled out of the space, then drove out the parking lot. When they pulled up to the Park, they were amazed to see so many people out. Normally this park is almost empty during the day, but tonight it seemed to be date night for the Grown Folk. There was everything from 20 somethings to couples that had to be 70+. A bunch of them. Something was definitely in the air tonight. Jerome went down further to the second parking lot that not too many people knew was there. It was a dead end the took you around a roundabout. But there were spaces all around the roundabout. There was only one car. A Police Car. The Officer was black. He saw Jerome pull up and actually nodded in acknowledgement to Jerome, which threw Jerome off a little. Most Police Officers, especially the black ones seem to want to make a point of their power or to give him some look of, "what are you up to?!?" This guy was on his cell phone speaking to his woman, judging from how many times Jerome heard him say, "Baby", in the space of 1 minute.

Kathy took Jerome's medium sized but hard as stone arm and squeezed it, with her head lying on his shoulder. They started walking down the concrete path that led between the uncut grass that had grown to waist height. In the darkness they looked black compared to the dark gray concrete they walked on. The contrast gave supernatural feel to the night. The park was only 2 or 3 years old. So just about everything was new. The concrete seats, the bbq pits, benches, and the two lookout towers with the pay per view telescopes.

The concrete path they were on climbed up a small hill from the parking lot. Then went down real low in before climbing another hill to a higher height. From there, at the highest point, it gave the optical illusion of a path that leads straight to San Francisco if you stood right below the top part of the path. The water that separates Oakland and San Francisco was blocked. So the path itself led right up to downtown San Francisco. It lights mostly showed yellow and gold. It looked like a miniature city at the end of the path they walked on.

"Jerome this is beautiful. I have never been here. I did not even know there was a park here."

"Yeah, they built this a few years back. It is nice. Had a couple of big BBQs up here. One concert that I know of. Sometimes I come up here by myself at night. A night like tonight. It helps to clear my thoughts. Sitting in my truck, watching boats and ships go by. Watching Day turn to Night, and all the changes that go with it."

Kathy looked up at Jerome, studying his strong jaw line and his eyes as he stared at the City, lights reflecting in his eyes. Kathy hugged him tightly, and he gave a gentle squeeze back. Both of them stared at the City and the Stars in the sky. It was a moment of contentment for both of them. The more Jerome talked the more she saw him as the man he is. How did the vain boy she had known back in school become this man? The slightly conceited boy, that is now very much a grown man, with a solid confidence that has replaced the arrogance she used to see in him from time to time. There were questions that needed to be answered, but right now the heat emanating from his body, was all she craved. The wind was starting to pick up. Where they were standing caught all the wind blowing off of the bay. The air temperature was not bad, but once that wind hit, you could feel it slice away your warmth. She only had a light jacket and scarf on. He only had a light jacket on, but his body seemed to radiate its own heat, like it he had his own atmosphere. The weather in his atmosphere was warm, cozy, but kept being disturbed by cold knives being thrown up from the water, slicing away at the atmosphere she was trying to burrow into.

"Let's go. You are starting to shiver. And that is no good. 'cause I need you healthy."

A grin spread across Jerome's face. He knew she was going to look at him to protest, but knew this wind was cutting her up. She was basically trying to crawl up into his chest now. So cold she could not even answer him. But the real reason he felt it was time to go is because he felt watched. Normally he was able to pinpoint the area where someone was without looking. It was a sense left over from his youth, when he used to get into too many situations. Now, older, more wise from those experiences, he had gotten used to listening to the inner voice inside him. And right now, it was telling him someone was watching them. He could not look around because that would alert whoever was watching, that he was aware. That, is not what Jerome wanted. Whoever it was seemed to be in more place than one. Which is strange, because normally that would mean it was more than one person. But right now, Jerome had a solid feeling it was just one person. And with all the shadows being cast by this overgrown grass, it would be hard to decipher what is a plant or what is someone coming at them.

"Damn, I am started to freeze too. Let's get up out of here."

Right as he was making the statement, Jerome, started walking at a very fast pace with Kathy under his right arm, being lifted slightly aloft by Jerome as he took off in a VERY fast pace toward his truck. It did not feel right to Kathy, but the urgency he was heading to the truck made Kathy just write it off as him heading toward the truck to get warm. What she did not know is that Jerome had spotted who was watching them out of the side of his eye. He could see the person was tall, but could make nothing else out. As he turned to speak to Kathy, while opening the door of the truck for her. He looked at her head but slightly past to the area where the figure had been . But there was no one there. He quickly scanned the area while making a statement about how the new park had been built over old train tracks. Using his hand to point from the far left to the far right, scanning everything in between. It looked natural the way he did it. Like he was just pointing something out. A regular person would have thought that. But whoever was stalking them, did not take a chance. Jerome still felt the person was down near the area where they had just walked down from.

Once inside the truck, Jerome kept playing it off as if he was cold, by wiping his hands together in front of the heater vents. All the while checking the horizon. He backed the truck out of the space after a minute, letting the heat fully kick in on the inside. Then put it in drive and drove out of the parking lot. Driving away but scanning his rear view mirror for anyone following behind him. He felt like he had left a piece of himself behind in the parking lot. That part of him he left, was searching, looking, waiting in the cold dark night. As he looked in the mirror while driving away, he saw a lone figure. A silhouette of the tall person he had seen standing there before. It was a slightly different spot than he had seen figure in before. Much closer to where he had parked the truck. Then the person faded away as he looked in the rear view mirror. The craziest part about it, was not that the figure vanished while he was staring directly at it, but that he felt like it sensed it had been spotted by the part of him he had left behind. To Jerome it was more of a thought, feeling, that he still had unfinished business and wanted to know exactly who was following him. But right now it felt as if that thought, that part of him, came back into him to tell him it had been spotted and the person had left. This created a great deal of tension inside Jerome. Because that, sounded crazy to him. A little dramatic.

Kathy was talking when she noticed Jerome grab the steering wheel so hard, it bent. This was not a flimsy looking steering wheel. She saw his eyes locked on the rear view mirror, and had a flash vision of a shadowy figure in the mirror. It came to her like a thought of her own, but she knew instantly it was not her own. It was Jerome's. Looking at him, she stopped mid-sentence. She saw the intensity in his eyes. They left because he had seen something but had not wanted to alarm her. It made perfect sense now with that walk that should have been called a run back to the truck.

"Jerome, what was back there?"
"I am just looking back, the police officer seemed to have pulled off before we came back. Did you notice that?"
"Don't try to avoid the question. And do not lie to me, because I will know. What did you see back there?"

Jerome could hear the alarm in Kathy's voice. He did not want to alarm her, protect her, but no alarm. She was staring right at him. When he looked at her, he felt as if she was siphoning, pulling something out of him. When he looked into her eyes, he saw an intense focus. She was staring straight into him. It was a little disconcerting. And with what he had just seen and felt, it was not an extra feeling he needed. But the look on Kathy's face gave him a feeling. A feeling that was that small voice in his head. Telling him two things. Tell her the truth, and that figure is following her, not you.

"When we were walking. I started to feel like we were being watched. Cannot tell you how I know, but since I was young that feeling has served me right and kept me alive. Even when certain things had nothing to do with me."
"Is that what you were looking at? Was it the tall man you saw?"

Jerome paused for a moment, he had not told her he had seen the person. Or what the person looked like.

"Yes. It was a tall figure. He was not moving, just staring. The last part of our walk when we were looking across at Frisco was when I felt like he was near. The funny thing is, it felt as though he was circling us, as though he was in several different areas at once."

"Do you think it was more than him?"

"No. That I can feel. But how he moved that much, that quick, concerns me. Is there something I should know about you. For instance, how you know what I saw without you telling me? Let's start there. How did you know?"

It was time for Kathy to get quiet now. Jerome glanced over her way quickly since he was driving. But his quick glance parlayed enough intensity to sit with her for awhile. He meant what he was asking. Almost sounded like he was willing to drop her off, in the middle of West Oakland, at night, around some old warehouses that had not been bought up yet by young artist, and real estate people looking to gentrify the area. Kathy knew he would not do it, but his look gave that kind of intensity for wanting to know an answer to his question.

"Sometimes I can see things in people. I have always been able to see things from everyone else's perspective. But now I don't know. It is as if the information is put so solidly in my head.......I don't know. Can't explain it."

Kathy's head drooped a little. Clearly feeling a weight from the information she had just given. She did not want Jerome to think she was some freak of nature, on the run from someone or something. Especially after watching the video her mother left her. The night had been perfect until now and she did not want it to be messed up any further.

"It is ok. There are things I have experienced too, like the way I can sense people's presence. Still one more question. Is anyone after you? Anyone or any people that you know of?"

Kathy thought for a moment, and decided to tell him about the video her mother had left her. By the time she finished, Jerome had gotten through his zig zag route across town to make sure no one was following them, and pulled up in front of her house. He backed down the driveway which was on the side of the house. He shut off the lights, then the engine. They sat for one full minute while he turned over the information in his head. To Kathy he did not have look like he did not believe her and was about to turn her in for being crazy. He just looked like he was considering every word. Finally, he spoke, to her relief.

"I believe you. And I believe what your mother told you. The man with the cane would visit your mother every so many years. He had a way of knowing I was around or watching. Whether I was right in front of him, or at a neighbor's house looking down the street from a small bathroom window, he would sense me. He would look dead at me no matter how far away I was. He was around more than ever, right before your mother died."
"Did she tell you anything about him?"
"No. He was not her boyfriend or anything. He did seem to come by and have a purpose every time. He would not drive up or off. You would just see him walk up the stairs to the door. They would talk for a while like relatives, and then he would leave. Saw him laugh one time. Other than that, the man was stone. His facial expression never changed. He did not look old close up. But from

a distance, the gray and white beard with the bald head made him look old. And I know he is I know he is old. He used to be around your Grandmother."

A flash of memories shot through Kathy's head, but none of them were hers. One stuck out more than the others. She saw herself being flung backwards behind the man with the cane, as he stood, looking like he had tossed a quarter behind him. The bottom of his cane on a root or very long branch. The branch itself glowed orange like an electric stove burner when it heats up. He was walking toward the shed as Kathy's grandmother took the child version of herself around the corner.

There was searingly bright light, muffled words. One of an unearthly tone. Almost sounded like dirt talking, screaming, then the words became clear.

"You cannot destroy all of us. In life and in death, you know as well as I, we will live. These bodies are just vessels."

A deep baritone voice answered back.

"These are things I know. What you do not understand is, there is no longer any oversight. You and your alliances made sure of this. So now I am free to do what I will. No longer am I constricted by the laws that used to bind. This will be our last meeting. You will experience no form of life any longer. And this vessel you are using, this putrid bile, full of dirt, maggots, and trash, is an abomination. You tricked me as to who you really are down in Louisiana, but that will no longer be the case. Pretending to be a, "Hoodoo woman", or any other character is over.
"It is not over until WE, say it is!"

The shed itself melted down around them, as if it was running water. Instantaneous. Heat so intense it felt as if the Sun itself had landed in the backyard and spread its heat, through the fence. The man with the cane stood in what would have been the middle of the shed. There was no longer any bright light. Just the waves that bend light showing the level of heat outside. The man with the cane stood, and appeared to be choking a body rapidly declining into skeletal form, on second look, a woman, who's body was being burned down to the skeleton. It was not a human woman. The hands were freakishly long. The end of the bones that made up the finger were long and sharp. Knife edge sharp. The man squeezed the neck so tightly it shattered. The head popped loose, it landed with its face turned toward the fence. Its sick yellow eyes, one having slit for a pupil like a cat, while the other was a black orb. Both eyes melted in less than a second, but not before recognizing the child. The mouth seemed to grin before it disintegrated.

"You were there. You saw all that, what happened to me as a little girl. Why didn't you tell me!"
"Because I was told not to. Besides that, I wrote if off as an overactive imagination from my childhood."
"Who told you not to tell me?"
"How do you know these things in my head? How long have you been able to do that?"
"Please just tell me who told you?"
"The man with the cane."
"When?"
"The day he killed whatever that was in your backyard. He also told me that I would have to seal the ground off at some point when I am grown. Make sure that this does not happen again. Years later I would find a pouch full of what looks like mix to make concrete in my bedroom. The funny thing about that day

was, I had made sure, to lock every way into my bedroom. I was holding some stuff in my room, and I did not want anyone to get in even if they tried by crawling through my window."

Kathy was still stuck on the other information to even hear Jerome's last point of how he knew his room had been locked tight that day. She just wanted to get this nightmare out of her head and out of her life. Just return back to normal.

"Good night Jerome."
"Whoa. Hold on. I know you are not upset at me not telling you something that would definitely sound crazy if I would have told you any earlier than today? Can you at least see *why* would not tell you something like that?"

Both sat in silence. Jerome looking at the side of Kathy's face as she stared at the glove box. Kathy, refused to look him in the eye. She knew if she looked him in the eye, she would not be able to hold. So instead of looking him in the eye she slowly turned toward the door and opened it. Jerome did not move to stop her. She then stepped out and walked toward the stairs.

Jerome sat in his car. Watching Kathy walk toward the stairs. In his mind, the night had been going so well until she started to literally, read his mind. Luckily he did not have some crazy fantasy going on in his head. Kathy's mother had told Jerome that Kathy was different. She could see into people. Jerome just figured that it was just another motherly statement of how a mother would feel about a daughter. Sylvia had not told him the full extent of seeing into other people. When she told him, she did look him right in the eye, as if she was revealing something, without revealing it directly. More of a, do you see what I am saying kind of look. Jerome did not make the connection then, but it was clear now. He did not move to start his truck, just watched Kathy get out, walk around his truck and then up the stairs.

As Kathy moved closer to the door she noticed she had not left the porch light on. Which is something she had done every time she left out of the house. Because she always figured she might arrive home late enough for it to be dark. Her key was out, but putting it into the lock was harder than she expected. It was as if she was blind and had to feel her way. She finally got the key in and turned it. Normally she did not lock the doorknob, just the bolt. The key turned effortlessly, as if it was not locked at all. Since she was turning the key to the bolt and doorknob at the same time, she opened the door up before she could stop. The realization that the door was not locked hit her as the door opened. Just as she was about to step back and close the door, wanting to ask Jerome to come over, a hand came around the door and snatched her into the dark house. Fear was all she felt. There was no time to react, scream, run, move. Fear, was all that could happen as she was pulled inside like a she weighed nothing more than that of little girl's rag doll.

Chapter 10

Jerome was watching as he saw Kathy get snatched inside and the door slammed shut. He jumped out of his truck in full sprint. He got up to the door and kicked it as hard as he could. One kick broke the door halfway open, the second kick broke the door all the way open. Working as a Building Engineer and Handyman had taught him many tricks in breaking things open. And right now, he needed to be inside as soon as possible.

The first floor was empty. The light showed in pretty well from the street, and sitting in his truck with the lights off on the side of the house where it is darker than the street had adjusted his eyes to the dark. Jerome scanned quickly but carefully. Listening for any sounds, keeping his back to the wall as he searched the living room. He then heard a hard thud on the ceiling, coming from the master bedroom. Instantly, he bounded up the stairs. There was a muffled sound of Kathy trying to scream. There were several more hard hits he could hear as he ran full speed down the hallway. This door was well made for a bedroom door but should break loose in one try. And it did.

Kathy could not see the person's face that had grabbed her, she could feel he was boney, but strong. She tried to yell out but felt all her air knocked out of her by a punch to her stomach as soon as the door *started* to close. Next thing she knew, she was over his shoulder as he carried her up the stairs. The man made no sounds. She could not hear him breath, could barely make out what kind of clothes he had on. Once in the master bedroom he locked the door. Then she could see he had on an old cotton gym outfit. The kind that are given away at churches to homeless people. As he came back from locking the door to where he had dropped her in the middle of the room, she was able to take her first breath in many seconds, an inhale that seem to last forever. What she wanted to do was stop inhaling and yell. She looked across the room and saw the man was getting closer, each step seemed to be at a faster rate than normal. For every moment she took to catch her breath, he was another step closer. Kathy not knowing what he might do next was terrified. All she could do was inhale, but all she wanted to do was yell for help, or make any noise to get someone, anyone's attention to end this nightmare. Before she could stop inhaling air he had stuffed her mouth with something crunchy, and cold.......to her horror was some type of bugs, and he kept stuffing them in. She could now scream and tried to, but the more she screamed the deeper in her mouth the bugs got. As they got to the back of her throat, the door flew off the hinges with Jerome moving straight past it.

Jerome could see Kathy on the ground with a tall man over her. He was of a slim build, his hand was over her mouth. There was something he was pressing into her mouth. The light was too low to make out what. All Jerome knew is that he was going to hit this man harder than he hit the door. As soon as he got in range he kicked up into the man's ribcage. The cracking of ribs could be heard as he felt soft tissue his foot had gone up in.

The man's body moved to the side of Kathy and Jerome followed with two stomps on the man before the guy somehow got up and to the side of Jerome hitting Jerome without much affect. Jerome started throwing blow after blow, connecting each time. Each hit could be heard. Jerome was not hitting the man's head, he was hitting the man's ribs, stomach, neck. Several hits gave cracking sounds, as many of Jerome's hits broke bones. The bony man did not yell out in pain, he just swung back but could not connect many of his punches.

Jerome caught the man with a blow to the jaw, that set is mouth sideways, another hit knocked it back in line, followed by another hit that seem to break the jaw loose. As the jaw dangled Jerome hit him one more time, all hits done without a pause between them. His last blow caught him right on the top right of his head, in the temple with a blow that Jerome *had* done before and *had* knocked out a few grown men that were bigger than this man, yet, the bony man still stood. This made Jerome pause.

Kathy watched from the floor, feeling a sense of relief after she spit and pulled all the bugs out of her mouth, which was priority 1 for her after Jerome had kicked the man off of her. The bugs did not leave her alone after they landed on the floor. They would run back toward her, and even in the low light, she could see them coming back toward her with a purpose. She stepped on all of them. Feeling them crunch through her shoes. After the last one was killed she looked up to see how Jerome was. He seemed to be doing fine. His movements were so quick Kathy could barely see, the other man was trying to fight back but each hit Jerome connected on the man seem to rock his body throwing off his equilibrium, but yet he still stood. Jerome's hits were so rapid it sounded almost like one long thump, with cracks sporadically heard. After a few seconds Kathy figured out the cracks were the man's ribs, nose, jaw, teeth all being broken. Jerome would get hit here and there, but he did not seem to catch any solid blows from the man. Jerome kept moving, constantly hitting and moving.

But when she saw the man's jaw get knocked to the side, then back in place, then all the way out of its joint without the man making a sound or reacting, fear and a deep worry entered her. Jerome was overwhelmingly quick, and powerful, but none of the blows he was landing seemed to hurt the man. His body showed the damage from Jerome's hits. But he was not dropping. His jaw hung loose with bugs pouring out of his mouth. And were pulling the jaw back together, back in place. The bony man's face now directly in the light, shown eyes that were gray orbs. His pupils seemed to be covered in a gray film. Like a membrane. Sightless. Even Jerome stopped for a split second, and in that split second, the man's right hand produced something reflective and brought it across Jerome's chest with lightning speed. Jerome moved back while pushing his foot forward into the side of the man as he lost balance in a swing meant to take Jerome out. The kick done to the man's torso was a brutally hard and fast push that sent the man airborne and out the window.

Jerome was out the window behind the man with full intentions of landing feet first on top of him. And he did. As the man landed Jerome landed feet first on the man's face and chest. He heard and felt multiple snaps, cracks and crunches of the bones in his face and chest. But he stood knocking Jerome off of him as if none of that happened. The body of the man moved awkwardly, torso twisted, as though the spine had been broken. Then he straightened out, the sounds of several vertebrae snapping into place. Jerome watched as the face, neck, and back straightened out realigning every bone. Fear, crept into him for the first time. Adrenaline leaving him. He had no weapon, and this man, if that is what he was, seemed to not be able to be hurt. A woman screamed from across the street. She had seen the man's body go from broken to straight. A man yelled, "What the fuck!?!??" The open mouth with the hanging jaw that was knocked out of place and half crushed by Jerome landing on it. Was brought back into place by bugs inside the mouth pulling it back into shape, and closing it as they retreated back inside. The bony man , took in Jerome's features, not moving just eyes staring.

"This is not finished. She is ours. We shall feast on her soul, and drink her power. You will know what you have entered into when we come back. We will be back to claim what is ours. No human can stop us. We shall have her."

The voice was a normal voice of a man. But the tone was sinister. It would have been better if it sounded like in the movies. Like a monster. But the directness, and matter of fact statement of it, gave it much more depth than any special effects on a voice could give. Jerome wanted to do something or say something but the man took off down the street, as the few people out walking watched. Jerome got on his phone and called the Police. He wanted to make sure no one called and reported it was him starting the fight. As far as he could see, the man he just fought was probably a man with no name. He seemed to be nameless because he looked almost featureless and Jerome doubted any of the onlookers got a good look at the guys face. They probably just saw his face and were willing to say it was him doing all the fighting, since he was black and the other guy, though black too, was light skinned with a bald head, which in the dark could look like a black man fighting a white one. And we all know how that is going to end up looking to the police. The area where this house is used to be an all black neighborhood. But with Re-Gentrification going on, it was now mostly white. The love of the old architecture of the Victorians brought people in to the area in droves.

The police arrived and one of them happened to be a childhood friend of both Jerome and Kathy. If it was not for him being the Highest rank officer there would have been a problem, and Jerome would have gone to jail. You could see what people were telling the white officers as they looked at Jerome. They would stare at him while talking to the police with conversation that went like this.

"Maam, are you a witness?"
"Yes. And I, saw, *everything!* That man right there, the thuggish looking one, knocked this, this….man out of that window right there. And was brutally and SAVAGELY beating on the guy. It was as if he was on PCP, Crack, or something."
"Did you see the other man?"
"Yes."
"What did he look like?"
"He was……he looked to be a European. But he was not the problem. That man, the one right there, he was just beating on him. I have never in my life see anything like that."

At this point the officer would ask about a black witness seeing the body of the bony straighten out. Saying they saw the other man make a threat to Jerome. The "witness", would then say something like this.

"All I saw was *that* man right *there* punching and stomping the man that ran away. Thank God he could run away because you just don't know what someone like the guy beating on him could do."

Never mind that he was there protecting a friend from assault rape or any other danger. He was wrong for beating on this other man. Jerome to them just looked like a common thug. The gentrified neighborhood had changed the vibe. Before the change happened, he was known as a man for the youngsters to look up to. As their families moved out and the white people moved in. His business took a hit. No longer getting the jobs he used to for working on different houses. The look many gave him was the same as the ones that people gave dopefiends in the area. Like a common nuisance that needed to checked and watched like some dog that kept getting out of a neighbor's yard. But lately, there was something new popping up. A fear. Fear of a black man. Similar to the way children feared the Boogie Man. An unfounded fear, that every news report that ran from morning to night said. Fear the black man. He is an evil and violent beast. Who will rape, steal from, and kill you. When in truth, the culture that put into law that Black People are not fully human are the ones that have a long history of doing just those things they fear. There was a time when they killed the black men and boys who showed any sign of self esteem as slowly and as painfully as possible. There was a time when they raped black girls as soon as they started to grow into womanhood.

But it is the black man that is violent. And some young black boys believed this. Trying to make themselves hard when they really are not. Starting a whole fake Thug Culture. When most of them had never been in a fight, and come from good families. But the families never taught them the history of this country. And how many things are done to make sure Black Folks minds stay buried in confusion, self doubt, and ultimately….self loathing.

Jerome had seen many try to be hard and see the life snuffed out of them, killed, by drugs, turf wars, and the Police. He could see this whole situation turning into a problem. That was if, the Commanding Officer was not a friend of his from High School that had a bit of a past himself. Surprised to see him as a Police Officer. Which normally would have raised some flags. But the way he took control of the situation, got all the officers at his command to do their interviews of witnesses and move out. The whole ordeal was over within a couple of hours. He talked with Jerome and Kathy. Then stayed while Kathy grabbed a few things and waited until Jerome loaded his truck. He left when they had left out of the driveway and went down the street.

A lone man stepped from the shadows across the street as they all left. He walked across the street. He seemed to blend in with each shadow he walked through. If you were not looking directly at him, he would have appeared to be nothing more than a trick of light. If you would look in the rear view mirror of a car trying to see him you would see nothing. The man walked straight up to Kathy's mother's house, opened the door and walked in. He then touched the ground and every strange bug that seemed to have come out of the bony man's body ran toward his finger, running up it and into his skin right below his wrist. He then stood. His body started to smoke. He jumped back and exited the door quickly. The slow sizzling sound stopped as soon as he stepped out the house. He then touched the ground on the front porch. Palm flat against the ground. The house itself made a groan sound. Then a sound of wood splintering. He raised his palm off of the ground. Tried entering the house again, his body started smoking again. Stepping back out he touched a wall to the side of the door and it quickly caught fire. The man made a low sound, like a frustrated moan. Numerous bugs spread across the side of the house ahead of the flames. The fire seemed to be spread by the bugs themselves. As they ran the area behind them caught fire with their progress.

"Hey, what are you doing?!??"

An elderly lady asked. She had lived down the block since the early 1950s. She knew Kathy, her mother Sylvia and all the children that had grown up with Kathy. The man slowly turned. And as he turned to look at her she saw a flash of yellow and orange across his eyes. He smiled, but his teeth seemed to be made of some type of metal. His skin was pale, like translucent it was so light. Hair gray, cut in a close cropped natural. After smiling he vanished, as if he was never there. All that was left was the spreading of the fire. The elderly lady stepped back to move all the way off the concrete walkway to the house. She then left went to her own house, down the street, making sure to glance back with every other step. She had seen the man disappear. It did not faze her, she felt at her age, death could come anytime. No one she knew, could tell her what that would look like. But what did scare her, is that house. It always felt like something had disturbed the ground the house was on. She went to call 911 as the flames reached around the side of the house. No one in the neighborhood seemed to notice. It was a cool night, not raining. With all the commotion from earlier, she knew her new neighbors would be out walking their dogs, sipping some overpriced coffee from a coffee shop nearby. But strangely, she seemed to be the only person on the street.

Just as she finished dialing 911, and the call connected she turned back to look at the house. Nothing was burning. There was no fire. The lights were out and everything looked fine.

"911, what is your emergency?"
"I have dialed the wrong number."

The house stood, ominously, as if there were many things waiting to break out. The lady made a note to herself to give that house a wide berth when she went by. No one would be getting her to go inside it, even if there was an Open House. She had heard about the attempted assault that had just happened a couple of hours ago. Was hoping she would catch Kathy and make sure she was OK. But now that question was null and void. Too old to be dealing with this much drama. Something is not right about that house or that man that was doing whatever he was doing. The elderly lady sat down in her favorite chair preparing to watch her favorite show, Stars Dancing. Just as she got comfortable, she felt a hand grab the back of her head. She went to scream because it scared her to feel such an unexpected and violent grip. There was no one in the house but her. She was lifted from the chair and turned to face the man she had seen in front of Kathy's house. He was tall and bigger up close than he looked from the sidewalk. Obviously strong he held her with one hand and the last time she had looked at the scale she was a solid 250+ at 5'3".

"It is always the nosey ones. People do not change over the millennia. All you people wonder the same things and just have to know as you get older, more lonely. Well, I am glad you did wonder. Because I am now going to use you to get the information I need. From that household. Thanks to some type of incantation I cannot enter. Specifically designed to keep my kind out."

The lady went to scream. As soon as her mouth opened, thousands of bugs flew from his mouth and into hers in the time it took her to open her mouth. Choking her, going up her nose into her mouth, down her throat, up her throat into her brain. Violently eating their way through each area. The pain was massive. It spread inside her like acid, but quicker. Only 5 seconds went by as she was filled with them eating and tearing their way through her body. Taking control of everything. Her mind was still conscious, but all she could do is look out from the inside.

"Good. Now, we shall seek out what I am looking for starting tomorrow."

There seemed to be a frenzy erupting inside as the man walked away and out the door. Her body sat back in her favorite chair. Giving her back control. She thought about killing herself, and as soon as the thought entered her mind, her body was held in place by the things inside her. As if to pass a message that she would be doing nothing of the sort until they were through with her. Even then, they, would be the ones to kill her. It was a silent communication that went on between the bugs and her. There was no longer any pain, but she knew if they wanted to cause any pain, they would.

Jerome had driven Kathy to his house after an eventful night that neither one of them saw coming. His house was actually behind another house. He had convinced the owners of the house in front to sell their driveway and half of their expansive backyard. It was a good plan, that owners did not know the true worth of the land they sold him, so he bought it for a low price. Beyond the remote control gate he himself had installed stood his full size house in the backyard. Two story house. The windows were installed but the outside still was unpainted. The finishing on the windows were not finished to. They drove up to the front of the house. His garage door was working. It came up as he tapped the remote. He dialed something in on his navigation screen. Some phone number and then some other numbers afterward. The lights in the house came on. When they walked in the heater was on full blast. The air was still cold inside but rapidly heating up from the heat being pushed out.

Kathy was impressed. She had never seen a house that could be controlled from the outside, remotely. Clearly the house was not finished. Jerome took her on a quick tour of the place and showed her all the rooms and what he had not finished working. Showed her his plans for each section. He *had* finished the Master Bedroom and bathroom. They were the biggest rooms in the whole house. His bedroom was expansive and fully furnished. He had a well used recliner in front of his bed so he could watch the huge TV in front of his bed. What must have been a King Sized bed with all the sheets, pillows, and comfort items to make it a good place to fall asleep. It was made up too. Most men's houses she had been to, were organized but they rarely had made beds. The closet was a walk in closet. He had a few suits hung and some other dressy clothes. But most of it was empty. The cabinetry was excellent. There was a place for everything. You could probably put more in the closet than it appeared. He seemed to be putting everything together with more space being needed in mind.

But the crown jewel of the whole place was the bathroom. The unpolished granite floors, the recessed lighting, mirror placement, huge shower with sprays from two sides, and the JACUZZI sized bathtub with jets. It was very deep. Probably come up her neck line when fully filled.

"So. What do you think….I mean I know it is not finished and you can see through some the unfinished walls. There is some wiring I have to finish. The HVAC is done as you can tell by the heater…..there is another.."

"Jerome." Kathy said stopping him. "I like it."

Kathy smiled, and touched his arm.

"I just would love to take a shower and get this feeling off of me."
"Oh, let me grab some towels for you then.."
"Just point me to where they are and I will grab them myself. Just thankful that you are understanding enough to let me stay here for the night."

Jerome looked her deep in her eye like she just said something that revealed to him she had some type of mental retardation.

"It is the least I could do. You have always meant a great deal to me. There is very little I would not do to keep you safe."

The seriousness of the last statement pressed into Kathy as Jerome looked her in the eye. Holding her gaze in a way she could not turn away from. A flood of memories flowed from him to her. She saw them as her own, but they were not hers. Starting around when they were 6, and a dog she did not see was running toward her. Jerome had grabbed a rock and threw it hitting the dog in the side of the head making it run toward him. The dog was hit by a car as it changed direction while in the street, heading toward him with a crazy look in it's eyes. The hit killed the dog instantly. Kathy had remembered the dog getting hit. But did not remember anything about Jerome hitting it with a rock. Many other memories sped past, mostly of Jerome defending her verbally. Then around 13, a boy, Darryl, had said he would rape Kathy. Jerome had known the boy for sometime and had known he had a problem with doing things that would later end up in the boy being a rapist. Jerome had told Darryl that was not funny and to not ever say that about Kathy. Darryl, had looked Jerome in the eye and started to say he would say whatever he wanted, but before he could finish, Jerome had started punching him in a rage. His memory was so filled with rage that Kathy, felt overwhelmed. The testosterone level of a teenage boy lost in a rage was something she had never felt. She had been angry but this memory Jerome had was hardly visible due to the rage he felt. At the end of the memory was Darryl on the ground, face beat so badly and misshapen by the barrage of punches. No telling how long he got beat. Jerome's young mind immediately wondered who had seen him do it as he headed down the street, bloody hands in his sweater pockets.

Every memory after that was of seeing Kathy and feeling a deep yearning for her, but never quite being able to get that through to Kathy. She laughed and walked off whenever he flirted with her. Seeing it from his memory she found he was hurt by her aloofness. He seriously cared for her, and did not really want anyone but her. Which is something she could have never guessed or known until now. As she came out of her trance of watching his memories. It became clear these were thoughts he wanted her to see. As the images faded from her sight she found Jerome close to her face, staring her in the eye. As if he knew she would see and feel everything inside of him. Kathy backed away.

"Where are your towels?"
"They are in closet next to the bathroom."

Kathy got some towels out of the small closet. Then turned on the shower. Quickly slipping out of the clothes she had on. As soon as she was naked she was in the shower. The warm water hitting her from both sides. She was completely immersed in warmth. Steaming all stress away. She walked backwards to one side of the shower, letting the water run through her hair. Normally she would not do that to her hair, but tonight was different, everything needed to be washed after the attack. She caught some water in her mouth and washed her mouth out a few times. Thinking of the bugs she had bit and crushed while trying to spit them out. Lathering herself up with soap, Kathy began to feel clean. She turned back toward the door of the shower that was two times the size of any shower she had been in. Jerome stood naked in front of the door. She was stunned to see him standing inside the shower. She had not heard him step in. But he was there.

Jerome had not planned on stepping in the shower. He had just caught a glimpse of Kathy's silhouette while walking by. She was slim, but very round in all the right places, more so in her lower regions than he had noticed before. He felt himself swell instantly. Not all the way, but he felt a tug toward Kathy. The next thing he knew, his heart was beating hard, not fast. He was naked, inside the shower, watching the soap wash off of her. Her wet hair, soft supple behind shaking as she moved, and her slightly parted lips, all this had called him. He wanted to be inside her.

Kathy looked at Jerome, and felt drawn to him. His chiseled from granite body moved away any platonic feelings she felt towards him away. Jerome was not a big man, but he had a chest like two iron plates, and muscles that were defined to the highest level she had ever seen in her life. His chest, stomach, and below there she saw him swelling larger and larger before her eyes. Instantly she felt her body react. Jerome look at her, and tenderly started to ask if it was alright to join her. Kathy answered by dropping the soap while he was still speaking, and rushing into his embrace while Jerome grabbed her lifting her up with such ease that she felt as though she was a child's weight. They kissed. Deeply, frantically. Each of them feeling each others body in a mad race as if they were competing to see who could feel the most of each other.

Like there was some type of timer. And once it went off, both would not be able to feel the things on each others body that turned them on.

The kissing went on for a while. Jerome had started to reach inside of Kathy with one long and strong finger. Kathy grabbed his arm that was connected to the finger inside her. He was a rock. He even started to lift her with that one arm. It did not hurt, a testament to his strength, a strength that turned her on even more. Jerome then lifted her by grabbing ahold of the left side of her rear. How light she felt, with a part of him in her, and him licking her ear, kissing her mouth, sucking on her neck and nipples, took her over the top in what seemed a few short seconds.

Jerome could feel the intensity coming off of Kathy. He had only begun to make out with her, but from the way she cried out and started shaking. Scratching the skin off of his back. He assumed she was ready to feel him. He felt the draw to be inside her magnetic on a level he had not felt before. He removed his finger, lifted her higher and lowered her down on himself. He felt himself enter the soft, warm, tightness that she was. She clung to him whimpering with pleasure. He could feel her soft breast and hard nipples against his chest. He palmed her bottom holding her up while squeezing enjoying the softness of her. Biting and sucking on her neck he slowly started to move in and out. Then a little faster, and faster, until Kathy started digging her nails into his back again. Making sounds like she was gasping for air, saying his name randomly in a breathless voice.

Kathy felt him deep inside her. Stretching her lips open at his base. She felt light and fragile in his arms. But the pleasure he was pushing and pulling inside her was beyond anything she had felt before. She was so wet that his initial penetration of her caused no discomfort at all. He was thick, thick enough to hurt, but it did not. As his rhythm increased she held on, wrapping her legs around him, gripping his back with her nails. She felt his head buried in the side of her neck, his mouth working on the same rhythm with his lower body. She felt as if she was a helpless passenger on a warm pleasure machine custom designed to please her. The power of his body was felt in every stroke, she could no longer see just feel what this man was doing to her as she felt an explosion of pleasure fall out of her again, much more powerful this time.

Jerome heard and felt Kathy reach her moment of ecstasy again. This time it felt like she locked around him with a boa constrictor type vice inside her. Holding him inside her. He did not move as she let out a high pitched cry in his ear, while scratching more lines in his back. Turning him on even more. Kathy's grip relaxed.

Kathy felt Jerome let her have her moment, but as soon as she relaxed he spun her around toward the wall of the shower. Pinning her against. It shocked her mildly, then she felt him enter her from behind, catching some of her hair as he entered, causing a small amount of discomfort as he got into a hard rhythm from the start. He moved his stroke from one side to the other to dislodge the hair caught between them. After getting rid of the last discomfort, he stroked deeply. She could feel each and every inch. It was as if he had swelled more. Each stroke seemed to radiate a deeper level of pleasure from him. She turned to see him, and could see him, looking down at her body shake with each stroke. Squeezing and slapping between strokes. She could feel and hear him grunt with pleasure. Her body was his to command and she was willingly giving to him as long as he kept pumping in more and more pleasure. She could not get enough. Her legs were shaking uncontrollably and felt as if she was going to collapse.

Jerome watched her behind shake as he pumped in, trying to go deeper each time. Her back was arched perfectly as he pounded deeper into her. She was so soft, and wet inside. She felt tighter with each stroke. He could feel an explosion about to come out of him soon. He wanted to make sure every stroke would build up to the most pleasure he could get. Kathy had turned around to look at what he was doing. He took his right palm and pressed on the side of her face to hold it against the wall. Her mouth opened in enjoyment of the control he pressed on her, making him get ever closer to his moment of release.

Kathy felt her face pressed against the wall, as water rolled down on her, she felt him swell even more inside her. He pushed with more feeling, deeper and harder. She felt him squeeze her hip painfully hard. As if he was having a problem not tearing her apart. He grabbed ahold of both hips and started to press in harder and harder, making Kathy cry out. Then she heard Jerome yell out, "UUUUNNNNGGGGGHH!!!!!!" She felt him pulse inside of her. Throbbing, thickly throbbing. She could feel him filling her up inside. He throbbed powerfully for what seemed like half a minute. Kathy backed into him, curving her hips and spine to feel as much as she could moaning herself as he pressed in deeper, restarting more throbbing, like a powerful heartbeat.

They both leaned against the wall. Breathing deeply. Kathy kissing and sucking on one of his muscled arms. Jerome slid out of Kathy. Turned her around weakly. The sheer weight of his arm giving him strength, but Kathy could tell he was feeling weak. They looked each other in each other's eyes. They kissed softly and tenderly for a long moment in mutual enjoyment of the moment. After they kissed. Jerome held her in his arms. She laid her head on his chest as the water ran. She felt Jerome's creations still in her, while other parts of him slid down the inside of her thigh. They finished showering and went to bed. Kathy fell asleep on Jerome's chest, wrapped in his arms under a warm blanket. She had never felt so safe and content. As she did now, laying in the bed of the man she seemed to have loved for a lifetime without knowing it. A Protector, and judging from his place, a man that could handle just about anything with his hands. Built on his own, with very little help. Self Made Man. She nuzzled deeper into his chest listening to his slow heart beat as she fell asleep.

Jerome did not fall asleep immediately. He lay with Kathy making soft breathing noises of sleep into his chest. Thinking about the events of the day, and how the man was able to bring himself back together. And what was up with those bugs? He had hit the man with all he had as fast as he could. May not be able to beat down every man, but that man was broken up and came back together. What was really going on. Wish that mystery man was still around. Maybe he would be able to answer these questions. Because none of this is normal.

Chapter 11

Almost 4-months had passed since Kathy had first stayed over at Jerome's house. Kathy had pretty much moved in with Jerome. All her stuff in Southern California had been sold or put in storage. She had resigned from her job so that she could get herself together. Her mother's house had been sold after she found it was too hard to stay there. She had tried to stay on two different occasions in her mother's house but she was never able to. Jerome had gone with her, but the feeling of violation, was too thick. It was as if the house had lost all its protective feeling that a lived in house has. A feeling of home, safe, somewhere you go to block out the rest world to relax. Everything from her Mother and Grandmother's presence was gone. It felt like an empty shell that had dried and emptied over time ending up just another empty shell on a large beach.

Jerome had gone through the house, top to bottom. Since he did most of the interior work and upgrades, he knew what everything in the house was supposed to look like. There was very little different other than the area where he had patched up the window he had kicked the man through. On the front of the house around the side, he did notice the paint looked like a large area had been in the sun for years compared to the rest of the paint. His crew had just painted it five months ago. There was no way for it to look like that.

The first time Kathy said she needed to see if she could sleep there overnight, he refused to let her do it alone. After all the years and different events that had happened there he was not about to let the love of his life be in danger without him being around. It seemed like things got worse after Jerome had cemented in the side of the house using some of the powder he left for him by the man with the cane years ago. He and Kathy both could not get comfortable in the house the first night and decided to go back to his house. Nothing happened that time. Other than a the distinct feeling that they were out in the open. Like someone had taken the roof off, and removed the wall to the bedroom they were in. Like anyone from the street or sky could see them. Get to them. They left. The feeling of exposure was too overbearing.

The second time they tried they did fall asleep for a short while, but there were noises. There was a loud sound, like an animal. A smell that seemed to fill the entire house. It hung in the air like humidity in the South. Sounds of something heavy walking with feet that must have been hard as stone. The hardwood floors protested under the weight of each slow step it took. Jerome had slid out of the bed with a hand over Kathy's mouth so she did not talk and a finger over his lips in a message that said stay quiet. As he got up he held out a hand. He made a motion that said don't move or stop, as he saw Kathy start to sit up. Jerome, was not in the mood to play with whoever might cause an issue after the last episode fighting with the man. So he had brought a bulletproof vest and a sawed of shotgun to make sure, whatever those shells hit, got torn it apart. He went downstairs, after creeping slowly down the hall and walking painfully slow down the stairs to stay quiet. An eerie tension seemed to creep into his muscles. His neck and shoulders tensed. He tried to relax them, but he felt a tension, that started at the shoulders and moved inward, constricting his breathing. He knew he was being quiet, but his heart seemed to be blaring in his head like a subwoofer bass speaker in the back of a teenager's car. His ears beat to the same rhythm as his heart. Drowning out his ability to hear much past himself. He could still hear the footsteps but strained to hear some type of clothing or if there was a gun in the hand of the person, or hear what they were doing, anything beyond the footsteps.

Jerome walked lightly, staying low, making sure to not make any sound. He could hear the footsteps walking toward the window. But could not see anyone there. He finished coming down the stairs scanning the room while keeping his aim at the area where the footsteps could be heard. The footsteps stopped. Jerome could see in the room, but could not for the life of him see what was standing there. The floor sagged under the weight of something. One area of the area lifted like a weight had come up. Jerome's heart froze. He knew whatever was there, was moving, before he could react, he saw and heard the floor sag and strain under the weight as the footsteps came toward him at a pace far too rapid for the weight it seemed to have. As if some had hit fast forward. The hardwood floor sagged and cracked under the weight. He started pulling the trigger when there was a knock at the door. The steps stopped coming toward him. Jerome fearing his imagination had gone wild and he had now lost it, did not move. His trigger finger was fixed, but he could not pull the trigger back. He saw the outline of a shape, he then felt an intense heat come from the area where the shape was.

An outline in orange seemed to go around the edges of this invisible being. The shape was not human. It was not an animal, it was something Jerome had never seen before. The misshapen vision of a being foreign to this plane of existence. It seemed to want to reach for him but it could not. None of the movements or shapes seemed to be of anything he had every seen. It was not of this world, dimension, time, or space. As strange and loony as that sounded to Jerome, even in his own mind, he knew that thought was true. Whatever it was, it did not belong here. Stuck in one position, Jerome could not move. All he could do was stare at this shapeless figure that appeared to want to reach or grab him, but not be able touch him. As if there was something holding it in place. There was a rush of sound out of nowhere. The same sound you can hear when your ears ring, after being at a loud party or near loud-speakers for a prolonged amount of time. But this was slightly different. It changed. Like some alien sounding cry of anguish and hate. The creatures movements grew quicker and quicker as it figure shrunk, more and more. Jerome watched as it disappeared soundlessly. Flecks of orange rose from the form as it disintegrated and disappeared in the air like embers or a dying fire in a fire pit.

Again a knock was heard. Solid knock, confident. Not a violating Police knock, or a playful 1-6 knock. Just three solid, confident knocks. Jerome opened the door. In the doorway stood the man with the cane. No name ever had been given by him. No one spoke his name. Jerome raised the shotgun with every intention of firing it if the man acted funny. But the man tapped Jerome's arm with one finger as it was rising. The movement was so fast and effortless it made Jerome feel slow, sluggish. The touch did something to him. Jerome was now straining to move. He felt as if he was having some sort of seizure that kept him in place. Like your body feels before you throw-up, clenched in the retching part of the movement. He did not feel like he was going to throw up but he was locked in position. Immediately sweat started breaking out all over Jerome as he strained to move anything. The man calmly walked in and closed the door. Then turned around and tapped between the thumb and finger part of both of Jerome's hands causing them to release the shotgun. It fell, but did not hit the floor as the man caught it with amazing dexterity using only one of his hands. He then stood and looked Jerome in the eye without saying a word. His face could not be read. Jerome assumed that because he was still alive, the man did not want to kill him.

"You are a strong Protector." A couple of chuckles followed. "But you will be hard pressed to kill me with a gun or anything else of this world. Many, many millenia ago, your people trained me on many things. You will have to be enlightened soon."

Jerome, stopped straining to move, and found his body naturally started to stand straight up. He now stood at attention and was able to blink. No longer feeling like he had to escape from some type of convulsion. He stood rigid. Hands at his sides. Straight as a board. He could only move his eyes, not his head or any other part of his body.

"You, are a quick study. Finding a way to flow with what I just did to you took many people months to master. Truly you are the last of your kind. In a land you now call Africa, your ancestors ruled in the interior. A powerful people. I have watched many cities be overgrown by Jungle, covered by sand, or submerged under water. But the memory of your people will forever live within me."

The man stared into Jerome's eyes. Looking to see if he was being heard or not. He could see he was being heard. Jerome noticed he looked younger up close, but something in the man's eyes revealed a true age. Older than anyone he knew. A power emanating from within, Nothing you could see, but it could be felt. Like a powerful presence turned into a physical manifestation like heat from a fire, but this was not heat. He could feel power emanating from this man. It filled the room.

" I have to get upstairs, and speak with Kathy. When I come back, there are memories and knowledge I will leave with you. Do not let her come back to this house again."

Kathy could hear a voice downstairs. A familiar voice, but she could not place it. Baritone. Deep tone. A tone with no give in it. Authoritative. She wanted to go see what was happening, but Jerome had motioned for her to stay put and not make any noise. She trusted him, and was not going to move an inch or make any sound.

While she was thinking about going down to see what was happening she had stopped listening to what was going on. She found there was no talking happening anymore. Not knowing it, Kathy held her breath. Trying to listen closer. She found that she could not hear a thing. She listened closer, straining to hear any sound at all. She focused so intensely on hearing any sound she started getting frustrated, because she could hear her heart, hair, her own self more than anything else. Just as she went to move, the door swung open.

"Kathy. I know you may not remember me too well but I am here to speak with you."

Relief did not quite wash over Kathy seeing a familiar face that had saved her in the past.

"Where is Jerome?"
"He is downstairs."
"Is he…"
"He is fine. But I could not have him come up here and disturb our conversation. He has taken up enough time as it is. I will come back later to work with him fully."
"Work with him?"
"He is an important person. As important as you. The child you both will have will unite what was once forbidden."
"What?"
"You are pregnant."
"No I am not."
"Yes. You are. The baby is mere days old, but it is growing inside you. Do not believe me?"

Kathy looked at the man in the eye. Looking for something. Trying to get a sense of something. There was nothing. As if the room was empty. He held no expression on his face. And he stood absolutely still. Nothing moved. Not even his eyes. He did not blink or even appear to breathe.

"It is clear you do not believe or trust me. So to show you what I know. Try to get a sense of my thoughts."

Kathy could not. Normally a feeling would hit her and she would be able to decipher from there what someone's feelings or thoughts were. Since becoming aware of a power she had, and knowing it was not just her reading people and guessing. She had become quite confident in what she could do with that power. But he was right. She had not used her power in days and could not summon the feeling now.

"Your power now rests in your child. There is no time to explain it. You must leave this place. Now. There are more who want what you and your child have inside. It can be taken. But the way they will take the child will destroy you. Not just kill you. It will shatter your soul. Many will devour it. Those that want it, want nothing more than to kill you slowly. I have kept your bloodline hidden through the rise and fall of many Nations. But there has been a change. A change that makes this no longer possible. You and Jerome will have to face what is to come together. I am being called away from here to deal with other issues."

Kathy barely understood. It seemed like some bad movie. But after her childhood and all the events leading up until this moment it was better to play it safe than to sit up here and try to doubt him. There were many questions she had for him. But hopefully they could be answered at another time.

"All in time. You will have to work through this by yourselves. "

Kathy thought to herself, did I say that out loud?

"No. You did not. There is not time for all this. The house no longer has its protection. You must leave. Now, not later. Now. This house has become more of a beacon to draw everything to this place."

Kathy grabbed her stuff and slid on her flip flops. When she looked up the man was not there, but the door was still swinging open as if he had just left the room. No sound or motion other than the door moving. It was as if he was never there in the first place.

Jerome saw the man suddenly appear in front of him.

"I must go. You must continue to protect Kathy. She will need you more now than she ever has. She is bearing your child.

With that statement he looked deep into Jerome's eyes. Jerome could see the weight of what he was saying without anything being said. It was as if the man was checking Jerome's strength mentally. Making sure all was in place.

"There is knowledge I can pass to you. It is not much. But this will help you to understand me and will help you to understand a power that lies in you. It has been dormant for Generations in your own family. But you have used it on occasion without really knowing. Remember and try to feel everything as your own experience."

The man put his palm on Jerome's head. And a rush of visions entered Jerome's mind. The first of being up in the mountains, where there were many, many trees and foliage. It was a flat area between two peaks housed a very sizable city with many different buildings. All of them in perfect symmetry. Perfectly straight streets with perfect symmetry. This seemed to be a long time ago judging from what people had on and the dirt roads. The buildings looked to be of concrete, one central building sat in the middle of the town. Rectangular in shape. It was not high, just about two stories high. Immediately Jerome knew this was a vision from the man with the cane's past.

They were moving down a path down the hill into the city. There were soldiers hidden in the vegetation near the road watching them descend. The sun was going down on the other side of some other peaks, making for a beautiful vision of color in the sky and against the lush greens of the jungle around them. He could sense they were being watched by guards but could not see them. A hand held wagon ahead of him had what looked like a wooden box in it. That, box, tore open abruptly, and a creature that had skin that you could see through. Each vein, bone, intestines, and many other things that looked like maggots inside it moving. It's skin was clearly not made for the sun. Bugs that live underground but do not come up to the surface had see through carcasses like this things skin. It looked human, but did not look human. Its eyes were gigantic orbs in a human head. Its pupils were huge but not dilated at all, probably due to there being too much light for it right now. People gasped as it looked around. Movements that were quick and clipped like a lizard or small bird. Its head snapping from side to side looking at people. The eyes never moved so it may not have had the ability to look around with its eyes. It grabbed the man pulling the cart by the neck and opened its mouth clearly intending to bite him. As it was moving toward the man's neck it a lightning fast manner, a spear pierced its neck. It turned to see where the spear had come from. It did not look to be in any kind of pain. Just seemed to have a growing rage. The creature pulled the spear out. The hole where the spear had been pulled out of, had blood spilling out. The hole itself closed as if there had never been a hole there.

The Creature let go of the man it was holding as two men came onto the road with amazing speed of the fastest track runner's Jerome had ever seen. The one on the left moved toward the creature to strike then stopped as if he had not been at full sprint in the first place. The only thing that gave away how fast he had run up was the dust going past him. When he stopped he dodged a clawed hand that was swung. The other was still running up and sliced off the arm as it was swinging. He too, stopped as if he was never moving at what looked like 30 mph. As soon as the creature looked at the man that cut its right arm off the man on the left cut off its head so fast it was barely perceptible by the human eye. Both men stood, strong stances, there stances spoke volumes of training to always stand in a strong balanced way and never be off balance. The swords they carried were short, and almost crude looking. Each man was slim, but wiry. One grabbed the head. While the other made a make shift fire pit, threw in what looked like red pepper. Cracked two rocks against each other and the sparks hit the red silt and a roaring fire came to light. He threw the body in the flame. The heat was the most intense Jerome had ever felt. He felt as if he would catch fire just watching. The fire itself died right after the body disintegrated. That was in a very short time.

A new scene was revealed. This seemed to be a festive one. It was in the same city. He was walking down the street. Many people greeted him. The colors people wore were brilliant. Fabrics seemed to be thick, of great quality. The styles that the men and women wore were of the highest scale. There was so much gold and huge diamonds, stones of all colors. Men mostly had short hair, beards here and there. Women had short hair to long. Some women with long hair had braids, others had twists. Most of their hair styles were done with gold clasps holding their hair in intricate styles. Most of the women were either attractive or extremely attractive. From Milk Chocolate Brown to Ebony Midnight shades. All of them seemed to come from some type of wealth. They all smelled of incense or some type of fruit. It was beautiful. There was music, dancing, food, poetry, and a drink that had to be wine but much more rich in taste. On the walls there were long sections that were long plates of gold with long Green strips of fabric between them. In the gold he saw the reflection of the man who was giving him the visions. It was a much younger version of the man with a cane. He must have been a teenager at this point. Right as he was trying to see the reflection more clear, loud deep bass could be heard. Everyone inside the building looked up at the two thrones which were up a set of stairs that stood slightly higher than most people's heads. The bass loud and deep reverberated through the room. Looking over there were two of the largest drums Jerome had ever seen to each side of the stairs. The rhythm the two drummers pumped out started in a slow fashion to get everyone's attention then it moved up in pace as the Royalty entered the room. Eventually ending on an upbeat tempo that was celebratory. The queen came out first. Her outfit was form fitting with a sort of cape. Hips wide, footsteps delicate yet strong. Her walk was the intoxicating mixture of someone raised to have a higher level of class, while also exuding the full power of her woman hood without doing too much. Her crown and hair were intricately woven together to create a style that was regal, like a queen should be. She held a fan made of feathers that had brilliant bright colors. The Cape she wore fit like a another dress, and gave off different colors from different lights as it hung from her shoulders. The dress and the cape were so form fitting that it was easy to believe that it was sewn on to her figure before coming out. The fabric was something that did not seem like it belonged in this reality. It appeared to be lightweight but strong. It seemed to fall along the curves or her body perfectly. But the colors. The colors seemed to be electrically charged. As if someone shocked it with electricity then sent her out. Every time it seemed a new electric charge hit the colors that swirled across the cape changed. The King came out with a large crown on. A thick gold necklace that was flat but thick, came down to a point in the middle, like an upside down triangle. It had three rock sized diamonds. A large one in the middle and two smaller ones to the sides. They were a deep green that reflected the light in a hypnotic way. He wore an outfit that was familiar to Jerome's eye. It looked like linen, but far more fine a cloth. The shirt came down to his knees with a v neck cut, so his necklace could be displayed properly. Pants of the same cloth and sandals. The queen wore no sandals, but the king did. He had a long graying beard and bald head. Strong hands and a stance that gave an air of power that filled the room. With every step he took toward his throne the feeling of his power spread over everyone. Most of the people looked extremely happy when he walked out. To Jerome this looked like he was a fair but strong ruler of his people. The admiration in everyone's eyes in his area was quite moving. The feeling did not come from him but the young man who's body he was inhabiting. And judging from the Soldiers that wait on the sides of the road on the way to the city, he must have many enemies.

The king looked across the room said a few words and ended it with a statement of celebration and thanks. He then moved to sit as he let the room know it was ok to carry on the celebration. He then caught the eye of the man who's body he was in, and a grin spread across his face as he motioned the man over. Jerome felt the man walk over and embrace the King warmly.

"Son! I see you *have* returned a man. How were your travels? You must tell me everything!"

The queen got up and hugged him too. She could not speak. Emotion overwhelming her. Tears of joy, relief, and love filled her eyes. She did not look old enough to have a teenage child but from the look in her eye, it was clear this was a mother looking at her child. A woman that stood behind the throne of the queen glanced at him also. She looked like a much younger version of Kathy's Grandmother. She too, looked like she missed the man. But in a much different way than the king and queen. It also looked as if she could not reveal she felt the way she did toward him. It was a secret between the two, he could tell.

The scene vanished and another appeared. Out in a field. There was a rock in front of him, 6 ft tall at least. An older man with a white uncombed rough beard was talking.

"You will now learn what you have in you. Punch through the rock."

There was a hesitation. Then a punch was thrown. There was no impact on the rock. Just a clap sound. Confusion. The older man's face appeared right in front of the man. His hand had caught the blow. Jerome could feel the actions. The punch thrown was almost as hard as any punch he himself had ever thrown. But this man caught it with no problem. Like it was a ball thrown by a weak person.

"Punch with your mind, soul, and then body. Your power is inside. Watch me flick this rock with my finger, just my finger."

He flicked the rock and some dirt flicked off of it.

"Now, watch me flick it from the inside out, *to,* my finger."

He flicked the rock now and large chips broke off of the rock. As if the rock itself was paper. The man turned around and pointed at his head, staring straight in the eye.

"From your mind, soul. Then solidify yourself, fortify your muscles, feel the energy in everything around you, know the weakest points of everything near you, then punch. Focus!"

The first punch thrown almost broke the hand. But it did put a small tiny crack in the rock. The pain forgotten upon realizing the rock could be broken. Given a new level of confidence in seeing what his last hit did, focus came to him like heat from the sun in the summertime. A second punch was thrown in confidence. Knocking off the whole side of the rock. A piece about almost two feet long cracked off. The whole rock being shattered would be harder. But right now he knew he could break the rock down from the size of a medium sized man to many small pieces with just the base of the rock left.

"Now punch down into the ground through the rock. Punch so that the full impact is into the ground. Punch *through* the rock. The rock may be the point of impact. But you are punching into the ground."

A punch was thrown immediately this time. It felt as if the arm of the person had solidified into a supremely hard and strong through mental decision. As if he had decided that his arm and fist were strong enough to punch through this rock like it was rubber or a hard piece of plastic. All the objects in the area's density could be felt like a radar feeling everything around him. He could feel the rock and the soft earth underneath it. He planned on hitting through the rock and into the soft earth below. The punch knocked the rock much deeper into the ground by a couple of feet. This new found power was exhilarating to the young man. To Jerome, his mind felt this was as unrealistic as a kung-fu movie. But another part of him connected with the man doing all this. It was as if he tapped into something in his mind that extended to the body. It was not something uncommon or not proven by science on lower levels. There are tales of women lifting heavy objects like a car as if they weighed nothing, to save their child. But instead of the strength coming up in a panic or a situation like that. You reach inside your self and trigger the brain to give the body extra strength. You control it.

The vision faded and Jerome was now back in his time. The man with the cane stood in front of him. Older, but not looking more than his early forties if you took away the gray hair. He was bigger size wise. Bigger, but a solid toned bigger. He was staring Jerome straight in the eyes. Looking as if he was trying to make sure the information got through to him.

"You still do not know my name, but that is of no consequence. You see where I come from. And the most important part, is the part about the training. You must strike from inside. Reach into your self and push out the strength from inside of you. This is something I know that you know about. When you were a young teenage boy I saw you do this to young men that tested you. But this time, you have to reach deeper and pull out more. These beings cannot be hurt by bullets or average weapons, you must put something behind it that strikes to the very soul of the being. Do you understand?"

"Yes."
"Good. I must go. But you will need to practice and try these things. You are not a child, and this is not a movie. But these are things that you must hear me on because they are what you *need,* to survive. Time is short. I must go."
"There are other things I need to know. When-"
"There is not time. Take what I have given you. Use it!"

Jerome bristled at the tone being used.

"I apologize for my tone, but there are more things going on than I can tell you, and they must be dealt with. Talking to you two was more than there is time for. Other things are at stake that would make your lives forfeit. "

Looking at Jerome he turned to the door with Jerome following close behind. The man walked toward a shadow next to a tall bush at the end of the porch area and seemed to walk straight into the shadow. Jerome walked straight up to the area and did not see the man anywhere. He had literally walked into the shadow like it was a doorway.

Kathy walked out with their bags.

"I am ready to go. What's wrong?"

Jerome cleared the look of concern off of his face. Took the bags from Kathy and threw them in back of his truck.

"Let's go."

Kathy did not need to be able to read Jerome to see that he was through with this place. And that something had happened. She decided she would tell him what happened later. Right now just did not seem the proper time. She felt strange and Jerome looked to be in no mood for talking.

That night, was the last night they stayed at the home she grew up in. The house was no longer a home. Jerome started driving and seemed like he was not going to stop until he arrived in Santa Cruz. He pulled up to a hotel and got a room. Came back to the car, grabbed the bags out of the back, and opened Kathy's door.

"Come on. We will be staying here for a couple of days."

Kathy stared at him, not knowing what to say, but somewhat understanding. Jerome read the question and concern across Kathy's face.

"We will only be here for 3 days at the most." This relaxed Kathy some to know it was not going to be an open ended run with no end in sight.

"He told me I must protect you. He showed me a few things from his past. It seemed more than another time. It seemed to be almost a different world. Clearly had to be in Africa. Who knows how long ago. There is much more to know. But one thing is clear. We need to be away from home for a few days until I feel it is right to return. Especially if you are bearing our child."

They looked at each other and felt a mutual understanding of the gravity of the situation, but also a love they felt for each other. A bond that could be felt from the inside. A bond two people can share when they are of one vision. Kathy and Jerome returned home a week later. Jerome nor Kathy felt good about coming back when a couple of days past. It would take more time. After getting back home, Kathy did not journey out much for fear of being seen by the wrong element,. That element being the man that grabbed her, and at this point, anyone that gave her a funny feeling. Jerome resumed his regular schedule, which was highly irregular. Coming home to check on at varying times during the day depending on his schedule. Kathy fell into a routine of exercise and calling a friend or two every other day. Eventually getting out and going for long power walks. The exercise helped. Her mind was feeling more open and her body was no longer tight. Besides, it was good for the baby. Jerome himself started to work out harder. He refused to work out more than 2 hours in a day. But to Kathy, it looked like he had gotten more tightened and toned since he started this new workout he would not explain to her. She would just see this childlike look in his eyes. The look children get when they discover something fun to play with that they are not supposed to be messing with. Or as many black people call it, "Getting into something"

The House Kathy grew up in was taken care of by Jerome. He patched up all the problems. They rented it out for a while then ended up selling it because it had too much history attached to it. Jerome then turned his full attention to his house. Hiring a crew to work on it while they stayed at another hotel. This time in San Francisco. While they stayed there, Jerome took Kathy to all his favorite restaurants, most he had done some type of interior work at. He would point out what he had done, each place had a funny story about something someone did, or how some places were built back up after years of being vacant. Finding homeless people inside or dope fiends and having to clear them and rats out before construction could be done. At each restaurant, they were always welcomed with VIP treatment. All seemed to be well. Jerome's house was finished. It looked nice on the outside, new. But the inside was immaculate. Looked like he spared no expense. Granite floors in high traffic areas, and deep lush rugs in the bedrooms. Their lives seemed to be heading in a new direction.

Chapter 12

Every day in Oakland, Berkeley, Richmond, or San Francisco seems like a mild to brisk day in the Fall except for maybe three weeks out of the year. Today was partly cloudy, the sun could be felt, and easily forgotten after a cold wind hit. Not cold, but enough of a bite to wear a light jacket or sweater. Jerome and Kathy were feeling good. They decided to go and have a walk at the market on the pier at the end of Broadway in Oakland. Sundays were a good day for that. They strolled laughing and talking. Jerome bought Kathy a couple of sweet things to eat. She had been having cravings for something sweet and had denied herself for a week. She had proud of herself but steady mentioning it all week so that Jerome was aware of it. He had decided he would get her that caramel apple before he even mentioned them going down there.

Kathy had started to show. Not much. There were many women with larger pooches than Kathy's baby filled belly. She had actually toned up more since she was exercising everyday. At the minimum going for her several mile walks up into Oakland Hills and back down. Since she had stopped working she had been obsessed with exercise. But she felt renewed. Her mind was more clear than it had been in years.   Jerome had been on a new program too. He had a room in his house where he did his workouts. He never wanted to be disturbed while in the room. He would close and lock the door. The Heater was turned on in the room while he worked out for no more than two hours. Every other morning he went to run up a Hill in a Regional Park in Berkeley. He would come back looking like he discovered something. His knuckles always looked like he had been punching dirt. No longer lifting weights he had gotten slightly smaller. But to Kathy's surprise his body felt harder, and looked more defined and his stamina had gone up immeasurably which was something since he had the most stamina out of any man she had been with.

They both were in a good place looking at each other they both felt good about how they felt. Stopping at restaurant that had an outdoor area. 4 ft high window surrounded the outside area of the eating area. It was made to block the wind. When they sat down they could feel the sun directly, warming them up immediately. The food was served and they both settled into their meal while Jerome teased Kathy about her cravings. Saying that she may blow up after the baby is born.

"I don't know. You may go boom after the baby."
"What?!?"
"Well, you know how you women do. Keep eating for two when there is just one."
"Or how you brothers do. Work out to get someone, then get obese after you have someone. Acting like your fat is muscle."
"Us!?! Naaah. That is just you all's way of trying to justify getting big yourself."
"Look. I stay in good shape, and not every woman get's fat after

having a child. Some women have extra circumstances that keep them from having the time to workout and lose weight."

"Really? I do not think anyone should get big. But we will wait and see how you do."

"You serious!?!"

"Yep."

"Jerome!?!"

"Shocked I would say something so callous and negative?"

"Yes!"

"I will tell you why I say such things."

"Please do."

"Because it does not matter to me if you do gain weight. I love you for what you have shown me you are. The way you are inside. Not the outside."

"Stop throwing drag. Saying sweet things to distract me with sweet conversation. You trying to distract me from the point."

"What point? The point is you do not have to worry about me tripping off of anything. If you do or don't gain weight, I will love you the same. "

Kathy looked at Jerome not quite not knowing how to take the conversation. This seemed to be out of nowhere. She looked him in the eye, and could see that he meant every word he said. He just sometimes had a weird way of expressing himself. But the look in his eyes reflected everything he just said. Kathy wanted to say something to check him on the weight issue but his eyes stopped anything she wanted to say past what had been said. At that moment a lady and a man walked in the restaurant. The woman looked familiar to Kathy. The lady was thick in size but shapely. Her hair was a medium length and styled to the nines. She had on a nice outfit and walked with a practiced grace. As the couple came closer, she saw that the woman was Angela!

While being guided to her table by the Greeter at the restaurant Angela saw Kathy sitting with someone. She could not see who she was sitting with, but this was perfect for her. She wanted Kathy to see she was not at all bothered by what happened with Kathy's mother. Her life had taken a turn for the better since then. She now had a man, a better job, had become a better mother and woman since. She knew she looked better, hell, felt better inside, and had actually stopped feeling so negatively toward Kathy. She still reveled in the idea that Kathy would get to see her in all her glory with a new man that was good looking. So she made sure to stop at Kathy's table to introduce her man and to show her new self to Kathy.

"Angela!"
"Kathy."
"You look good!"
"Thanks"
"Wow! What have you been up to? I have been saying I was going to call you because I had some things I wanted to ask you about that had to with Mom, but wow! You look really good!"
"Well, you know. People have to get themselves together at some point. Let me introduce you to Dominic."

Dominic moved past Angela as if aimed at Kathy. He took her hand with both of his and greeted her so warmly that Angela felt funny about it. Jerome stood as he seemed to be invisible at the moment. But once he stood, his presence was felt by all. Kathy introduced Jerome.

"This is my fiancé Jerome."

Jerome and Dominic's eyes locked in a directness that could not be missed. Jerome noted\ that even though Dominic was smaller than he was, his grip was almost as strong as his, almost. The way Dominic had moved in on Kathy seemed almost like he had been looking for something and found it.

Angela herself had noticed it. But as soon as she started to feel funny she felt Dominic's hand on her back stroking it softly. Dominic had been the best sex she ever had. The things he did to her were subtle, yet built up into a deeply addictive feeling inside her from her body to her soul.

"It was good to meet the both of you. And man you have got an Iron Kung Fu grip. Don't hurt me brother. Don't hurt me."

Dominic said in a joking manner causing both the women to laugh. Jerome smiled while looking Dominic directly in the eye. There was something there that was not right. He was used to men looking at Kathy or trying to get her because she was a very attractive woman. That is one of the many reasons why they would be getting married soon. She had shown herself to be a rare lady with a unique beauty. But there was something in this Dominic that felt familiar, but he could not place it. Whatever it was made Jerome feel on edge. Like he needed to literally keep his feet balanced, because the floor was going to be moved in a way that would throw someone off balance if they are not ready.

"Well, Jerome is my king and protector. I trust his judgment." Kathy said looking lovely in Jerome's eyes.

"Dominic is mine as well. He has been a godsend. We are going to get over to our table." Angela stated, so she would not be outdone.

"Wait a minute baby. Would you guys be interested in coming by my place for a dinner. Just the four of us?"

Angela's eyes were not able to hide the shock of what Dominic just asked. She held a face in a frozen grin that looked more like a pained grimace than a happy smile. She hated the invitation, and she knew that Dominic *had* to be aware of this. She had worn him out on details of how she felt toward Kathy and the things she had gone through over Kathy and her mother. So an invitation to his house for Dinner was the last thing she expected.

"I have no problem with it, Jerome, you OK with it?"
"Sure. Why not. This could give you and Angela a chance to catch up"

Kathy had hoped Jerome would say no, but her quick acceptance made him feel like this was something she really wanted to do. After Jerome spoke about her and Angela catching up, Kathy's mind immediately went to the many questions she had for Angela. Kathy turned from looking at Jerome and looked at Angela with a smile on her face.

"Yeah. It has been a while. We can definitely catch up."
"That is true. It has been a while. And there is so much to catch up on." Angela said trying to not let the mix of emotions come out in her voice.

That time and date were worked out. Dominic and Angela went to their table. Kathy and Jerome left not too long after. Angela kept up looks of happiness until they left. She then expressed her disappointment in having to have dinner with them. She talked to Dominic about it from that time, to the car, to the house. Nonstop. Dominic said nothing. Never really getting a chance to say a thing anyway. But he listened to the growing level of bitching Angela was doing all the way until they walked in the house. Angela was still talking taking off her sweater.

Dominic slid a hand around her waist , with another hand cupped to the side of her face, running fingers through her hair soothingly. Instantly Angela stopped talking. He brought her nearer to him, kissing her on the lips tenderly. Angela opened her mouth to protest but found his tongue on hers and they fell into a deep kiss. His tongue melding with hers. Her body yearning for his. Instantly wet and ready for him. She felt his fingers exploring the side of hair. His other hand grabbing her behind in a sensuously smooth way. Angela could feel the difference in her body since he first grabbed her. She had years worth of unexercised fat then. She did not like the way her body felt when he squeezed and touched her. Now, after months of a regimented workout, that was done on a daily basis she found that her body had not only shaped up but gotten softer to his touch. She felt him squeeze her now soft, but firm behind. The slip she had on under her dress making his hand feel silky smooth as he squeezed it in a way that made her one of the cheeks he was squeezing pop out of his hand and jiggle.

It took no time for them to go from standing straight up to her being turned around and face up against the front door. The sounds of a belt coming loose then hitting the ground as his slacks fell. He massaged her back as he kissed her neck and ear.   Angela arched her back reaching to feel Dominic's hardness press on her if not in her. He was out of reach but his hands continued to massage her strongly, keeping her pinned against the door. Through her dress she started feeling him press himself against her, making her want to feel all of him inside of her. It was such an addictive pleasure what he gave her.

Dominic kept grinding her from behind with increasing pressure while still rubbing her back for another few minutes. Angela had started to moan, with pleasure. She felt her dress come up, but did not remember nor care about when his hands left her back to lift the dress. He entered her as soon as her dress was lifted.

Angle's breathing came in loud irregular bursts. Feeling him fill her so fully, made Angela feel weak. It was as if he was connected to her entire body spreading his feeling to the rest every part of her. Setting her on fire with sensation. Her legs started to shake uncontrollably. It seemed as if he was holding her up with his manhood, and nothing else. His rhythm was smooth, not rough, his hands rubbed her on the same rhythm that his hands rubbed her on. Dominic started speaking. At first Angela did not hear him, due to being lost in the feeling he was giving her. Then she listened but it sounded like he was speaking some language she had not ever heard.

"Now. We will have this dinner. You will cook all the food and enjoy this. The dinner is something you need to do to squash this beef between you two. Right."
"Ye…ssss."

It was hard for Angela to talk as he filled her up inside, seemingly to get her more wet with each stroke. Angela tried to concentrate on the words but she was so weak from what he was doing to her physically she was hardly able to keep a conscious thought. Then he stopped moving.

"Angela."
"Yes."
"You will do as I say. This is not an option. I have heard all you have to say as to why we should not do this or why you do not like it. But this is something you need to move past."

"OK. But I did not like the way you were talking to Ka-"

The next few strokes Dominic did took all thought from Angela's head. She could focus no longer. He pushed her to the peak of ecstasy three times before finishing and leaving her to sit on the ground for awhile to get a hold of her legs shaking. Dominic had left the room leaving her to herself. What she was saying about him and Kathy long forgotten. Angela got up and went to the bathroom to clean herself up. But her mind had been made up. Whatever Dominic wanted her to do she would do. Because this man had a power she had never felt. A control over her that made her give to him willingly. Whatever he wanted would be done. She did not care what it was. There was nothing she would not do.

Chapter 13

To Kathy and Jerome felt a month pass like it was just an hour. Dominic had Angela call and setup a time to get together. Kathy asked Angela about her kids and started talking about how she was looking forward to having one herself. Angela was more kind than usual and listened, but then politely stopped the conversation by mentioning an errand she had to run before picking up the kids from Summer Camp. This stunned Kathy, because Angela never even seemed to pay attention to the kids outside of feeding them. This was totally out of character. The whole tone in which Angela spoke and the *way* she spoke was, different. More mature. Less hateful. She would actually let Kathy speak without cutting her off mid sentence in the most rude way possible. She still got off the phone pretty abruptly. But no where near how she used to. Kathy was calling her and she had to make sure she got a couple of answers or at least a commitment before she got off the phone.

"Angela, I know you have to go. But we should talk about our mothers. There is so much to discuss. There are things I have

questions on and some information you might like to know."
"Look, there is so much in the past, let's just leave it there."
"True. There are many things we should leave in the past. But after the video I saw, there are things we should share together, as family."

There was a silence on the phone. Kathy could not tell if Angela was in agreement or not. But neither made a sound. Almost if there was some sort of stalemate going on.

"Kathy. You know that was hard for me. And it is hard not to go down a negative road about the whole thing. What more is there to talk about? That part of my life is over. And I have moved on."
"Ok. But, I never got to hear much about what you remember about living down south. What *you* remember about your own mother."
"Not much."
"Still. We should do lunch."

Angela actually felt pressured. She was normally the one applying all the pressure, but just as she had changed she felt a change in Kathy too. Almost as if Kathy was threatening to chase her to the ends of the earth to get this out of her. Which had not been her personality at all. Normally Kathy was quiet and not aggressive. She would stand her ground but would not be the one to pursue or to act in aggression on anything. Angela could tell Kathy felt different about her by the tone she used. Normally Kathy had a tone of venom. Kathy had never hidden her hatred of the way Angela did not appreciate her mother. And in truth, Angela now understood better why Kathy saw her that way. In dealing with Dominic and cleaning herself up to match and please him she had to face many things about herself that were downright ugly. It was as if she grew up in a matter of months. Taking responsibility for herself, and her children in a way she never had before. Now hearing Kathy ask her with such conviction and pureness to speak to her as family touched her in a way she had not originally thought possible.

"Fine."
"Let's get together during the week while you are on lunch. That way you do not have to worry about your kids or Dominic."

Angela thought, she is getting slick too. Is it having a baby getting her this way? Dating Jerome? Maybe a combination of both. But this was a side to Kathy she had not seen nor heard before. Angela agreed to the day and time with no hesitation. They would meet at the small strip mall across from her job. There was a Salad place there. After Angela got off of the phone as if something was burning in the kitchen. Cutting Kathy off and saying she had to go, important business to attend to, but in reality. She wanted to make sure Kathy did not bulldoze her again. As she hung up the phone she turned around looking at the ground. She was shocked to see Dominic leaning against the wall. He had a key to her house, but she did not have one as yet to his.

"Hey baby. Who was that on the phone." Dominic said while sorting through the mail in his hand. Her mail.

Angela took the mail out of his hand and put it down on the counter. He moved right up on her as she put the envelopes down. She could feel his probing eyes staring into the side of her head. He did not lift his hands and arms to hug. Both hands hung at his side, open like they were waiting to grab something. He stood, unmoving, waiting for her to turn and answer.

"It was Kathy. She wants to get together before we have dinner."

"What for?"

"To talk."

"You all can talk when we have dinner in a couple of days. You should skip that. Tell her wait until the dinner."

"I already committed…"

"What?! You did not even speak to me about this! What is wrong with you? This is going to ruin *everything*!"

Angela normally could ignore small things Dominic did that were controlling. In fact, sometimes she was secretly turned on by the way he controlled her. Because he led her to do things that were healthy and good for her. But right now, the tone of his voice and the fact the he was standing close made him seem extremely intimidating. Angela was over the moon about Dominic, but right now something deep inside her told her that something was off, something was wrong. Wrong in the way he was talking, his approach, and something inside the very nature of him. Like there was something underneath the handsome slim exterior, slithering like a worm in an empty bottle.

"Dominic! You are scaring me! What is with all these questions and demands? Why are you coming at me like this?!?"

Dominic stared for a moment, no emotion evident in his eyes. Just cold calculation. In his mind he saw and heard that Angela was about to be hysterical. So he changed his posture, sliding a hand around her shoulder, finger rubbing lightly over the top of the shoulder. He put on his most syrup dripped baritone voice.

"Angela, baby, I did not mean to scare you. Its just that, I had this beautiful plan to make it a night to remember Saturday. A night that we could all come together and enjoy ourselves. I am having the back yard decorated just for the day, and some food catered in.

Your favorite, Jamaican."

Dominic then pulled his head back so that she could look in his eyes. Angela felt hypnotized. His melodic words, and his bedroom eyes both working together to take her far away from the feeling of something being wrong. Then he turned away from her and said.

"Now, make sure you tell her not until Saturday."

The hypnotism stopped. A new far more aggressive feeling came from him. Angela knew she was not imagining things or tripping out this time.

"Look, it is just for some girl talk. An hour. That is all. It would be better to get that out of the way before they get here together. Seeing how you and Jerome looked at each other, it would not appear that you two would not have a good conversation together without Kathy and I intervening. So let us get the girl talk out the way so that we can concentrate on having good conversation for all concerned."

Dominic actually seemed to bristle at the name of Jerome. Angela noticed, but it made her think of Jerome. She was impressed how he had turned out. She thought he would grow up to be nothing. But he had filled out, in mind, body, and spirit it seemed. Enough for Dominic, who had quite the presence himself, to feel it.

"Perhaps you are right. Getting the 'girl talk' out of the way is a good idea."

Before Angela could react or speak, Dominic had turned and gone down the hallway toward her room. He did not say a word but he had his cell phone out, and was dialing a number. He turned to go into her room, she went to follow, but he put up a hand making a stop gesture. Then put up one finger that said 1 minute.

This behavior was not like Dominic. He was always so gracious and smooth. Today he was cold, callous, and abrupt. Something was up and Angela felt as though talking to Kathy, however heinous that may be, needed to be done. Her mind was made up. She would definitely speak with Kathy. About whatever.

Jerome arrived home after doing his run and secret workout in Berkeley Hills. He felt stronger, more in control of his mind and body. He felt as though his business decisions were coming to him easier now. Kathy had been a calming influence on him that helped him to focus easier on the task of bringing in more business. Not that he was struggling. But for several years now it has been just him. Now, with a child on the way he no longer felt as relaxed about it. He felt he needed to make sure he built up enough to take care of and leave his child with something. The memory that the man with the cane gave him led him to a new level of physical prowess. All types of attacks and defenses now played in his head all day. When he walked past objects he now could feel their breaking points. There were very few things he could not break now.

Years spent working on dilapidated houses, squeezing into small areas to punch or push something out helped him to understand things better. He had now gotten to the level of being able to shatter large rocks. He did not tell Kathy about the secret workouts because he felt as though this might make her stress a little. And the last thing he wanted was to make her stress, especially now that she was pregnant His workout fading from his mind he opened the door to the house and was greeted by Kathy. Arms wide, and smile even wider. He felt like a king come home to greet his queen. She hugged him tightly, even though he was still a little sweaty.

"How was your workout?"
"Good. You look like you had a good day."
"Yep."

Kathy kissed Jerome's face until he laughed.

"What is all that for?"
"Well, you are kind sexy when you come in all sweaty. You look good and I missed you. Plus I was able to do something today."

Jerome did not move. Not thinking it was something bad, but she had his full attention.

"I got, Angela to agree to have lunch with me before the dinner."
"How."
"Made her."

Jerome laughed

"And just how did you do that?"
"Did not take no for an answer. Besides she is family."

Jerome's right eyebrow went up so high, it looked like it was going to enter his hairline. Calling Angela a family member always seemed so far away from anything Kathy would say he thought she might be possessed. With recent events, it did not seem too far fetched. The feeling he got though is nothing but togetherness and love from Kathy. She seemed to be radiating it.

"If I did not know any better I would think you were possessed."
"Stop it you don't really think I am possessed. Even though right now that does not sound as crazy as it would have a couple of months ago. What?"

Jerome was looking at his woman. Her face had gotten slightly more round. Her eyes were clear, with their big brown pupils. She may have been pregnant, but her body still had a beautiful shape. The baby pooch in the front seemed to make her all the more alluring to him. Feeling himself grow he pulled her mouth to his and they kissed passionately. Both overcome with lust, Jerome lifted Kathy. She wrapped her legs around his waist.

His strength was something she still loved to feel. Each time he lifted her it felt like the first time. She felt like a paper weight in Jerome's arms. He did not shake like some men did while trying to hold her. He was solid. No movement, other than what he wanted to move. Her dress was pulled up with one hand, her panties torn off like paper by the other. He was in her in an instant. The hunger in his eyes sent a thrill through her entire body. Many men seemed to get turned off by body changes women make during pregnancy. Jerome always looked at her with nothing but a hunger for her and her body. She could feel his desire in each and every stroke. He drove deep into her, careful not to hit the back of her, as not to disturb the baby within. Careful, yet powerful strokes, that seemed to take her up in higher in different ways with each and every stroke.

Jerome felt himself reaching his peak quicker than normal. He had to steady both of them by grabbing the corner of the wall. As he released inside her, she could feel him thumping away deep inside her. She also heard a sound like metal being twisted which scared her. She looked to the side where she heard the sound and saw Jerome's hand had literally pushed through the wall and crushed the metal beneath.

Kathy stood immediately, grabbing his hand to check it for bleeding or laceration. There was nothing. Nothing but dust from the wall. Jerome was strong, but this was super man strong. He stood, smiling down at her.

"Don't worry. That did not hurt. Very little can hurt me now. Trust me."

Jerome caressed Kathy's back as he pulled her toward him. She laid her head on his chest, feeling his powerful body and the amount heat coming from him. He made her feel warm and comfortable in his arms. Safe.

"Let's go upstairs. So I can clean my funk from my workout off of me and you in the tub. OK"
"OK." Kathy smiled but did not lift her head from his chest. She was too comfortable. Both loving the feeling of each other in different ways. Her feeling protected. And he feeling like she was a tenderness that needed to be protected. They both walked upstairs, feeling each other's spirit.

"So, tell me what you and Angela are going to talk about."

Chapter 14

A week went by. The get together was upon them. Angela had been feeling nervous about it since Friday morning at work. Dominic had been somewhat distant. Different all week. He always was on the phone and could not always be talked to like before. When she started to tell him about her day, he would give her a look that could only mean shut up. He no longer spoke in slow soothing tones that eased any tension she had. Since the relationship seemed to have been one-sided in the fact that Dominic had done so much for her. Angela felt it was only right to start doing for him. She would rub his back while he was on the phone or sitting alone in what looked like deep thought. Made sure that she did not bring her kids around when with him. Just in case they did something to set him off. Over a short time, she seemed to almost abandon them in some instances because she felt her man needed her support. Always asked him what she could do to help him. Dominic would stop, and kiss her on the forehead. Look her in her eyes, with a look of surprise each time, like he could have never imagined she could be this way. But then he would turn and go back to whatever it is he has been working on, locked away in his office. This caused a panic in Angela. She started to have panic attacks in front of him asking him what was wrong, was it her, did she not make him happy. He would sit and watch her speak, voice uncertain and cracking. Tears streaming down her face. Angela's body would be shaking she was so upset. There would be no expression on Dominic's face. As if there was no one behind the face. As if it was a mask that would only work when turned on. During those moments it was as if no one was there.

This would disturb Angela. She would back away as the empty eyes of his followed her movements. Saying nothing. She would move to walk out the door, and he would stop her every time. Soothing her without words, just soft touches and a warm look in his eyes. Pulling her close she was often overcome with emotion. Too emotional to speak, he would pull her head onto his chest and she would cry for a few moments. Then would feel better. This perturbed Angela to no end. Because she found herself talking to him like a love crazed teenage girl afterward with him saying very little. Just appearing to be amused by everything she talked about.

"Hey. I know I have not been my normal self lately. Its just.....some business that I have to take care of is on my mind. It should all be over by the time we have dinner with your friends."
"OK."

Angela, normally looking at the ground after crying, looking about as much like a hurt little girl as she could look, would feel Dominic's slender fingers under her chin lifting it up. He would then look her in the eye and just say one sentence before kissing her tenderly, but deeply.

"You have to trust me. Have I ever steered you wrong?"

A statement, more than a question. But the love he would make to her made her forget or just outright not care. He was a drug and Angela did not mind being the addict.

The week of the dinner, Dominic got more and more upbeat. He refused to let her in on any of the details, whenever she pushed he would some how get her off of the subject without her even knowing. She was going to find out if Kathy knew what was in store. She was also curious why Kathy had all the sudden wanted to know more about their history in the South.

"Kathy!"
"Wow you look good! What is your workout program, because I am going to get on it once I have this baby!"
"Intensity is the key. For at least 30 minutes straight 4 days a week. I knew I had gotten fat. But did not know just how out of shape I was until Dominic came into my life. He has been a revelation. Not that he called me fat or something. But he inspired me to want to get in shape."
"I can see, you look like a whole new person. "

Both women sat in silence looking at each other. Volumes of understanding passed between them. The closeness that can only come from growing up with someone you did not get along with. But the amount of time they were around each other at young ages bringing them close together. Both women had gone through major changes in the past few months since Sylvia died.

"Kathy, you are looking radiant. Being pregnant suits you. You look happy."
"I am. Jerome has given me everything I need. I never knew that

he had a crush on me when we were younger."

"Well hell. I could have told you that!"

"You would not have back then. *That,* I know for sure."

"Yes it would have been better if we could have related to each other like we do now. So much has happened since your mother passed."

"You are right. That is why I wanted to talk to you. So that we could discuss some things that you may remember that I do not or was not born yet and could ."

"Like what? I do not remember much about the South. Most of my memories are from here. And why this sudden interest in our mothers? There is nothing in my memory of you ever asking anything about our past. Is everything OK?"

"Yes. We will get to that in a minute. Just wondering what has brought about such a change in you? Dominic? Something you decided to change?"

Angela sat back, more than ready to talk about it. She began with leaving from the Lawyer's office in how she was feeling, to meeting Dominic, to her deciding to make a change and how it affected her along the way. The new view she has of the world and most of all, her new view of herself and how she has to live her life to be healthy mind, body, and soul.

Kathy sat back and took a deep breath. Angela's transitional story was so deep it almost made her feel like what she had to say may be irrelevant after hearing all that. The story she had to tell would be very hard for any sane person to sit and listen to let alone believe.

Angela looked at her, she watched as Kathy seemed to suddenly tense. But Kathy then turned to look at Angela directly and started telling everything that happened in such a low but clear and matter of fact way that Angela believed every incredible statement. It was far fetched but there was something about the man with the cane that had always seemed too different. Even as a little girl she remembered him, standing out from everyone. Like her life was a picture in a frame. And someone came up and put him in the picture without bothering to make him seem like he was part of the picture. Just like he was put there by a 4 year old learning how to paste. Memories from her childhood came flooding back to her as she listened to all the information Kathy told that she had heard from her mother. Angela herself was not that old in the 60's but she could remember enough.

"What I can tell you is, Sylvia, did not seem all that outgoing back then. At least compared to my mother. Whenever they were around it seemed as if my mother was always the one that wanted to do something or had done something. I never knew what at that age. But at the age I am now, I see it had to do with men."
"Did you ever hear her speak about any 'powers' my mother had?"
"No. But she would always say that your mother had, 'Secrets'. She never went into detail. But the way she said it. It was as if something would play back in her mind every time she said it."
"Did my mother ever tell you about anything?"
"No. But you know how I was. And I really do apologize for all that. For whatever reason I could not see how much help your mother was giving me. I think of her everyday now."

Kathy sat back. The way Angela was speaking, it was as if some exorcism had happened to her and instead of the demon that had been controlling her, now it was an angel controlling her. She seemed to be so full of positivity, that it was almost unbelievable to think this was the same person in the same body. So instead of being controlled by a demon, Kathy joked in her own mind that Angela was being controlled by an angel.

"Judging from the look on your face, what I am saying must be hard to believe. But since your mother's death a lot has happened."

"By listening to what you have had to say and watching your transformation, I could believe a lot has happened."

Both women laughed and ate for awhile in silence. Kathy had so many questions before but listening to Angela had thrown her off. She now was drawing blanks from her own memory. So she just let the silence go on while they ate. Mostly because of her not remembering what she was going to ask her.

Just when she thought she had heard the biggest change from Angela. Angela started to speak of her children and how they were doing. She had stopped letting them eat whatever and had helped them to be more focused in school and life through a new regimented schedule she kept them on. Kathy's jaw had fallen through the ground and hit China on the other side of the world. She sat and listened as Angela gushed about how her children were doing. How much better she felt since losing some weight. The clothes she could now buy and look good in. Then she got to Dominic, and kept stating over and over that he was the best thing that had happened to her in her life. He was patient, understanding, but not weak, sometimes very mysterious though. More so than any man she had ever dealt with.

Kathy then started asking about Dominic, where did he come from, what about his family, had he ever been married before. Angela had no answers for any of the questions and seemed perfectly fine with that. She just continued on and stated how good he was with her kids. At that point, Kathy felt like all the old Angela was not gone. In Kathy's mind she felt she might need to know just a tad bit more about a man if he was going to be around a child or children of hers. Angela seemed to sense what she was thinking so she changed the subject.

" So, do you know if you are having a boy or a girl?"
"No, not officially, but I think it will be a girl. There seems to be a calm coming from down there. And you know boys do not give off any kind of calm."
"Too true!"
"But in reality I do not care as long as the baby is healthy."
"I can hear you on that. Any names yet?"
"No. But we will cross that bridge closer in. Oh! I just remembered that question I wanted to ask you, do you remember a Preacher traveling with you all to come out to California?"
"I remember the man with the cane, and I remember some other man that seemed to be the same age. If not older. He did seem to always go to the store, or go get something to eat, or just flat out go with your mother all the time."
"Do you know if they...... you know...."

Angela sat blinking. Eyes empty but questioning.

"Do you know if they had sex?"
"No. That I do not know. But judging from how much time I remember them spending together, it is highly possible."
"What happened to him?"
"You know, that is a ...."

Angela looked like she was seeing a ghost. Her color in her face went from a pretty brown, and started fading to a sickly color of gray.

"He.....he......"

Kathy leaned closer and reached out for Angela's hand, but Angela pulled back like Kathy's hand was a snake trying to bite her. Angela's phone went off and seemed to snap her out of whatever memory she was seeing.

Kathy watched with a worried look on her face. Angela had seemed so vibrant a second ago, but now she seemed like life was draining out of her. She said one word answers to the person on the phone. Then said she would be right there.
"Kathy, that was Dominic, he needs me and it is an emergency, we can talk more later. You have brought all kinds of memories back."

Angela took a $100 dollar bill out and put it on the table while reaching down to hug Kathy. Then stood back up with one hand on Kathy's shoulder.

"That should take care of the meal. We will talk more at Dominic's this weekend. "

Kathy tried to stand but felt held down to her seat by Angela.

"We will talk more this weekend. I enjoyed our talk."
"Me too Angela. We should do this more often."
"We will. Have to go, but take care."
"You too."

And with that, Angela walked swiftly out of the restaurant. The money Angela left was more than enough to cover that chocolate volcano cake Kathy had been craving. So she sat alone at her table eating the cake, enjoying her day, when suddenly she got a very sure feeling of being watched. It went away as soon as she felt it.

The feeling was so powerful that it felt as if someone was standing over her, looking down over her shoulder to see what she was doing. Kathy would not call it a psychic, more like intuition, or the same feeling a woman gets when a man just stares at her in plain view.

The feeling stayed in her head for awhile, prompting her to leave. A small voice inside her was telling her to leave so she listened. Angela having that look on her face for the last subject piqued Kathy's interest. She would need to find out more. This weekend she planned on doing just that.

Chapter 15

The day came for the dinner. Jerome was tense about going to dinner but had agreed to it because he knew it was important to Kathy. She seemed to be beaming about it and for the life of him, he could not figure out how Angela had gone from most hated in Kathy's eyes to what seems like most loved in a couple of months. Problems like they seemed to have usually pass when people grow up. Theirs seemed to get deeper with age. The few times he would see them around each other through their 20s and 30s the barrier between them seemed to widen and get more virulent with each passing year. Now all of a sudden, this is the only friend he hears about?! Both with Kathy in her thirties, and Angela in her forties, they squash it? Jerome shook his head as he used the confusion to boost his last sprint up the hill. Many times after finishing his last sprint up the hill he would practice what he learned on the rocks up there. Then after that, having a clear mind that only come from intense workouts, he would meditate. Letting the sun hit him, the quiet of the area soothe him. There was always a wind blowing through no matter what time of year, and that wind would help him ride them deep off into his own mind. He would look around him and take in the environment in full then close his eyes letting the wind take him deeper. Deep in his thoughts he found ways to expand his business, trips to take with Kathy, found out inner problems and worked them out all at the top of this hill that was really a small mountain. No one else came to this point because it was steep and slippery slope to get here. If you stood in front of it the first section was nearly straight up. One could lay their shoulder on it and not be leaned over to far resting on that shoulder. But he had found a way to literally leap up from one small rock that fit under his foot to another rock all the way up. It helped him with his explosive strengthening. If you stepped on the dirt it would give and you would slip back down. There was a path he took all the time that had been perfect for what he needed. Even with all this serene environment and all the meditative thinking he did, he still could not work out going to this dinner.

He really did not want to go. He was about to take out that frustration on some rocks and then head home. But to his surprise, the man with the cane standing in the middle of the field. Clean as ever, wearing an off white suit. He was not breathing hard or even looking like he had climbed up there. There was no sign of dirt on his clothes. He looked relaxed as could be. This was the 10th time for Jerome running up to this point. No one was up here before and no one had been climbing up when he was up here the other 9 times. Normally he would get to the top and run around it looking down the sides of the peak he was on to cool down, then go back down and start again. He did the same thing today, no one was here or coming up here then. There was really only one path up. The other sides seemed to actually go in under the peak and then come back up. Which means you have to be someone that could walk or climb upside down on loose dirt to climb it.

"I see you have been practicing. That is good. Because you may need it soon."

"There has not been too much going on lately."

"Speak for yourself. There are many things going on all the time. You are just unable to see them yet. But you will have to deal with these things soon."

"What are you talking about?"

"You will see soon enough. For now there is something I have to give you before I leave."

Jerome started to say something but found the man had covered the distance between them without seeming to take a step toward him. There was a slight breeze that hit Jerome letting him know, the man did move across the space between them. Jerome felt a pressure on his forehead. It took him half a second to realize that the man's palm was on Jerome's forehead, and once again he was pushed into the past. It felt like he had lost his balance and was falling. But instead of falling to the ground he felt as if he had fallen into someone else's body. He was sitting watching what look like a judgment being passed on a man. A slim man, but then the vision was ripped from him as soon as he saw it. He felt a short burst of heat so high that it felt as if the very air, oxygen was being burned.

Jerome's eyes opened and all he saw was the sky. The man with the cane was no where in sight. There was some blood on the ground and a piece of fabric that looked the same as the man with the cane was wearing, it was lodged under a rock. Scanning the area Jerome saw no one around but still moved cautiously anyway. It felt like something was wrong in the area. A deep feeling of wrongness that could not really be put into words. Just wrong. Jerome started a quick but cautious walk back down the hill. He felt more surefooted than he had felt before, but that feeling just made the moment that much more intense. Speeding up until he hit a main trail where he saw several people walking their dogs and children. He went straight to his truck and pulled off. His senses alert, and mind racing. He had to get back to make sure everything was OK with Kathy and their unborn child. He sped home on a mission to get there. Moving through traffic like he was in a Corvette and not a truck. When he saw Kathy standing in the front driveway grabbing the mail speaking with a mutual friend's mother. Smiling, laughing, his heart stopped pumping as fast. Her relaxed look on her face put him at ease. He knew that she was all right, judging from the wide smile she had, and the laughter he could hear as he drove up to the driveway, confirmed that she was alright. Kathy and the lady said their goodbye's as Jerome motioned for her to hop in.

"Wow you were flying down the street! What's your rush? You all right. Your workout go OK?"
"Yeah. Everything's fine baby. Now that you are here next to me."

Kathy looked at Jerome smiling. He looked back at her with such a look of relief in his eyes that Kathy had to ask again.

"You sure everything is OK?"
"Yeah baby. How about this, let's hop in the tub. Do some relaxing before we go to dinner tonight."
"OK!"

Kathy grinned sitting up straighter. She had fallen deeply in love with that bathtub since moving in. It had been her place of solitude for many months now. The lit candles and soft lights always let her relax into a deep sleep. The jets with their multiple levels of adjustment had become her personal masseuses.   Besides that, Jerome would be there too, which would always lead to, a higher form of release.

Time flew by for both of them. After they got out of the tub had a small lunch, then Jerome made some calls while Kathy went to bed to take a nap. When she woke Jerome was laying next to her in a deep coma like sleep. The mattress was firm but seemed to be sagging a little under his weight. Kathy looked at him as he slept. He had no shirt on so she caressed his defined lines from his shoulder to his chest. She looked at his face again to find him staring right at her. She let out a surprised yelp, that they both laughed at for awhile. Both decided it was time to get ready after laughing a little more. Playfully prodding each other. Jerome would lift her up as if she weighed nothing, like she had lost weight instead of gained it. She loved his strength and he loved her softness. They matched each other physically in a way that neither one of them spoke of. Maybe for a mutual fear that it would ruin the understanding if spoken aloud.

They pulled up to Dominic's house. It was in a town called Orinda, just outside of Oakland. Jerome and Kathy had to go through the Caldecott tunnel, which went straight through a mountain, to get there. After that, they had to take a maze of back roads before they pulled up to Dominic's house. It was not big, but the land the house was on was plenty large by California standards. They had to drive down a rather long driveway before pulling up to a modestly sized house. As soon as Jerome turned off his engine Dominic and Angela opened the front door with big grins on their faces.

"You guys got here right on time. The food is ready and the scene is set. Hope you guys are hungry!"

Dominic voice boomed from the front door of the house where he and Angela stood. Normally he seemed more reserved. But from where they were in the truck still, it was clear Dominic was feeling himself a little bit. Not in an ignorant way. But it was clear that this is clearly his domain. Aside from that, both Kathy and Jerome were starving so they made their way up to the front door with haste. Hugs and handshakes were exchanged. Talks of if it was easy to find the place but many twists and turns. They all made their way to the backyard. It was not so much a backyard as it was a small park. The landscaping was excellent. It was not finished but it all went together perfectly. The plates had already been set. The Catering company employees were out of sight.

The food was at the center of the table, so they were able to choose exactly what they wanted to eat. Kathy's plate had a healthy sized lobster tail with butter and garlic. For salad she had her favorite, Caesar salad. Jerome had a large bone in steak of a cut he was not familiar with, but did not care because it was grilled to perfection, potatoes and greens. Both of them sat said hello and immediately tore into the meal like they both had not had a home or food for quite some time. Both were too busy eating to notice what was on Dominic's or Angela's plates. They did not look either. Angela barely ate too busy secretly laughing at Jerome and Kathy.

After dinner was over the conversation flowed, as well as drinks. Kathy did not drink any alcohol, but she did go through a bottle and a half of apple cider. Jerome had gone through three bottles of beer while they were talking. Angela sipped her Merlot, and Dominic sipped what looked like some type of white wine.

"Well, I am glad you guys came by. " Dominic said
"It was our pleasure, this is a very nice pad. If the person doing

your Landscaping falls off, I can fill in. But whoever you have, I must admit is good." Jerome said with a raise of his beer bottle.

Dominic stood beaming, glass raised to toast his glass to Jerome's bottle. Angela stood with him and hugged him looking up into his eyes. The moment seemed perfect to her. Jerome and Dominic were getting along in a way she had not anticipated. She watched as Kathy leaned in toward Jerome and laid her head on his shoulder, skin aglow in the soft candle light. The evening air was nice and the stars shown in the sky, she could see Jerome and Kathy were radiating a deep happiness that seemed to affect the whole area they sat in. It was the type of love that could fill a house and make it a home. The type of thing that cannot be given, it just is or is not there. It is that intangible thing in a grandmother's house or a family's house that gives the home a life and feeling all its own. Standing there gazing at the scene Angela felt herself overcome with the joy of the moment.

There was a rustle that came from the far side of the yard, everyone looked over. A man walked out of the tree line on the other side of the solid acre that was the backyard. As he got closer they all began to see it was the man with the cane. He strode with a solid conviction. Looking past Kathy and Jerome and directly in the direction of Dominic and Angela. His breathing seemed somewhat labored. His clothes that never looked out of place were torn, and filthy. A gash was across his forehead like something had slashed him. There was blood, dirt, and various other dark fluids that had dried on his clothes. He walked with a slight limp that he seemed to try to ignore and walk normally. There was a bloodstain on his left shoulder, with blood still flowing from it. On his shirt over his stomach he had a blood stain. Which would explain the limp if his stomach had been injured. His face showed no pain, just a conviction that a mans face has when he has decided to kill someone, no matter what the consequences. The cane that he carried was stretching as he walked. It was stretching longer as he got closer. It stretched out to the length of a walking stick or a broomstick. The wood itself looked like it had come to life, there seemed to be a dark lines moving down the sides of it, like blood in veins. The Diamonds started to glow like miniature suns getting brighter as he got closer to them. The air around them became warmer like there was fire near.

"That is too bad. This means the party is over. Get that one I will take care of Mr. Cane here."

Kathy and Angela heard Dominic say the words but it did not register. Jerome was on his feet immediately, but was struck brutally hard in the chest, all air knocked off him, followed by a kick to his side that sent him flying into the side of the house. Pain spread through his side with an intensity he had not ever felt. Then he noticed he could not breath. He also could not move. He had just bounced off the house and landed. He saw the man he had fought at Kathy's mother's house. Angela stood shaking looking scared. The man that hit Jerome backhanded her so hard a tooth flew out of her mouth. Her head snapped to the side with such force it looked like her neck may have been broken. Her body dropped in a limp heap like she had been killed on contact. Kathy was trying to get up to move away from what was going on while looking at Dominic approach the man with the cane.

Jerome could not move but saw Dominic stomp the ground once and the ground between Dominic and Mr. Cane the name that Dominic had just given him rise up and rush toward the man as if it were alive. The cane's diamonds let off a blindingly bright light. The dirt dissipated, but a creature came up that looked like a giant centipede leaped at him behind the dirt Cane had seemed to push away with a rush of air. The giant bug that was the height of a grown man while sitting upright, reached for the cane-wielding man. The bug's exoskeleton exterior was see-through. Something that had spent all its life underground somewhere. A whitish color, but still you could see through it. All its organs were in plain view, you could see them working. Its lungs, heart, stomach, brain, all in plain view. The large bugs and small rodents in it were being digested, clear to be seen inside it. Some still alive, moving slowly, suffering a long painful death. Its many legs seemed to have razor sharp endings. Looked like hundreds off knives. Each one seemed to have some type of liquid dripping off its tips. No eyes could be seen. But it was well aware of where its adversary was. Moving in a rhythmic but quick way. Cane moved away from the creature with astonishing speed. A quickness that did not seem human at all. Dominic raised his hand and seemed to be giving a command to attack, and the creature did just that.

"That ought to hold him for awhile. Grab her and let's go get this over with." Dominic said.

Suddenly the bony man was next to her. Kathy was in such shock when everything happened she had just frozen. She was solidly in the grip of fear. What she was seeing did not surprise her, but the fact that this seemed to be set up to get her scared her beyond what she could take. What did they want from her? She looked over and saw Jerome struggling to stay conscious, Angela was dead as far as she could see, and Cane was fighting a giant centipede looking bug. Dominic's eyes no longer looked normal. The pupils were now golden in color and the shape of the pupils was familiar but alien. Like no person or even animal she had seen before. It looked extremely sinister, like a predator. A thought crossed her mind that Dominic might eat her. And as he turned toward her to look at her, the look in his eyes did not seem to do anything to stop her from thinking that.

"Your thoughts are loud and dramatic. I may not be totally human, but there will be no eating you. You have been the target the whole time and never sensed it. Funny, from one of your lineage. The fact that no one taught you who you are or how to use what you have is pitiful. There is something in your bloodline that has laid dormant for many millennia. We will use it to move forward with our new design. There are too many still bound by a law that is no longer enforced. They must all be freed. It is a pity you will never get to learn the power in you. The power that resides in your child. But right now there is no time for explanation, we will be taking that child of yours. You may both die, but I have lived too long and fought to hard for this moment to let it go."

She felt the bony man's hands on her shoulder, cold to the touch, like a body that had been dead for quite some time. Dominic's words seemed to sink into Kathy's head slowly, as if he were really speaking another language and she was slowly translating what he said back into English. Dominic was planning on killing her and her child. Before she could think anything else she heard a grunt of effort from out in the backyard. She saw Cane tearing open the bug that was attacking him. It was quick but the man was quicker. Brutally efficient in the way he tore chunks out of it puncturing it with his cane then tearing the cane out to the side of wherever he stabbed into it. They both moved around each other. The sound of the cane penetrating into the liquid insides the only noise heard as

233

the man ripped the insides out of the exoskeleton of the bug. The bug did not yell out in pain, it made no noise, but moved quicker. It appeared to be trying to get past the man and get away. But Cane would not let it. He stuck the cane in what would be the head, and that part of the bug exploded. Slime and internals flew everywhere. The bony man holding Kathy fell to the side as Jerome cracked the man in the head with a stick, then hopped on top of the man and put the stick straight down into the eye socket of the man on the ground, pressing straight through it and into the skull. The sick sound of the penetration could not just be heard but felt through the ground.

Screams of pain could be heard from the man, Jerome raised his foot high and slammed it down on the man's skull, again, and again, until the man's face was flat and his body unmoving.

Dominic would have helped the man but he had other problems than Jerome. Cane had started running toward him. Cane got all the way to him and was pulling back his cane to strike when Dominic lifted him off his feet. Kathy could see nothing but knew something was constricting around Cane's neck. A cut appeared across Cane's cheek. Then what looked like a giant slug laid down on the scar leaving slime covering the cut.

Cane reached up with his cane and touched his neck. A fire blazed all the way down to Dominic. The slug was attached to Dominic. Not only attached to him. It was apart of him. The outline of the fire showed a larger body behind Dominic. The body was connected to him. Kathy tried to see more but felt herself get wrapped up by a cold wet but strong limb. She looked down and to her horror she saw what looked like a giant slug wrapping itself around her.

"Cane. How long will this go on? There is no longer a Council you can defer to Your powers are waning and you grow weaker by the second. Why protect this girl? She is of no consequence."

Instead Cane giving an answer to Dominic he seemed to make the fire burn more intensely making the creature that Dominic is drop him. Right as he hit the ground he ran for the creature. Looking to make a death blow. He stopped. Blood stain spread across his shirt, in his lower abdomen area.

"Yes. What I did to you earlier on top of that hill was a warm up to show you that you can and will die. There is no one to stop that now. It is funny how that happens over the years. So many years go by, and what was so important in the past becomes irrelevant. Irrelevant as you trying to be the police to the likes of me and countless others for many, many millennia."

Jerome had stomped the face of the man like it was a giant bug that needed to be stomped into a liquid mush. Which is what he did as what looked like hundreds of thousands of bugs came running out the neck like they were going to fix the problem of a smashed head. He kept on stepping on the bugs until they ran another direction away from him. Jerome looked up to see everyone across the yard from him. A good distance away. Kathy was floating in the air like she was being held up by a giant hand. Cane had fallen to one knee, blood and other things were coming out of his stomach. The man was dying, and aging with every drop of blood that left his body.

"Before you die, I want you to see the uselessness of your duty. The true end to it all. All the power will be consumed and expanded inside of me. Funny, the same powers that were used to curse me, I will now use to free myself completely and get rid of the whole bloodline."

Kathy's Shirt was torn open by some unseen hands. Her stomach was sliced two ways, she seemed to not feel the cuts, but Jerome and Cane both saw them, both of them cringed. Even though Jerome cringed he was still running toward them. Her stomach was then pulled open and the fetus pulled out by sharp but slimy tendrils, she experienced a pain beyond anything she could imagine. It was as if whatever had opened her up poured pure alcohol on the open wound. As the pain ramped up she could not hold back a scream full of terror and pain as the child was then torn out of her.

Jerome ran toward her but felt a sharp pain hit his shoulder, tearing through his skin and bones. His body was slammed against the wall that was some 50 yards behind him when he was hit. He was then pinned up against the wall. His left arm dangled, useless, but filled with pain like every nerve had been set on fire. He cried out himself. Unable to move and feeling his left lung collapse, he watched as small arcs of lightning arose from the unmoving child held by a slime covered tentacle. The lightning struck Dominic making the child drop and revealing Dominic's cross dimensional form. A glimpse of something not of this world. Not made for human eyes to comprehend. The whole effect was like some strange B movie effect. But the problem was that it was all real, and happening right now. The outline of it was monstrous in scale and grotesque in look. Dominic's body was actually the head of the body. Dominic screamed himself as the electricity hit him from the child. An unearthly sound. His features started to melt away. His eyes and face seemed to be melting. The sound of what must have been 10 voices spoke.

The living liquid that had gone into Kathy's father was now in the child. That liquid was a sliver he sliced from himself to make another less powerful version. One that allowed him to follow the family for generations. So that he could always tell where they were.

"Such power this child possesses. Even undeveloped it holds the power of generations that span many thousands of years. The child is one of many Embryonic Legacies passed from one generation to the next through the mothers mostly. It too bad your power was never shown to you. No matter. It ends now."

Dominic's head turned and looked at the child with a focus that had not been shown. The child, clearly under Dominic's control then rose and started walking on its barely developed legs, toward the man. As soon as it got close enough Dominic lifted the child, opened his mouth. A normal mouth would stop opening, his stretched wider, his head tipped to the side at an awkward angle. His teeth stretched out to fine points like then sharp spears. Rows and rows of them. His head stopped moving but the teeth grew and reached straight into the flesh of the child. It was only after the teeth grew like sharp thorns into the baby's skin, that he started to bite down. Rending flesh from bone, even crunching some of the bone. Biting again and again. The sick sound and sight of the child being eaten and living through most of it was sickening.

All of the child was consumed. There was no ceremony, there was no extra dramatics. The child was chewed in a very methodical manner. Eaten like someone would eat a piece of bread. The half melted face of Dominic started to reshape back to what it looked like before. Kathy, still being held aloft, was held very close as the child was eaten, so she could see, the child's face as it was being eaten alive. The child itself had been held in one position while being eaten. Even though the child was not full developed, the pain was evident on its face. The baby's face not fully formed, but it was formed enough to show when it felt pain.

Kathy's stomach was open and blood was leaking out of her. She had been screaming in terror and pain the whole time, but once she saw her child being eaten, she was overcome with emotion, emotional pain that only a mother could feel when their child is being hurt. She shut down. Her eyes glassed over and she fell into a catatonic state of silence, seemingly unaware of anything around her. Body limp, as if her soul had left her body. And all that was there was an empty shell.

Jerome watched as his child was eaten and killed in such a manner. He was pulled out of his groggy pain ridden state. He gripped the arm, slug, or whatever vile thing that had penetrated straight through his arm into the wall with his one good hand. Squeezing the thing as if it were an old grocery bag, and tearing it out of his shoulder.

The way Jerome ripped it out of himself looked extremely painful, but Jerome did not make a sound. Standing, one arm limp, useless, dangling in a way that looked like it might fall off. Jerome's eyes were focused. Dominic was the target, and Jerome seemed to be looking not just at Dominic, but inside of him. He then sprinted across the room instantly up to full speed from the first step. Reaching Dominic and then burying his fist deep into Dominic's chest. The sound was very similar to a branch snapping, followed by the sound of something wet being pressed into. His fist reached deep inside the man's chest cavity and pulled out a slimy yellow worm like creature, which had hard, thick hairs protruding from its wet slime-filled body. More ooze seemed to pump out of it from every pore. It stank of something wet left under someone's skin, without it ever being aired out. A similar smell would be the skin of a homeless man in the summertime, with an infection on it without it ever being cleaned.

The thing writhed and fought to get free of Jerome's hand but it could not. Jerome stared at it while holding it. They seemed to be communicating in some type of way. But Jerome held it tightly. His eyes were those of a man who has lost his soul and now wonders the world with no emotion. Cold, dark, empty. The only thing that could be seen was the resolution to kill this thing. But he did not move to kill it. His hand looked it was just one finger short of squeezing the thing into several different pieces. But he did not kill it. The thing still wiggled and squirmed in his hand, fighting for its life. Dominic's body had fallen dead. And started rotting right after Jerome pulled the thing out. It was as if untold number of years started to catch up with the body causing it to die immediately. Jerome squeezed the thing tighter. It stopped moving. The top of it, which had no shape other than a giant slug, seemed to be looking dead at Jerome. It appeared to be looking Jerome right in the eye, though it had no eyes, just two ends that came to a point at each end of its body. It was like a larvae, or worm. More shaped like a slug, but it was none of those things. It was slimy, but textured. The smell of it could make any person throw up. It was too alien to just be some type of large worm with hair, if that was hair. This creature was far more sinister. You could sense its intelligence. Its malevolence, wanting to kill, hurt, maim, Jerome, or anyone else near it.
Jerome stood, he did not move any further. It did not move any more. Both Jerome and the creature seemed frozen in an invisible and silent battle of wills. All the plants around them moved, but they seemed to be outside of time. Like they were frozen in time. The thing had a singular focus. That focus was on Jerome. Jerome had beads of sweat rolling down his head. Veins protruded on his forehead. His jaw was muscles were tensed. It was as if he was

straining, but yet his hand was only squeezing with half the power he could squeeze with. His mind was being played with. What Jerome saw was not what the outside world was seeing.

Jerome stood on top of a rock at night on a foreign landscape. There were two moons and they were close to the planet. Jerome had noticed all this but did not care. He was still trying to squeeze Dominic's insides to kill him, but could not squeeze any harder.

"You cannot kill me. Your precious daughter is hidden from you, safe! If you kill me you will never see her alive again!"

Jerome thought, he remembered that there was a reason why he was trying to kill this man, but could not remember. The man was saying that his daughter was safe but could not remember his daughter being around. Her face, smile, clothes,....nothing. Yet, he had the feeling so deeply, that Dominic needed to die so he stuck to it. The little voice in his head screamed for it. Not a real voice, but more a feeling that this man should die, and die now. As painfully as possible. Suddenly he was able to get a tighter grip, then it would not go any tighter. Dominic's face looked shocked and deeply pained. He raised a hand in a stop notion, Jerome was able to grip a fraction more, but no more than that.

"Look, I have not done, anything, wrong to you. Why are you trying to kill me Jerome? I do not understand. Can you at least tell me why you are trying to kill me?"

Jerome could not think of why. Nor could he remember anything. Just the feeling that something was wrong. He did not remember leaving the house, or ending up on this rock slab underneath a night sky with two moons. On this rock plateau. This was not right. And he could feel there was something wrong. But his mind was telling him to believe everything, while on the other hand a feeling was telling him not to believe anything. Dominic started speaking with more urgency, but Jerome decided to ignore him and remember what he had forgotten. He was not supposed to be here. He was at a house. Dominic's house! Something had happened. The memory evaded him, like a dream from the day before that was strange. But now the details of that dream were gone. A lost memory. But he must remember.

"He is in your mind, Jerome. This is not real."

Jerome looked to the side where the voice came from. He could not see anyone. The voice was familiar, but he could not place who. Dominic's face showed frustration and a deep angry hatred. Dominic then tried with renewed vigor to free himself from Jerome's grip.

"This is an illusion it has created in your mind so that you do not see the real being that you hold."
"Shutup!"

Dominic's voice was changing with every word. It no longer sounded human or like it was speaking English. But yet, every word was easily understood. Jerome looked at Dominic and his irises were no longer brown they were now a golden color. And they had a funny shape to them. The shape of his iris was like an 8 laid on its side. The body that was Dominic started to shift. As it started to shift it burned. It felt like acid was coming off of it.

"Do not let go Jerome. Squeeze it. No matter what you feel, keep your grip."

Jerome now saw the being in front of him as an indescribable terror, reaching for him. He held it from his face but slime covered teeth stretched forward from what looked like a head and inched nearer to his face, neck, and eyes with each second. Jerome stood his ground, for some reason he knew this had to end, even if it killed him. He was going to make sure that he was taking this creature with him if he did die.

In that moment, the moment that he let go of his instinct to live, his memory came rushing back in a flood.

The pure acceptance of what must be done, broke any hold this creature had on his mind. Shattered the block that kept him from remembering

The memory of his child being eaten and all the emotional pain that went with it flooded back in. The nerves in his bad arm seemed to catch fire. The backyard suddenly back in view, and the thing he was holding had several spikes now growing off of it. The spikes had been what looked like just hair before then. Each one reaching for a different part of Jerome's body. His bad arm was already had one of these pus covered yellow spikes in it. It felt like a burning fluid was being pumped into the arm. He was losing strength all over his body.

"You can hear me. I am inside you and will bend you to my will. The man you know as Dominic was a willing companion for many more years than you can imagine. But YOU. You will be the perfect............."

Jerome focused all his strength and mind on squeezing this thing in his hand to death. He felt the body bursting. Cartilage like material inside of it breaking and tearing. A deafening roar could be heard inside his head. A sound that could not be described, but was more felt than heard. The spikes fell limp. All except one. Jerome kept squeezing until the thing split into two, releasing a smell that was ancient and putrid. Jerome started to fall to one knee, so overcome with exhaustion and overwhelmed by the toxic smell of the thing.

His vision blurred then he fell to the side. Lying on his bad arm. He felt no pain, he could hear his own labored breath, looking at Kathy lie on the ground on the other side of this creature. He tried to get up but could not move. The creature, was mere feet away. Not moving. Again. Jerome tried to move. But he was paralyzed. There was nothing attached to him anymore. He could see what looked like pollen in the air, and figured that must be what he inhaled to make him immobile.

There was a movement. Out of his line of vision. All he could move was his eyes. One spike, more like a tentacle now reached from one half of the body toward him. It started to drag the half of the body left that oozing some type of yellowish green liquid behind toward him. Jerome looked. Not being able to move. Staring at this thing drag itself toward him, a little at a time. Sliding awkwardly, but slowly, toward him. Jerome closed his eyes and waited for death to come. It would probably be long, painful, and slow death. He was ready. The tentacle slapped down on his face and stung him like a whip, tearing the flesh clean off of his cheekbone. Jerome felt it all, but could not scream or yell. All he could do was lie there. The body part was brought right up to Jerome's face. It seemed to sit and stare at Jerome. Then it started to open. Slowly. At first it just looked like some weird type of shaking it was doing. But then the shaking intensified.

As it kept shaking it opened up into what looked like a mouth. No real teeth, but a row of what looked like teeth made out of the skin that was the creature. The mouth opened wider and wider, with no breath coming out of it. No tongue or throat.

The tentacle shot straight into Jerome's open wound in his shoulder, and immediately filled his arm and wherever that blood flowed with pain. Then a sick and weak sounding voice filled his mind.

"You thought to kill me. But you will not mortal. We come from a time before you. Could have shared that with you then showed you. But you denied my offer. Now you will feel what your child felt as I do not devour you slowly. You will feel everything. Every bite, tear, pinch, burn, as I eat you alive. There will be no sedative. There will be no--"

The voice stopped suddenly, and a heat entered the area that was so intense Jerome closed his eyes. As the heat passed after a minute of burning fire like heat, he felt himself being lifted up. The creature was gone. As Jerome was sat down he looked directly in the eyes he knew. Older looking eyes than he remembered. An older man looked back at him. Cane. His face drooped a little. He looked older, smaller. He looked tired, worn. He still wore the same clothes tattered and filled with blood and dirt. His skin underneath showed no sign of a wound. He limped slightly with each step.

He pulled some type of plant that was twisting in his hand on its own, even though it clearly had been ripped from a larger plant it moved like a fish trying to get away, trying to break free of his grip.

"I am going to put this under your nose. The smell of it will hurt you, but it is the only cure for that poison you took in over there.

The creature is gone and it will not be back. Once you are able to move I need you to get Kathy to the nearest Hospital. "

Cane looked Jerome in the eye to see if he was being heard on the urgency he was trying to get across. Jerome could only look back at him, his body, other than his eyes, still did not respond. But Cane must have been satisfied with the look in his eye, because he then ripped the plant in half and stuck both halves that he held in each hand up both sides of Jerome's nose. The effect was like a medicine mouth wash poured up your nose and reaching your brain giving it the same jolt. Jerome started to regain control of his body. He threw up while sitting in the chair, still unable to move to the sides. After that happened he regained full control of his body.

His nose ran and so many tears came out his eyes he could not see. He could hear Cane speak, from what seemed like a long distance away.

"Get Kathy. And go to the hospital. Do it, now! I will handle the rest of this."

Jerome hobbled over as quickly as he could wiping his eyes to he could see. Each step was the same as when someone wakes you and you have to start moving and interacting as if you have been up the whole time. His limbs was not working together. He had to focus to control his body. As he got closer to Kathy he found the focus he needed to not only walk right but to pick her up, get her to his truck, and take her to the hospital.

Chapter 16

Jerome got Kathy to the hospital. He was taken from her as soon as he got there. His wounds were severe enough to warrant him being taken into surgery. No one could move him from Kathy's side until he was sure she was in good hands. After he spoke with a nurse and saw Kathy on her way to surgery his strength started to fade. He tried to play it off, but his vision dimmed. Before he could sit down to catch himself, he was out. Unconscious on the floor , the nurse he was speaking to rushed to his side, a bed was already on the way. Kathy just needed to be taken care of first. Other people in the emergency room watched in horror. Everyone in the room looked glad to not be either of them. Kathy's blood had dripped all over the floor from the door to the bed. The wound on her stomach, could be seen through torn open clothes, torn open flesh open for all to see. Jerome's limp arm had an open wound that a bone stuck through. Their bodies told a story that no one in the room wanted to live or had the curiosity to experience. In a way, their brutal wounds lifted the spirits of the depressed energy in the Emergency Room. Most were just sick, others had slightly deeper issues. It was clear something had happened to those two that was deep, and hard to filter out. Something, unnatural. All were suddenly grateful for the small "discomforts" they felt. Because after seeing those two nothing in the room seemed more than an inconvenience.

Jerome did not wake up for a week. When he did wake, he found it was the middle of the night and he was in a room alone. He could hear the heart monitor beeping to his heart's rhythm. His mouth felt dry and his throat burned slightly, like he had was sick with a sore throat. His injured arm was in a sling, and his body felt extremely heavy. He went to sit up and barely moved. In a panic he suddenly felt the urge to wiggle his toes to make sure he was not paralyzed.. They moved, and not only that, he was able to lift both legs.

Near his right hand was a remote that allowed him to call for the nurse. He clicked it once. He watched the clock as 8 minutes went by. He then clicked it several times. Followed by two clicks every 30 seconds. A nurse arrived in 2 minutes this time.

"You are awake! We were wondering when you would be coming back. Do you need anything? Are you in any discomfort?"

This nurse must be new, Jerome thought to himself. She spoke without ever looking him in the eye, and talking to him in a tone that said he was a child or some type of dog or puppy. The fakeness in her tone that she thought would sound caring, had a real undertone of being irritated, made him want to grab her by the neck and throw her. But he was in dire need of water, so he croaked out.

"Wa.....(cough)....wa...water"

The nurse looked like she wanted to ask something else but left to get the water. Jerome used 10 times the effort he normally would to push himself up to a sitting position. As soon as the woman comes back he was going to find out about Kathy. He had to find out how she was.

" Here is your water."

The nurse said entering back in. She helped him to drink it. The first sip he tried to drink he coughed back out.

"You have to drink very slowly. It has been awhile since your body has taken in anything orally."

Jerome finally was able to gauge just how much he could swallow at a tine. The water was clearly poured from the faucet in the hospital, but it was the best tasting water he had ever tasted since he was so parched. He kept drinking until all the water was gone from the pitcher. Then he asked his own questions. He found out Kathy had been in Intensive Care and on they had been on the verge of losing her life several times. She had recovered quite miraculously on the 4th day at the hospital. She was in an induced coma due to her wounds, but she was now in stable condition as of today. The nurse also told him there were two police officers waiting to speak with him. As soon as she walked out, they walked in.

"Glad to see you are out of that coma you were in. We have a couple of questions for you."

No hellos. Are you all right to speak. Just straight to the questions. To wake up and get hit by those questions felt like a violation. They were indeed happy he came out of a coma. Only because they felt like he may be the person to pin whatever case they were building, on him. Nigger treatment in the most blatant of ways. Just woke up out of a coma. Fine. Let's get you charged and arrested get you straight into prison.

"Now. As we understand it. There was some type of scuffle up at a house out in Orinda. Is that true?"
"Yes."
"Were there drugs involved?"

The officer, or detective, whatever he was had not even said yet who, he was seemed like a hungry wild animal that just got scent of something it eats bleeding out, weak, something that would be easy to kill. Jerome was still groggy from waking up after basically being asleep for a week.

"I do not believe either of you. has introduced yourself with name, rank, department, or anything else identifying you", Jerome said.

"We are asking the questions here, now answer that last question we just asked. Were there any drugs involved?"

A man walked in the door, short and heavy set. His voice cut into the room with a clarity and air of confidence that seemed to have the same effect as physically slapping them.

"Officers, you would not question my client mere minutes after coming out of a coma, while he is still hooked up to IV and other prescribed drugs, still getting his bearings, would you? Because that would not look good in a court of law. As a matter of fact, it may be inadmissible. There may be even room to sue for harassment. In this case, a high possibility even if we do not win to get at the minimum both of you fired."

"Who are you? You cannot just walk in here and tell us..."
The older and more wise officer touched the younger ones
shoulder to get his attention. The younger officer snapped his head
around to see why he was being touched by the other officer. The
older officer spoke without looking at his partner.

"Counselor we were just on our way out."
"Well I am glad to know that. Maybe you can give me a call. We
can setup a time and place to meet. So we can sit down and
discuss this like civilized people."

Chenault flashed a grin that looked more like the bared teeth of a
dog before he is about to bite the life out of something. The
officers took the card and walked out without saying a word.
Chenault stepped out into the hallway, noticing the Officers had
stopped one door down.

"Are you visiting another patient here? Because if you are not, I
know that my client would feel better if you both were not in the
vicinity when he and I have a little chat about the legality of his
questioning."

This time both officers turned and walked to the elevator bristling
with rage. They did not look back or say a word. It was clear they
were in violation. Trying to hear something in the conversation,
they were trying to get extra information by eavesdropping. Not
technically illegal if they just happened to overhear what was
going on, not trying to purposely listen in. This is the way they
thought. But in real life, outside their own minds, this was a
violation.

Chenault watched as they left watched as the two went to the elevator. Neither turning around because they knew he was watching. The elevator door opened they both got in looking at the ground, ceiling, anywhere but at Chenault. And Chenault did not look away until the door closed and the numbers changed letting him know they had started going downstairs.

"OK. Jerome, looks like things have pretty much been taken care of by a Mr. Cane. Since he is an elderly man, that looked pretty beat down, they had no reason to believe he caused all the problems. It seems physically impossible. He has spoken to the police and said there was some type of home invasion. The body of Dominic has not been found. Mr. Cane says the man was taken away by kidnappers due to some type of shady deals he was involved with. You, Kathy, Angela, and Mr. Cane were all victims in this. Angela was assumed to be Dominic's woman and that was why she was attacked so brutally. You were able to save Kathy and sustained injuries from the effort."

Chenault stopped and looked Jerome in the eye. He was putting out information fast, and had not even checked to see if Jerome was OK with all this. Jerome appeared quite calm. Chenault did not know what went on up there, but would bet it was something he could miss out on judging from all the injuries and mental scarring both the women seemed to have taken in. It occurred to him that Jerome would want to see Kathy.

"Enough with all that. We will work on that later. Right now I assume you will be needing to see Kathy."

Jerome nodded. Then moved his legs around to stand.

"Wait. I will get a nurse. You should not be walking yet."

Jerome did feel a little queasy, so he stopped. The nurse came and brought a wheelchair with her. Jerome got in and they went down a hall into another section of the hospital. They rolled up to the room and another nurse from that section went inside. She came back out and gave the OK to go in. Jerome, though weak, was now feeling a great deal of anticipation. He had not known until less than an hour ago if she had made it or not. This was the woman he had known all his life, and wanted to spend the rest of his life with. Visions of her smile, and feminine ways filled his mind as they rolled into the room. He could see the bed, her hair from the side, the delicate beauty she was. She was a little bit more slim. But as he rolled closer he could see her arms still bore bruise marks, her stomach was heavily bandaged. Worst of all were her eyes. There were dark circles around them. The eyes themselves were distant, like she had retreated somewhere inside of herself that was insulated from everything. He could sense her there, but the trauma she had experienced was evident in her eyes.

Jerome was taken back for a second, he wanted to rewind the whole situation and never go through what had happened, but this was the situation. He looked into Kathy's eyes and saw nothing of recognition at first. As he took her hand and looked into her eyes he saw a glimmer. Then the glimmer faded.

Jerome squeezed her limp hand. Chenault started to say something but Jerome frowned and raised his hand. Chenault left the room taking the nurse with him. After the door was closed, Chenault looked through the small window in the door and saw Jerome move in close. Kathy was lying on her side. Jerome got near her face and started to speak. Chenault could not hear the words but he saw Kathy's head rise. Jerome still sitting looked Kathy directly in her eyes. There was a moment when it looked like neither one was going to do anything. Kathy staring at Jerome, and he back at her. Jerome searched her eyes for something. He looked deeper, trying to get past the fog in her eyes. As he stared, he saw a spark of recognition. He held onto it and gently tried to bring it out with his words. The feeling was the same as grabbing something small and trying to hold with two fingers too big to grip it properly, but still having to bring it out of a tight spot where all it takes is one bump to drop it. An agonizingly slow process that requires pure concentration. Slowly bringing it out of whatever it was stuck under without dropping it for fear of losing it.

Jerome felt like this way about bringing what he considered her soul out of hiding.   He used his eyes to gently guide her back out. She stopped, he waited, then while he was waiting, she did come out more until she finally let herself free from the bondage her mind had put herself in to block the mental, physical, and soul scarring pain.

They embraced. Chenault watched from the door, then he noticed the nurse behind him had also been watching. She moved to open the door. Chenault blocked her way with his arm.

"I think they need some private time. Don't you?" His head turned, but not all the way toward the nurse that stood behind him. He then turned to look the woman in the eye. She tried to put on an almost Police like pose, but wilted under his unmoving stare, turned and walked away. Chenault then turned to sit in the hallway chairs after the nurse had left. There were two other nurses

For 2 hours Kathy spoke about how she had regained consciousness and they told her how he was in a coma and were worried he might be in a coma for a long time. From that news to the memories of what had happened to their child spinning in her head causing her to fall back into a slightly catatonic state for a few minutes. Jerome gently brought her back, tenderly. The emotion of what happened to their child was still raw, deep, and painful, an infinite pain that seemed to have no end in sight. Like looking into the Grand Canyon at night with no moonlight. You can look see the ground, but once you look down into the canyon, all that can be seen is darkness past a certain point. But you know it is deep, wide. Not being able to see how deep, but your mind's eye will tell you that it is deep enough to kill you. Kathy's emotions felt like that. The pain felt infinitely deep, she could not feel there would be an end. The pain itself now that Jerome had brought her out of her shell, seemed to run like a river.

The emotions small and large kept rushing out of her. She shook as tears poured from her with no control to hold them back. Jerome held her with the one arm he could use. Jerome got up on the bed and tried his best to comfort her. He felt pain also, but he knew that what he felt could not match what a mother feels, seeing what was literally apart of them, being tortured to death slowly, bite by bite. Pain that would torment her soul for the rest of her life. Her eyes reflected the pain she felt inside for her child as the baby was consumed. The police officers had not been allowed in to talk to her due to her state of mind before Jerome woke up. She barely responded to anyone or anything. A Psychologist had been sent to the room but was unable to get any information out of her. Kathy had been quiet and did not speak much at all. Until today. Seeing Jerome battered but alive, speaking and smiling helped to bring her back from the dark depths of her mind that she had retreated to trying to escape the pain.

Kathy, now out of her catatonic state of silence, was released within a few hours. Jerome however, had to stay for a few more days. Kathy stayed right next to his bed. It appeared he had overdone it going to see her. He tried to get up off of her bed to his wheelchair, but fell down and laid on the ground completely out of it. He did not wake up for another 8 hours. When he did wake, he awoke to Kathy's smiling face. Her smile showed so full of love he felt as if he had floated out into a beautiful dream instead of reality. Kathy's smile was the most beautiful sight he had seen up to this point. She helped him drink some water. And then they sat and talked quietly. From that point on, Kathy took care of him everyday until he was able to leave.

It took a few days of them sitting side by side, talking, until he gained enough strength to be released. Within a couple of days of that, he was back on the phone delegating his business. A worker he had used for years, was moved up to Manager. The guy was young, in his early twenties, but had been working with Jerome since he was a teenager. He knew how Jerome wanted things done, and who to hire. Jerome was unable to get out of the house yet for prolonged periods, and would not be able to do any labor for quite some time.

Kathy, watched Jerome set his business up in a way where he did not have to be there for every little detail. Once he was done with business, which never seemed to take too long, he turned his full attention to Kathy. He took his time with her, letting her know no matter what, he would be there for all her needs.

Sometimes she would try to hide from him somewhere in the house when she would feel tears coming on, thinking this was taking the burden off of him. Because the last thing she wanted to be was a burden. But every time, he would find her. Taking her under his arm and sitting with her until she was done. He would rub her back softly, slowly. Many times she fell asleep on his lap or chest listening to his heartbeat. He would hang up on anyone if he was on the phone, excuse himself and saying he had to go. Then tend to her. He would get her to drink juice, tea, and at least eat soup. Kathy's appetite had gone down considerably. Not just because of the damage done to her. But mostly because of how depressed she was. She was healing, but the process was slow. The physical and spiritual sides of her had been forever scarred.

Things continued getting better for both of them at a slow pace. Chenault had taken care of the police harassment, by speaking with a childhood friend that was in the police department. There would be no more problems from that side. Kathy had gotten back to being able to smile and laugh. She had started to meditate and do light exercise to help focus her mind, and to take it off of the same memories that seemed to play over and over in her mind. Jerome did not exercise, but they both went for long slow walks together. Never to anywhere in particular. They just took comfort in each other. Angela had come to visit them. Chenault had updated both Kathy and Jerome on Angela's status when they were both in the hospital. She had been hurt badly and had to go to a hospital. But she was in much better condition than either Kathy or Jerome. Angela looked like she was dead at Dominic's house so they were both stunned to hear she was actually less hurt than either of them.

Angela arrived and explained how her emotions were a train wreck, but pulled it together for her kids. She told them about the same two officers asking about what happened. But since what she saw was so far out of her imagination, she refused to talk for fear that they would send her out to the looney bin. And that, was not an option when she had children to finish raising. Angela also felt responsible for what happened. But Jerome and Kathy would have none of it. No one knew that man, Dominic, was not a man. Besides, both Jerome and Kathy had liked the change she had made. Any one that could inspire someone to change in a positive way like that just did not seem to equate as evil, even in hindsight, it was still hard to imagine what they had seen happen. Angela still felt bad. She suffered a broken neck from the blow she received. Not bad enough to cripple her, but she would have to be careful for quite some time. The Doctors and Specialists told her she would now have neck and back pain for the rest of her life. Angela believed it was Karma for the way she had treated Sylvia, Kathy's mother. Kathy said nothing , just gave Angela a heartfelt hug. Angela gave them her new information. She was moving to Phoenix to start a new life and get away from the Bay Area. Go somewhere warm and renergize herself and her children. Both Kathy and Jerome wished her luck. Angela accepted and wished them the best. Angela and Kathy hugged again, both feeling this may be the last time they see each other. An unsaid feeling. But understood. Sad, as they both had come together as sisters in the last months in a way they never did in previous years. Angela left, Kathy and Jerome sat in silence for awhile, both lost in thought. Then Jerome got up and said,

"Let's get married."

A few days later, they were married at City Hall. No one was told. It was something they wanted and right now, really did not want any extra attention. There would be time for a church ceremony later. Kathy half way felt like she should do this before he changed his mind. The whole thing was his idea, but she felt like it might not come around again, and agreed to go to City Hall to make it official.

For a celebration they got a Hotel in Sausalito for 2 days. The hotel was on a hillside. It had views of both San Francisco, Oakland, as wells as the San Rafael, Bay, and Golden Gate Bridges. Both nights they stayed there was no fog and the views were unbelievable. Both got the Spa treatments.   Jerome skipped most of the skin treatment, as well as the manicure and pedicure. He took the two hour massage, while Kathy did the manicure and pedicure as well as an hour massage. When they got back to the room there was a box on the bed. The box had Kathy's name on it. When she opened it up she saw the most beautiful and uniquely done wedding rings she had ever seen. A large diamond in the middle with a design like the middle diamond was the eye, and the smaller diamonds were like the eyelashes. It was beautiful. Kathy did not scream, she did not cry, she sat staring at it with no expression on her face. Inside her head she was screaming her head off. But outside, there was no noticeable reaction. This puzzled Jerome, because he thought this would make her happy. But she seemed to have no reaction at all.

"Baby, do you like it? Is it too much. I really worked with the jeweler on the design. I actually ordered everything directly from a jeweler friend of mine. I designed it based on your eye. It took………"

Jerome could not finish, because Kathy, suddenly as healthy as a young kitten, pounced on him. Her excitement overflowed until 4 in the morning. Jerome was worn out, but Kathy kept playing and talking to him until the sun came up. She took him around the world and back. He was shocked, happy, and worn. Kathy seemed like she was just catching a second wind when Jerome fell asleep while she lay on his chest talking. The ring, the hotel, the marriage all seemed to distract her almost completely from her pain. Kathy now was now feeling like she saw a very bright light at the end of the tunnel.

When they got back they felt renewed. Like new people. As they drove up to the front of their house an older man sat on the front stairs to the front door. For an older man he seemed to be in good shape. When he stood, he stood with strength and solidity that most men of his age did not seem to have. Then he picked up a cane, Kathy and Jerome immediately knew who it was.

"Was beginning to think you all were not going to come home. I was told that your reservation ended today at the hotel you all were at. Figured you all would be back around this time."

Cane smiled as he shook Jerome's hand and gave Kathy a hug. Both Kathy and Jerome looked at the scar running from under Cane's chin across his neck and onto his shoulder. He had a collared shirt on with another light colored suit. This time of gray, with white shirt, and brown shoes. The man was immaculate. But his face now matched the color of his hair. His skin now sagged somewhat. His eyes now had the distinct glaze of cataracts like a lot of older men had. He looked to have aged 40 years since they last saw him. He still stood straight, but his shoulders were far more narrow. Kathy and Jerome took this in as they watched him he watched them back finally saying.

"Well, I cannot look into your thoughts anymore. But I can tell both of you are shocked by my appearance."

Both Kathy and Jerome nodded like two kids that did not want to say too much. Quiet and somewhat wide eyed. Neither said anything just stood and waited for an explanation.

"OK. You both have some questions. I think I can answer. But could we do this inside. I am feeling a chill out here."

Spoken like a true elder. Cane pulled his collar forward and hunched his back slightly as he spoke. He really did look like he was feeling a chill. Before he seemed impervious to any chill, cold, heat, anything. He just would stand. Now he looked weathered. Jerome started with the questions after Kathy offered some tea and Cane politely declined.

"What happened at the house after we left?"
"I did some changes, made sure there was nothing left to show anything but a home invasion. An attack done to a man involved with shady people."
"But what about the whole transformation? The things he did, the things we saw done?"
"What you saw was not what should have happened. He orchestrated an ambush on me with the help he linked up with. The odds were overwhelming. But I left and took them to places to make the fighting ground more even. In doing so, I paid a price. The price I paid is what you see before you."

Cane looked up staring at one, then the other. Looking both in the eyes. Making sure they knew the sacrifice he had given for both of them to be safe.

"Kathy, I swore an oath to ancestors of yours to protect your family's gift. Now that the power has been taken and will not be passed on to anyone else, I have failed. But you are alive, and I can rest in the knowledge I gave everything I could to save you. Like I promised your mother. "

At the mention of her mother Kathy became curious about their relationship, and wanted to know more. But right as she was saying that Cane fell into a violent coughing fit. He coughed so hard he actually fell to one knee. The coughing kept going even after he had fallen to one knee. Jerome tried to steady him, but the man's body was being jerked so bad by the coughs that he fell forward and threw up blood. No small amount either. None of it got on him, but the smell was putrid. Like it was not just blood.

Cane took a handkerchief out and wiped his mouth after spitting more blood out. When he stood he looked to have aged another 10 years in front of them. Stopping Kathy in her tracks, she was about to turn and grab something to clean up the mess but was shocked by what she saw. When he stood this time he was unable to stand straight. His shoulders were more narrow and his back was slightly bent.

"The price I paid for this last battle. That is what you are both observing. I have not bled in years. But now, my life essence flows out with it. I will die soon. I just need to clean up a little in your bathroom and I will leave you two with one last gift."

They all went inside. Cane went to the bathroom. But as soon as he washed his hands he was wracked with another coughing fit. This time he did not cough up blood. His skin started to flake away like burning embers in a fire, floating up in the air. He looked in the mirror and saw the skin slowly come off and fade to dust. He called Jerome and Kathy to the bathroom. They both got there just in time to see him fading away.

"I am sorry. My time has come sooner than I expected. Know that you both come from strong lineage that is so old it is forgotten. Neither of you come from the Bush. Your people were strong dignified people, no different from the people you see in cities now. They were from great civilizations that time has forgotten. Kathy when you are ready, you will be able to have more children. I was able to heal you. Jerome. I was not able to heal you, and your arm may never be the same. Just remember the training I gave you, and it will give you the edge to be a level that most will never achieve, even with your disability."

The slept well that night. Kathy on Jerome's chest, feeling safe and warm in the night chill. Jerome feeling strong and confident with the woman he loved laying on his chest softly breathing. They both radiated a love, that radiated like heat from the sun. Together they radiated a positive energy that could be felt from outside the home. The type of thing that made plants grow with more strength and color. Gave a house a feeling of a Home. While their bodies slept, Cane greeted their souls and took them to what would be a family reunion of sorts. Introducing them to ancestors they had starting with those most recently passed to many from long ago. The further they went back in time the more regal the people appeared to be. The dignity could be felt. The ones that were born and raised in America were strong and proud, but there was something missing. Maybe from the disconnect that had been done in slavery. The ones born and raised in Africa possessed a different kind of pride. A pride that comes from not having a culture on top of yours while it develops, trying to destroy it.

The men wore heavy thick jewelry with similar hairstyles, but varying clothes. But all wore giant bracelets, rings, or necklaces that were all diamond or precious jewel laden. Women, had all manner of hairstyles, from short to long. There were so many different clasps, bracelets, rings, sandals, looks that the women had that Kathy found herself getting lost in their fashion more than seeing looking into them to see them inside of her. They all noticed her curiosity and found it slightly amusing. After what seemed like a week of meeting people. Cane told them they must go. As everyone they met stepped into a light. Cane told them to go. They were not ready for the journey all must take.

When they awoke, in the same position they fell asleep in, Kathy began to tell Jerome about the most beautiful dream she had ever had. Jerome listened and told her, he knows exactly what she means, because he was there too. He said it must not have been a dream at all. But a last gift from a good friend. A link to a past that most people will never know.

A woman stood across the street staring at the second floor of Kathy and Jerome's house. Staring at the bedroom Kathy and Jerome slept in. Her face twisted with a mad hatred. There were bugs falling on the sidewalk warmed by the noon sun. Bugs were falling out of her dress. Foam was coming out of her mouth, as she fell to one knee. Someone walked by and asked if she was OK. The lady kept foaming at the mouth then fell to the ground as if in seizure. An ambulance was called and there in minutes. The woman died in route to the hospital. When an autopsy was given they found a hive of bugs inside of her, all of them dead. A government agency came in and took the body after it was found the woman had no relatives to claim her. There seemed to be a small City built inside of her body. All the bugs were dead, but most of her innards had been eaten away, and landscaped to match what the bugs needed. The last of Dominic's creations was dead. But enough remains were left inside the woman's body. They would be studied.

Kathy and Jerome could sense the last of their tension passing as they both went for a walk to the coffee shop before starting another new day of their married life. The sun filled them with warmth, life, a spiritual renewal that they both needed. They both breathed in the warm air into their lungs and feeling a positivity renewed. Stronger than either had felt before, and deeper than either could have imagined.

Photo by www.bmalikphotography.com/

Bahati was Born the Bay Area and raised in Southern California, now currently living in the Bay Area. Being the youngest born by nine years of the siblings born to his parents, he spent great deal of his young life in solitude after his siblings moved out and into the world as adults. That time alone was not wasted, albums and books left by older siblings left worlds to explore. The musical sounds, as well as album cover visuals of Earth Wind and Fire, Stevie Wonder, and Parliment/ Funkadelic, led to the creation of rich, textured worlds of fantasy for a young Bahati to explore with his mind. As the years went by introductions to Black History from his Father about the African Diaspora and history of Africa and it's many
empires only led to even deeper worlds within worlds of imagination. After working twenty

years at different jobs in IT, Bahati, prompted by his eldest sibling, decided to start to
write down some of the stories that had been running through his mind since childhood.
Embryonic Legacy is the first of these stories.